True Stories of the (mostly) Flawless Penelope Hazard

by

J. Grant Fiero

To hear more awesomeness from Penelope, visit

penelopehazard.com

Chapter 1

Despite the implications of her last name, Penelope Hazard lived in the bubble. Things just seemed to work out for her and why shouldn't they? The caption of her life, as told through selfies, should be "#awesome." She was flawless and her life was awesome, except that she wasn't and it wasn't, at least not most of the time. High school was hard. Being fifteen totally stressful and her parents were clueless. She loved them both but they just didn't understand.

Penelope was still deciding how to feel about the latest development. She would shed no tears for the vicious high school scene from which her mom's most recent career move liberated her. Mean girls and stupid boys dominated the landscape. Penelope was not a mean girl. She could be. She chose not to be. The formula was easy enough to copy. She had the required looks and her family had the required money. Her only shortcoming was an utter failure to believe the world and everything in it revolved around her. It annoyed her that girls she had known for a long time had, during the ten weeks of summer, turned from normal girls to mean girls.

Penelope mostly managed to stay above the drama that swirls around mean girls, except when her world and theirs occasionally overlapped because of some beautiful, stupid boy. The beautiful ones were extra stupid and extra childish and completely vulnerable to the trashy charms of mean girls. Apparently, Penelope was a threat. She stared hard into the mirror sometimes, trying to understand why.

She was pretty. People told her that and some days she could see it. She had her mom's cheekbones and Father's long eyelashes, which she found more hilarious than he did. The fair skin and strawberry blond hair came mostly from her mom. Penelope was happy it wasn't as thick as her mom's hair. That must have been her dad's contribution. She had less body image baggage than most of her friends, which meant she hated her body only a little. She didn't wear mean girl makeup and her parents were a little fascist about skirts and short-shorts so she would never be accused of looking "hot."

Maybe she was a threat precisely because she didn't try to compete with them. Could indifference really be the key to life? Her mom said the mean girls were mean because they were horribly insecure about everything. Penelope felt insecure about just about everything, so if mean girls experienced a worse version of hell, she could almost feel sorry for them, almost.

The one thing that didn't bother Penelope about high school was the school part, which was the one part that counted for almost nothing to high school kids. Her parents assured her that learning and getting good grades were the important things. Clueless, they were. Clueless. Not that she wanted to be the kind of clueless the mean girls and stupid boys demonstrated daily in class. They had to be doing it to be cool. No one could really be that consistently stupid without trying, could they?

Penelope didn't feel smart. School was only easy for her when it involved remembering things. That was easy. The school tested her a long ago and decided she had a photographic memory, which really wasn't the case because such a thing doesn't exist. That's what her mother said. She had a good short-term memory, particularly for images, which was more like an eidetic memory, which she also did not have -- again, according Mother. Her memory of her own experiences was really good. They call that hyperthymesia or HSAM -- Mother again -- which, as a teenager seemed more like a punishment than a gift. Why yes, I do remember exactly when and how Trevor made fun of me that time in Algebra and I will probably always remember, thank you very much.

The only thing about her brain she found cool was her ability to make connections, to see patterns others missed. Penelope hoped someday that would come in handy in the real world. If not, she had fashion sense and so many people in the world clearly did not. Surely that would provide some sort of opportunity.

Her parents got absolutely no credit for liberating her from the hell of her Illinois high school because she knew her new school would be exactly the same. Different faces. Different fashion. Different mascot. Same crap -- mean girls and stupid boys. Maybe she would give the mean girl thing a try in Florida. Yeah right. At least the weather would be better. Her dad was ecstatic about that. He hated the Midwest winters. Mom was worried about the bugs but she traveled so much Penelope and her dad really didn't think she should get a vote about the location. Her two biggest clients were now in Florida and she could get to London, Berlin, Rome, Vienna, and so on, from

2

Miami, which was only a couple of hours away via something called alligator alley. It must not be as dangerous as it sounded.

Her brother, who was away at college in Oregon also did not get a vote and not just because he was a slightly older version of the stupid boys in her world. Having escaped Illinois, he wanted the family to stay there so he could come home and visit friends. Instead, he would have to suffer through winter break in the tropics with her. She couldn't really feel sorry for him about that.

It wasn't the perfect location for her either. Penelope thought they should be closer to Miami. Father said they chose St. Georges because the Gulf Coast had sunsets over the water -- superior to the watery sunrises of the Atlantic Coast. That seemed thin, as did the reason for selecting St. Georges over all other locations along the stretch from Naples to Ft. Myers. It seemed a perfectly pleasant gated community but her parents lowered the average age of the place by quite a lot. It was positively crawling with old people. Mother said that enhanced the property value because retired people liked to live around each other. She also liked the fact that they would have the smallest, by which she meant cheapest, house in the whole community. You always wanted to have the smallest rather than the largest house in the neighborhood, she said. Whatever. Father said the quiet neighborhood would suit his writing. Thin. Flimsy, actually. The result was the same for Penelope -- house after house with no one her age.

Father. He was what all those stupid boys would grow up to be. Why was she attracted to stupid boys who would grow up to be taller stupid, dorky boys with embarrassing body hair? She called him Father when she when she wanted to distance herself from his chronically dull and practical adulthood -- or when she wanted to be a pill. Penelope couldn't decide whether this writing thing made him dorkier or slightly less. Part of the deal he and Mother made -- same thing with calling her "Mother" except that Mother really didn't like it, which made it so much more fun -- was that Father could finally "retire" from his job. Nothing could really be less cool than working for an insurance company so "novelist" had to be a step up. He never really said what he did at work and she really had no idea what kind of things might go on inside such a place, but it all had to be tragically dull.

He and Mother traveled a lot, which was a constant inconvenience for Penelope. Mother's travel was better for Penelope, because she went to cool places and brought back good swag. In the summer Penelope would occasionally get to go along, which recently meant she would have the freedom of whatever city they were in during Mother's working hours -- Vienna, Munich, London, Brussels, Geneva, Milan. Sometimes she had a handler and sometimes she just pretended to stay in the hotel all day. Either way, she had a lot of unsupervised time in awesome places.

Meanwhile, Father went to exotic places like Omaha, Des Moines, Milwaukee, and St. Louis. Dallas was about as cool as it got for him. Anyway, when both of them were gone, and that happened too often, Penelope had no chauffeur. Totally unacceptable. Arrangements were always made for getting her to and from school and related activities but that was it.

So no more crap travel for Father and no more time doing boring insurance stuff in a big gray building full of indoor/outdoor carpet and beige cubicles. Actually, that had all stopped about six months ago. It happened kind of suddenly and Penelope wondered at the time whether he had been fired, not that it would matter to her unless her finances were impacted, which didn't seem the case. He started writing a couple of years ago, or at least he admitted it a couple of years ago. He said he spent so much time sitting in airports and hotels he started writing just for something to do. Mother seemed kind of surprised, amused actually, when he finished his first book -- shocked when someone agreed to publish it.

Mother mocked him playfully about his books. Penelope thought it was cute that he wrote spy thrillers. His protagonist was super spy Raglan Dunne, who worked for a secret international security organization loosely affiliated with the NATO countries but acknowledged by no government. The books all had lame titles based on the ironic punnery of the last name Dunne -- Never Dunne, Well Dunne, Hard Dunne By, and the like. It wasn't sad at all that the nerdiest guy imaginable wrote nerdy fiction about the super cool man of mystery he secretly wished he could be -- not sad at all.

It was mostly endearing because he loved him to bits. And actually, he wasn't the nerdiest guy ever. The insurance thing was uber nerdtastic but being a published author was interesting no matter how trashy your books might be. Also, his other hobbies were less tragic.

He liked to go to the gym, which was not Penelope's thing but he was maniacal enough about it to keep him from becoming a balding, pear shaped nerd in a cubicle. She found it funny and also fun that the stupid boys in her class were visibly intimidated. It was funny to her because he was such a softy. There just wasn't much mean to go with his muscles. Mother seemed to like them. She would sometimes paw on him in front of Penelope just to get a reaction. Eww! She didn't want to give her mom the satisfaction. It was just an involuntary response. Eww! Every time.

Of course Mother was rarely home long enough to get on Penelope's nerves. She wasn't exactly sure what it meant to be someone's personal lawyer, beyond the apparent need to jet all over the world tending to their lawyery whims. It did not escape Penelope that all her mother's clients were men of a certain age. They were all ungodly rich, so they no doubt had plenty of attention from young, dumb hotties. There was no need for them to get their lawyering and happy endings from the same women. Still, Penelope was sure Mother's looks and charm gave her an edge in bagging clients.

Penelope's stream of consciousness recap of her existence was suddenly interrupted by an annoying noise. The thing above her seat was dinging and the voice from above was saying they were beginning their descent into Ft. Myers. Winter was officially in the rear view mirror. Bring on the bikinis and sunscreen. It was summer in Florida.

Chapter 2

Penelope paid close attention to navigation as the car maneuvered from the airport to St. Georges. She would be driving soonish and wanted to get started learning how to get around. There were certain critical landmarks she needed to find and remember. Shopping was high on the list. It seemed unlikely their route would magically pass by a mall. Still, she couldn't rule it out. Eternal vigilance is the price of looking fabulous, after all. More important was the need to spot and map one or more Starbucks locations. She had been assured there would be an ample supply of fancy coffee in her new life in Florida.

Soon they were on something called Springvale. It was long, mostly straight, and utterly without redeeming retail outlets on either side until right at the end -- an outlet mall! It looked big, too. And now they were slowing down. Her heart jumped a little -- right turn then immediate left and they were into something like a neighborhood. They were almost there, which meant Penelope lived close to a mall! You would have thought Axel or Louisa would have mentioned that. Of course they wouldn't, because, yes, exactly, they are clueless.

The long straightaway passed immaculately landscaped trailer courts on either side. One left turn later and a few more glances at big palm trees surrounded by perfectly arranged flowering plants brought them to the gates of St. Georges. The guard was very serious. Penelope figured a furrowed brow and raised voice were probably his only weapons. He was -- how would she put it -- way beyond retirement age. Mother handled the discussion with him. She tended to handle most such conversations.

Through the gate and a sharp left put them on their new street, Fulham Road. A minute later they pulled into their new driveway. Penelope had seen pictures of the house. In person it looked bigger, more inviting. Objectively, it was about the smallest house in the entire community, which was less than a hundred lots. She heard her dad say that back when Mother was deciding if the house was acceptable. The moving trucks had arrived earlier in the day and the movers were already shuttling furniture from truck to house per her mom's written instructions. Most of the boxes were accumulating in stacks in the garage, organized by room, of course.

"Isn't this great Pea?" Her father asked. Pea was short for Sweet Pea, which was not the worst play on "Penelope" she could think of -- not nearly the worst the kids at school had dreamt up. "Watch your step, PeePee Hazard ahead," was her nickname low point.

"Living the dream, dad."

"Oh, come on. It's like paradise." He goaded her. He wasn't wrong. Everything she had seen of St. Georges so far was gorgeous. Their house only looked small because mini-mansion was the norm. Everything was lush and green and, at the same time, immaculately manicured. The vibe was nearly theme park perfect, without crossing over into creepy fake perfection.

"If paradise is a steam room inside a pizza oven full of bugs." Mother chimed in. "My hair will never look right in this humidity."

"I kinda like it frizzy, Lou. Very sexy."

"Daaaaad!" Penelope scolded.

"She's right, Axel. No little girl wants a mental image of her parents getting all hot and sweaty together."

"Stop!" Penelope stamped her foot on the driveway as her mother flashed an evil little smile. "I'm going to go find my room."

Penelope's bed was already set up in her room and she plopped down on it, one leg dangling off the edge. The ceiling was higher than she was used to, or maybe it only looked higher because the room was smaller than her old room. She followed the blades of the ceiling fan around and around, contemplating what she knew about St. Georges. It wasn't officially a retirement community like the trailer court they passed with the big sign out front announcing "+55" to the world. It really was, though. She remembered the very serious conversations Axel and Louisa had on the subject before they committed to the house. Nearly all of the residents met the +55 requirement. St. Georges didn't seem to need the sign to make the point. Interesting that Axel and Louisa failed to include her in those conversations. "Oh yes mummy, yes daddy, I'd love to live in a place where the only teenagers are the ones visiting their grandparents. That sounds perfect!"

She also knew most of the houses in St. Georges had some sort of water right outside the door, her house included. Of course the water outside her door was collected in a little drainage ditch running along the road.

There was a yacht club. Her experience with yacht clubs was limited mostly to movies. Her lone visit to one on Lake Michigan reminded her of Bushwood Country Club so her expectations were not high. To keep on the pretentious golf theme, apparently everyone in St. Georges had a golf cart. There was no golf course on the grounds unless you counted the Sunset Point course next door. Father said there was even a little gate between St. Georges and Sunset Point just for golf carts. He pointed it out as they drove by it on Fulham Road. He was really amped up about the golf cart thing even though he didn't play golf. What a nerd. Penelope liked the idea of riding in a golf cart instead of walking but she wouldn't go so far as to mistakenly say the ugly little things were "cool" like her father did.

Yachts, on the other hand, could definitely be cool, even if the "yachts" were actually just big boats. She knew all about the yachts of St. Georges. For the last several months, most of the time he had her trapped in the passenger seat of his car, Father regaled her against her will with talk of big boats. Blah, blah, GPS, blah, blah, Sonar, blah blah, cabin cruiser, blah blah horsepower, . . . blah, blah, blah. She remembered about three percent of it, which was only accidental and due to the way her brain worked. She couldn't always turn it off when she wanted.

Father made a run at Louisa to get a boat for the family -- all the other grownups will have boats -- what's the point of being in a yacht club if you don't have one -- it's actually faster to get to some places by boat down there -- we can take it to the islands instead of going on big vacations -- and Penelope's personal favorite -- it will bring us together as a family.

You had to give him credit for trying to win an argument with a lawyer. He tried everything. The problem was, he was the least nautical man on the planet. Father did not like to swim. He could do it. She had seen him do it. It just wasn't his thing. He wasn't even that into lying in the sun by the pool. Nor did he fish. He and Louisa had gone on a cruise once and came back gushing about how much fun it had been. That seemed his lone credential as a man of the sea -- five days of buffet lines and off, off, off Broadway entertainment on a floating hotel.

Needless to say, there would be no yacht. On balance that was a good call and not just because Penelope needed Axel and Louisa to save money for the small, gas-sipping, red convertible she would be ecstatic to receive on her sixteenth birthday, a little less than a year from now. No, her thinking on this subject was more generous. Father was a bit of a goof, particularly with mechanical things, and she could not see how handing him the keys to a fifty-foot floating condo with two massive diesel truck engines under it could possibly go well. In the end, Mother spared his feeling and based her entire defense on finances. The term "money pit" came up repeatedly. Her parting shot, while she stood over his mortally wounded body with her big lawyer gun, was "I'm sure you will find a friend with a boat."

That was Penelope's plan. By her calculation, at least seventy percent of the residents were grandparents. A lot of them must have boats. And the grandkids would only be visiting a few times a year. That meant there would be a lot of pent up grandparent energy. Penelope would be happy to give them an outlet for that. She was a constant delight, after all. Everyone said so -- well everyone over the age of thirty. One thing would lead to another and soon she would be lying on the deck of a big boat soaking up the sun as the breeze and salt spray washed over her. That might be her only social life this summer. It was only fair that she salvage something good from her parents' decision to cast her socially adrift in this not officially a retirement community, retirement community.

Chapter 3

Trish answered the door while her husband Will opened the big sliding doors to the lanai so they could do the required business while enjoying the view in the pleasant evening air. The bugs were less thick than usual tonight, so the foul smelling candles on the lanai were holding them at bay. The screens encasing the lanai provided an adequate barrier against most of the little flying carnivores but some, particularly the no-see-ums, always managed to find a way.

Will looked out on the marina in the dying light, soaking in the warm, wet air. It was always good to come back to St. Georges. The pastel sunset and gentle sounds of water lapping against the boats below lent the scene an innocent. It made him sad to think there was something unpleasant lurking in the dark just beyond what he could see.

"Will, how was your trip?" Commodore Riley asked as he and his wife, Lesley, took seats inside the bug cage. Will waived the Pattersons -- Roger and Doris -- onto the lanai as well. Robert was just starting his year as Commodore. Although it was not a requirement for election, he had the look, like he was born for the little black brimmed cap and navy blazer. He was tall, for starters, and the white hair, slightly barreled chest, and wire-framed glasses rounded out the yacht club stereotype. Physically, Lesley was all counterpoint. She was petit in every dimension, noticeably thin and reminded Will of some officers' wives he had known -- polite, gracious, a little judgy, and always perfectly groomed.

"Colorado is spectacular this time of year. The weather was perfection and I love the mountain air -- so crisp and clean. We took the cog railroad to the top of Pike's Peak. Beautiful."

"You know it was the views from Pike's Peak that inspired Katherine Lee Bates to write the poem that turned into the lyrics for America the Beautiful." Trish added as she carried a tray of tea onto the lanai.

"Yes we stayed at the hotel where she actually put pen to paper." Will finished the thought. "We would have stayed at the Broadview but the Elkhorn was more convenient for our business."

"Speaking of your business, was it a productive trip in that regard?" The Commodore asked.

"Yes, we had a very productive meeting. Trish gave a compelling account of our concerns." Will responded.

"Did you meet with the big man, himself?" Roger asked.

"No, he was indisposed. But we felt well taken care of. Say, are we expecting Jerry and Joan?"

"No, they had to go back to Maine on short notice -- something about unwanted critters in their place up there. They asked that we fill them in after we met with you." Lesley piped up.

"Tell me, did you get the sense we ruffled any feathers by approaching GSC directly?" Roger asked.

"There was no hint of that. Did you feel anything negative, Trish?" Will handed off to his wife. Will had a hard time taking Roger seriously. The reason was ridiculous and also powerful. He looked just like Leslie Nielson from the days of the Airplane movies. Trish had put that in his head the first time they saw Roger and now there was no way to get it out.

"Not even a little. If anything, I sensed an unusual disarray at the firm."

"Disarray, yes that is a good word. I felt it too." Will added.

"And after you made your compelling case -- our case -- what was the resolution?" Will was surprised the Commodore had been able to wait so long before getting to the meat of the issue.

"They agreed our concerns are not imagined and they promised to take care of everything." Trish started this time.

Will looked at his wife and wondered how their friends would describe the two of them. They had worked together so long he suspected they had begun to sound alike. That probably amused their friends. Will had always believed he looked German. He sometimes thought he would look a bit too natural in lederhosen. He definitely looked the part in a hunting jacket with the little hat with the feathers sticking up from the band and his thick silver hair pushing out from underneath. Trish would prefer to think of herself as French, which made sense to him given the deep, smoky eyes he had fallen in love with once upon a time. Of course, they were neither German nor French.

Will picked up as Trish ended. "More than that, they said we were merely validating something they had already identified and that the necessary wheels were already in motion." Will could tell the Commodore was unsure how to react.

"Did they share any ideas about who it might be?" Roger asked.

"Nothing beyond the obvious. We share a history, all of us here -- stands to reason it is someone from our past." Will responded.

"That was so long ago. Why now?" Lesley wondered aloud.

"We asked the same." Trish responded.

Will cut in. "They seemed equally confused, I have to say. All we got was something to the effect that 'the matter had been settled.'"

"I suspect the uncertainty is one reason we are getting such prompt attention." Trish added.

"That is all very reassuring I suppose, but what does it mean? What exactly are they going to do -- or, rather, what are they already doing, I guess?"

"I understand your concerns, Bob," Trish tagged herself in, "But you have to understand that discretion is an important part of what makes their services so valuable."

"Trish is right. Think about it. From their perspective, if they do a good job, it will all be taken care of and we will never be aware of what or how or who." Will added.

"And don't forget, based on what we told them, they can't rule out involvement by one of our own. So the less we know, the less chance we will inadvertently muck things up for them." Trish finished.

"I suppose. It just all sounds a little nebulous and clandestine." The Commodore grumbled.

"Look," Roger offered. "We believe St. Georges is under real threat at the moment -- from something beyond our ability to handle -- and we all agree the firm is our best option to take care of that threat."

"I know, Roger. I just don't like feeling clueless and helpless at the same time."

"Bob, seriously, you need to stop feeding me straight lines like that." Will chuckled, hoping to lighten the mood. The others laughed with him and the rest of their evening was spent in conversation on more pleasant thing like plans for the upcoming summer Gala.

Chapter 4

Two weeks of unpacking, organizing her room, and binge-watching movies on her computer had Penelope at her limit. She was nearly desperate enough to see if Father wanted to do something. Sadly, he was loving life here in St. Boring. He was happily consumed writing the next lame "mission" of his super spy alter ego. Whatever. At least it kept him out of her hair. It also meant he would likely turn down any request from her to be entertained, which was too tragic to contemplate.

Having no better prospects, Penelope decided to wander the grounds of St. Boring and resolved not do it with a fabulous casual style. She grabbed her designer sunglasses, slipped on an extra wide hair band, and squeezed into the tiniest shorts she could find after several minutes of staring "Where's Waldo" style at the scatter of clothes littering her floor. She tidied her room frequently but order never seemed to last more than ten minutes in her room. Penelope decided long ago that chaos had a secret grudge against her and would always win. Mother, of course, lacked imagination and felt otherwise.

Her house was at the edge of St. Georges at the border with a retirement village called Sunset Point. The house was wedged onto a tiny lot just as Fulham bent inward from a long straightaway to allow normal sized lots along the same road. It was far from the water, of course, which was saying something because the whole subdivision was clearly arranged to maximize the number of lots touching water. Most faced the little harbor carved out to support the yacht club, the open water of the Intracoastal Waterway, or at least bordered one of several small, mangrove lined canals that provided the illusion of proximity to water. Penelope's house didn't even have that, which was fine with her. The little bayous snaking through the property were narrow, dark, and full of creepy noises, any one of which might be an alligator. No thank you.

This was not her first walk around the neighborhood. Mother and Father dragged her along on a family walk the morning after they arrived. Penelope felt like an accessory that day, particularly because Mother insisted on picking her outfit. Grrrr? That walk produced several meet and greet moments. "Wasn't Penelope just a little doll -- adorable" was the theme. She smiled unconsciously through the ordeal. That walk also led to an invite for Father and her to kayak around with one of the locals, which is how Penelope came to experience first hand the mangrove tunnels of horror. At least she got that out of the way in the first week and would know to fake a migraine or a stroke or something if anyone ever asked her again.

Today, there were no parents to parade her through the village. Penelope could meet any human contact with a cute smile and polite waive, although it was the middle of the day in June in South Florida so running into anyone seemed unlikely. It was particularly hot and humid today, with the sun alone in a deep blue sky.

Penelope liked the heat in controlled doses. She knew it would be different if she had to actually work in the heat. There were several men putting tiles on a roof on one of the side streets. They were the kind of men who would say rude things if she walked by so she didn't turn down that lane. She could see even from a distance that they were hot and sweaty up on the roof. This kind of heat, she decided, was lovely for those who could trade it for air conditioning whenever they wanted.

She wandered past the club to a small parking lot serving the marina. The initial walk with her parents included a tour of the club, which mostly consisted of a little bar, nautically themed of course, and a large dining room. She had already experienced the dining room several times. The menu wasn't her style but the food was edible and, as Father pointed out, the location was perfect. The veranda just beyond the dining room looked out on the marina and on one end transitioned to a modest kidney pool rimmed by a spattering of lounge chairs.

Penelope walked along the dock. Some of the boat slips were empty. She had the impression there were no slips to be had for new boats, which meant some boats were out for the day. She had never really been around people who didn't do the whole Monday to Friday work thing. It might take some time to get used to people on perpetual summer break. Maybe she could skip the career part and transition straight from school to retirement. That would suit her temperament much better than growing up and joining the world of cubicle zombies. She would have to work on that.

The dock kept going past the rows of boats and along the edge of the water behind a string of big pastel row houses. She heard someone at the club call them "villas." To her they were row houses frosted with stucco and separated by just enough space to avoid sharing walls, but "villa" certainly sounded more exotic. She kept walking. At the end of the dock there was a walkway cut through the mangroves. She followed it up an incline to the back corner of the last villa in the row. The street in front ended at a big, perfectly flat lot rimmed by a freshly poured retaining wall on three sides. It seemed like a big house should be going up on the lot and probably would be soon. At the back of that lot was another walkway leading out through the mangroves to a point beyond the harbor. Penelope started across the freshly mown weed patch to investigate.

"Hello there young lady." The words startled her.

"Hello?" Penelope called out vaguely in the direction she thought appropriate, which was behind her. She turned.

"The fire ants are going to get you, you know."

This time she had a better fix on the sound. "What are fire ants?" She asked, looking toward the top floor of the villa.

"Well, ants, obviously. Tiny ones. The name comes from the way their bites feel on your skin. They love little girls."

"I have shoes on."

"Shoes only help a little. You've already been standing still too long. Better come back to the pavement. Hold on, I'll come down and spray your feet."

"Umm, ok, I guess." Penelope responded. Part of her thought "stranger danger" but there was something about the old man's voice that put her at ease. Besides, he wasn't lurking at a playground in a van with puppies or candy. She walked to the garage doors where she assumed he would emerge. The grinding of the door opening announced his arrival.

"Hi, I'm Penelope. We just moved in." She said as a figure emerged from the garage. He was old, of course, medium height, a full head of dark hair, with slightly rounded shoulders, and little bird legs sticking out from his khaki shorts.

"Yes, of course, the lawyer, the writer, and the teenager. I'm sure you've noticed you're just about the only residents under 55. Must be terribly exciting for you, in particular."

"Yeah, I didn't get a vote. Father seems happy, though." She smiled.

"Allow me to introduce myself, Penelope. My name is Harvard Merriam Bagwell."

"Pleased to meet you, Mr. Bagwell." Penelope thought he had the biggest, brightest smile she had ever seen. It was impossible not to smile back.

"Bags. Call me Bags. Everyone calls me Bags. I used to find it annoying but now I think it suits me." He said as he sprayed Penelope's legs with clear liquid from a little squirt bottle. "My own concoction. The ants hate it."

"It smells."

"Smells worse to the ants."

"You have a cool looking house." Penelope offered. It was big and a little boxy. Like everything else in St. Georges, it had an almost perfect quality about it.

"Villa. They call them villas so they can charge more. And thank you. I like the view."

"From up there," she asked pointing to the screened in lanai on the third floor of his villa.

He nodded. "I can see the marina and beyond it to the open water. I can see the boats coming and going and the dolphins when they come into the harbor to hunt. In the spring, when the eagles are here, I can see their nest with binoculars. Sometimes, I can see my neighbors through the binoculars too."

"Sounds magical." Penelope responded, trying not to sound snarky.

"The sunsets are the best, though. That's what makes the Gulf Coast superior, you know."

"So I've heard. Well thanks for the stinky spray. I should probably be going now."

"You're quite welcome, Penelope. It was a pleasure to meet you. Say, do you drive? I was thinking I might have some work for a young lady running errands for me."

"Oh . . . that's sweet of you to offer. I don't drive. I mean I do drive, but I don't have a license. I mean I don't drive without someone. I have a learner's permit."

"Oh, I see. Well how is the learning going?"

"Gas pedal, brake pedal, big round thing to steer with. It's really not that difficult."

"Indeed. Sounds like you have it all down. Maybe you can show me some time."

Penelope could see past him into the garage. She couldn't quite make it out but whatever was in the second garage stall was sleek, red, and very sexy. That was the kind of candy that might get her into an old man's van, she thought. He didn't seem to be going for that though. He just seemed lonely -- sweet and lonely, and old. "Maybe." She demurred.

"I've read one of your dad's books. I suspect he might like to go for a drive in my little convertible." He pointed over his shoulder. "I'll give him a ring and see if we can set something up."

"Ok, cool. Well, like I said . . . .."

"And come visit any time. I like visitors."

She smiled as she started walking. "Have a good day, Mr. Bagwell. I mean, Bags."

Chapter 5

Penelope soon learned that everyone in St. Georges knew Bags and loved him. Her dad knew exactly whom she was talking about when she told him their meet-cute story. He was apparently the unofficial social director of St. Georges. With Father's encouragement, Penelope spent parts of every day over the next two weeks helping Bags prepare for the Summer Gala. The entertainment was particularly important, he told her. Many St. Georges residents were snowbirds, migrating north at the beginning of every summer. The guest list for club events during the rest of the year filled quickly even if the entertainment wasn't likely to be good. There were enough members still around during the summer to fill a party. In fact, Bags and some of the other residents wouldn't have much social life in June without the Summer Gala. But to make sure it was a party worth attending, the entertainment had to be "top notch," Bags said.

Penelope thought it only a little sad that she had been drawn into his excitement. The plan was all very secret and she liked that Bags trusted her to be one of the insiders. It was going to be a murder mystery theme. Bags had written the script himself. He was quite proud of all the inside jokes. None of it seemed funny to Penelope, which was just fine. She really didn't want to become an insider in a group with a median age of 70. In fact, the whole idea of a murder mystery dinner party seemed a bit over the top. Bags disagreed. He said it could be a big hit if everyone in the "cast" took it seriously. The key, he said, would be the little details in the staging and the performances. Everything had to be "just so."

Bags used to do this kind of thing for a living, and did it well enough to make big piles of money, so she tried not to roll her eyes, at least not while he was watching. Besides, watching him fuss over every little thing was fun. Today he was trying to work out a realistic way to make a nine-inch chef's knife stick out of the murder victim's back. He wanted to call in help from a friend who did special effects. She overheard him on the phone a few days ago talking about blood packs and Bluetooth triggering devices. Very elaborate. The problem was the "talent, " as Bags called Harry, the volunteer murder victim. Harry had moved to St. Georges about a year ago and was viewed by most as a bit of an outsider. Bags considered it a coup that he was able to persuade Harry to take a prominent role in the production and Harry did not like the idea of dealing with Hollywood special effects contraptions. It had to be simple.

"Why does Harry have to be such a Diva?" Bags snorted. "Don't you dare tell him I said that." He looked at Penelope.

"What happens in the garage stays in the garage." She responded.

"Good. Now how am I going to make this stupid plastic knife look real without riling the diva?"

"Hmmm. He's going to stumble in through the doors to the veranda, right?"

"That's right."

"And he doesn't have to be in the room just before that."

"Keep going."

"We're going to cut the end of the blade off, I assume. Maybe we can rig it with gaffer tape to the back of his shirt -- two little flaps to hold the knife? Then we cut a slit in his tuxedo jacket and stick the knife through. We can use a little fake blood to hide the exposed tape." Penelope explained.

"Ruin his tuxedo jacket? He certainly won't let us do that. And even if he did, the fake blood is a definite deal breaker for him."

"We won't tell him about the blood. We'll just do it real quick. He'll never know until it's all done and by then he won't care because everyone will be telling him what a great job he did."

"Devious. You have a knack for this, Penelope. But what about the ripped jacket issue?"

"Please. He's worth like a bazillion dollars, right? I'll talk to him. He will say yes to me."

"Penelope, my dear, I have no doubt. Excellent. We have solved our last problem. All we have left is to rehearse. Now go see if you can find Harry before rehearsal tonight." Bags tousled Penelope's hair like she was a ten-year-old boy. She couldn't decide if it was annoying or cute.

She did as instructed. Harry's house was on her way home. The lanais at the back of the row of houses ending with the Bags Villa looked across the marina onto the back of Harry's place. It sprawled across two or three lots. Penelope had only heard descriptions of the inside. One wing, it seemed, was devoted to a master suite. In the middle were the common areas -- kitchen, dining room, party room, and the like. And the far wing was two stories of guest suites.

From the front the guest suites were hidden behind a drive flanked by two rows of garage doors -- at least eight. The man who built it liked cars, apparently. In the middle was a portico covering the front doors, which matched the scale of the house. The far wing housed the master suite and there were no windows looking out onto the street. Penelope wondered if that was for privacy. If so, it seemed ironic because the back of the master suite looked onto the water through floor to ceiling windows, which meant everyone at the club, on a boat, by the pool, or in one of the villas could see right into the master suite.

Actually, to see in, the shades had to be all the way up and the lighting just right. That apparently never happened with the first occupants but the word was Harry was not as attentive -- or didn't care. At least that's what "they" said. Penelope had heard enough about what "they" said back at school to know the anonymous rabble tended to be wrong a lot.

She rang the bell, hoping Harry would answer. Penelope had a plan for working Harry. It did not involve Harry's wife. While an unusual amount of time passed, Penelope mused what a burden it must be a to have a house so big it was a trek to the front door.

"Hello. And who might you be?"

"My name is Penelope, sir. I'm helping Mr. Bagwell with the Gala this weekend and I have a bit of a problem."

"Yes, of course, the young Miss Hazard. Well, it sounds like you better come in and tell me all about it, Penelope."

"Thank you, sir."

"Harry. Please call me Harry. I bet Bags doesn't let you get away with calling him 'sir' or 'Mr. Bagwell,' does he?"

"No, sir, I mean Harry. He does not."

"Lemonade? Ice tea? We might have some cookies. Come in and sit."

"Nothing to drink for me. Thanks, though." Penelope followed Harry into a large open area looking out onto the marina. She sat on the edge of an oversized chair. Harry was about the same height as Bags. Actually, he might be a little shorter but his posture was very erect, which made him appear taller. He had the same full head of dark hair. Penelope thought his features had likely become increasingly severe as he aged. She imagined he had been pretty handsome a few decades ago.

"Very well. Now tell me what problem Bags has sent you over to solve for him. He's quite mad, you know. All this bother over a little play acting is silly, don't you think?"

"A little, maybe. He just really wants it to be fun for everyone."

"I know. He's a born showman. Can't help it. Hard to say 'no' when he starts working on you, isn't it?"

"We both know the answer to that, don't we, Harry." She smiled. He laughed. "Here's the thing. My one contribution to this little party is an idea about how to make the knife look real while it's sticking out of you and Bags says you will have nothing to do with it."

"Not more of his special-effects-team-flying-in-to-fix-me-up nonsense! He's right. I'll have none of that."

"No, sir, Harry, I mean. I told him we could get the same effect by cutting the knife and taping it to stick straight out of your back. Then you stagger in, collapse on your face, and it's all perfect."

"But . . .."

"He says you're too cheap to let us slice a hole in your tuxedo jacket."

"He said that, did he?" Harry cackled. "It's not the cost. Not at all. I have more darn tuxedos than I need. I could just wear an old one and toss it the next day. The problem is the hole itself."

"What do you mean?" Penelope asked, caught off guard by Harry's tone.

"You see, Penelope, I have made a lot of money by making sure every detail in every plan of mine was exactly right, triple checked. In my world, everything has to be just right, perfect actually. When things feel not quite perfect, it gets to me. I like order, require it really, quite a bit more than is good for me, they say. So it's the hole. I don't wear clothes with holes in them -- ever. Clothes have holes, of course, but holes that are not supposed to be there. I just can't do that."

"Wow, I hadn't thought about that." Penelope said apologizing.

"Why would you? It's not normal. It's a terrible thing to live with."

"I can't imagine. I bet your room is all tidy and perfect, too."

"Hmmm, 'my room.' Yes, all my rooms have to be that way. I take it your room is not perfect?"

"I bet you would have a stroke just looking in from the hall. I'm kinda messy, which, come to think of it, makes us a lot alike."

"How so?"

"Well, your life is perfect and orderly, just like your house and your clothes. And my life is a total mess, just like my room."

"I wish you could teach me to be messy. I wish I could wear a tuxedo jacket with a silly little hole in it for you. I don't think I could even put it on. I'm sorry."

"Hmmm, have you ever worn a costume to a party?"

"Of course."

"I bet your costumes are always perfect."

"Well they don't have any extra holes, that's for sure."

"Could you wear a costume to the Gala?"

"I could. To what end?"

"What if your costume was a tuxedo, perfect in every respect, except for a large knife sticking perfectly out from your back?"

"I don't follow."

"Give me your old tuxedo jacket and I will make a costume of it -- one with a single, perfectly tailored slit, just the size of the corresponding plastic knife that completes your costume." Penelope offered.

"I don't know . . .."

"I'll do some stitching all around the edges of the slit. It won't be a hole. It will be a necessary opening. Without it, your costume will be imperfect."

"But a fake knife wound would never be perfect without some fake blood." He countered.

"Harry, if that's what it takes to make this perfect, then that's what we're going to do." Penelope smiled and made her eyes as wide and adorable as possible.

"Penelope, you are one clever young lady. I think this will be just right. I'll go get the jacket." Harry started toward the master suite. "Now don't let Bags think he had anything to do with me agreeing to this."

"Our secret. Promise."

Chapter 6

"Would you like another Shirley Temple, my dear?" Bags asked.

"Maybe. I can go and get it, though." Penelope pushed back from the table, stood, and draped her napkin across the armrest, excusing herself from the pre-dinner conversation. She stopped in the ladies room, mostly to check the mirror and make sure she didn't look silly.

It was hard not to look silly sitting next to Marika. Penelope guessed she was from somewhere in Eastern Europe; probably somewhere exotic like Romania or Bulgaria. She was kind of ancient, probably over forty, and she still managed to look scary hot -- not nubile, vacant, beach bunny hot, but more like walking out of the Paris street scene on television perched on impossible heels and dripping with diamonds, hot. It didn't matter what she was wearing, with her dark hair, green eyes and perfect curves, Marika always managed to make every other woman in the room invisible. Tonight she was actually trying so no one stood a chance. She would call it a little black dress. It probably didn't cost as much as Penelope's and she still managed to make it look like Coco Chanel designed it just for her. So annoying.

The stupid puberty struck boys at her old school would still prefer the mean girls -- because those boys were stupid and immature. Father, on the other hand, would have been sitting next to Marika leaving a big pile of drool on his plate. It was just as well that he begged off on the dinner invitation.

Bags was a bit more in control of himself. Only his eyes gave him away. Very sparkly tonight. Marika was alluring. That's the word. She was alluring in every sense of the word and she knew it.

Penelope headed for the bar, where, hopefully, she would not look quite so much like a 12 year old boy. It was quiet tonight. This was the first time she had been in the bar without adult supervision. Penelope recognized the bartender. "Hi there, Mr. Billings."

"That's 'Bud' to you, young lady." He flashed his trademark ear to ear, California surfer dude smile.

"Ok, Buuuddd," she drawled his name, returning the smile. Penelope wondered if all bartenders were charming like Bud, and handsome. "Can I get a Shirley Temple, Bud?"

"Sure thing, Miss Penelope. You here with your dad tonight?"

"Nope. He's home pretending to write -- probably watching TV. I'm here with Bags and Ms. Jones."

"Ms. Marika, eh? Bags must be feeling pretty smug about that."

"If you mean he must be behaving like a stupid boy, then, yes he is feeling smug about his little date with Ms. Jones."

Penelope wondered if Bud was as puppy dog infatuated with "Ms. Jones" as all the "mature" gentlemen that congregated around her at St. Georges. She guessed Bud was a little younger than Marika. Except for the age difference -- guys, particularly older guys, like in college, seemed to go for younger women -- Marika seemed like the kind of girl Bud might like.

She might like him too. With the square shoulders and sun-wrinkled face of a man most comfortable out on the water or in it, Bud was ruggedly handsome with just a hint of danger -- looks Hemingway would approve of, or rather, "of which he would approve." When he smiled, he had a touch of Bobby Cobb goofiness about him -- a little sparkle in his eyes -- that softened him just enough. Of course, Marika was way out of his league. Even a handsome bartender was still a bartender and Marika could do much better than that on any number of levels.

"A little jealous of the attention she gets, I take it."

"Ha ha. A little. I like it better when it's just Bags and me. Actually, it works best when she's not even in the same room with me. I'm sorry. That's mean. She's just so beautiful and elegant and sophisticated, blah, blah, blah."

"Yeah, I guess some men go for that kind of woman." He smiled and handed her the drink.

"How long has she been a member here?" Penelope asked.

"Oh, she's no more a member than me. Well, that's not technically true. I'm just the help. They let me in because I'm on the payroll. She's kinda the unofficial St. George's mascot."

"How's that work?"

"She's very popular with the members and not just the dirty old men."

"Really?"

"Yep, she leads an exercise class here two mornings a week and a lot of the women go to her yoga studio too. She gives massages and does Reiki -- and also nutrition consulting and natural medicine."

"Wait, what's Reiki? Is that even a thing?" Penelope curled up her nose.

"It's some kind of bullshit -- sorry -- new age, chakra, aura, nonsense."

"So yoga, massage, new age stuff, and herbal tea. And that makes her popular? Huh. How do you know all this stuff, by the way?"

"I'm a bartender. I hear all kinds of stuff. Part of my job is to listen and to keep the secret stuff secret. They call it 'discretion.' But Ms. Popular's list of services is hardly a secret."

"I've seen her around a lot."

"She makes house calls sometimes. And, like tonight, the members take turns inviting her to dinner. Bags takes more turns."

"Yeah, Bags is bringing her to the Summer Gala."

"Well you won't have to worry about her stealing attention at the Gala. Bags will be in the zone."

"Tell me about it. He's wearing me out with his big plans." Penelope sighed, shoulders slumped and elbows on the bar on either side of her glass.

"Yeah, I've heard you guys talking about it. You'll have to tell me how it goes. I have that night off."

"Lucky you."

"Yeah, the new guy will be working the Gala. The tips are crummy at the big events. Too much work not to get paid."

"What do you think of the lovely Ms. Jones, Bud?"

"Me. I'm just the bartender. I get paid to not think too much about any of my customers. Discretion, remember. Besides, I hear a lot about her but I don't really know her. She's not the kind of woman who ever has to go and get her own drink."

"That was a total non-answer, Bud. Come on, you see everything around here. You must have some opinion."

"Well, just judging by what I've seen, she's the kind of woman who causes trouble wherever she goes, never intentionally, of course, but trouble all the same. I'd be willing to bet she's caused a lot of heartache without even realizing it."

"Wow, ok, so I guess you do have an opinion." Penelope reacted, sensing Bud had a little heartbreak in his past. "Now that I have you talking, what other kind of things do you hear?"

"Usually, I hear way too much about people's business that doesn't involve or interest me."

"Must be kind of fun being the keeper of everyone's secrets." Penelope said, hoping he would dangle something interesting her way.

"Sure, more entertaining than a reality show sometimes. But sometimes you hear things you really didn't want to hear. Things you can't unhear. It can be unfortunate."

"Like what?" Now Bud definitely had her attention. It wasn't so much what he said as the way the sparkle in his eyes went dead when he said it.

"Well, see, if I told you, then you couldn't unhear. Also, it would violate bartender-patron confidentiality." Bud grinned.

28

"That's not a thing, though, right? I mean if someone told you about a plan to rob a bank or kidnap the president, you wouldn't keep that to yourself?"

"Depends. I might keep quiet if it was one of my big tippers." The grin got bigger.

"Whatever, Bud. You are not playing along well at all. You're lucky I need to get back to the table. I suspect at some point Bags might slip out of his trance and notice I've gone missing."

"You sure you're just a kid, Ms. Penelope?"

She smiled. "Wait let me go stand next to Marika and make sure."

"No one likes a bitter teenager, Ms. Penelope."

"No one but you. See ya, Bud. Thanks for the drink."

Chapter 7

Mother was out of the country the night of the Gala, which meant Penelope made it out of the house in a dress that otherwise would have been pronounced "not age appropriate," which was what her mom said when she was thinking "slutty." It wasn't. Mother was just out of touch.

Her dad cared only that she not expose skin too close to her girl parts and, in general, his standards were looser than Mother's, which was just one of the ways parental stereotypes seemed flipped in Penelope's family. It wasn't a scandalous dress, just calculated to allow her to pass for 18, or maybe even 21. Tonight was just a game of dress-up, anyway. Everyone would know her, although the new bartender might serve her anyway, just on the chance it might help things work out for him. He was a bit creepy like that, but very cute.

Too bad for him she really didn't like booze. Things rattled around in her head way too much as it was. Anything lining up against her in the ongoing battle to control her brain chaos was not welcome. Plus, she didn't care for the burning sensation of alcohol sliding down her throat. Penelope wished Bud was there tonight. Bud didn't treat her like a kid but also didn't creep her out.

Bags was flitting about the room when Penelope arrived. She caught glimpses of him here and there, never in the same place more than a few breaths. She stayed with her dad like the good daughter as he made smalltalk and worked his way to the bar. When he found someone sharing his disdain for smalltalk, Penelope paired them up at the bar and slipped away.

She found Bags on the veranda going over stage directions with his little cast of volunteers. Harry feigned disdain for the whole process but Penelope could tell he was enjoying himself, maybe more than he ever had at such a function. She hardly recognized her friend Bags. From the back, only modestly thinning hair just on top and a slight roundness to his shoulders gave away anything about his age. It was true, a good tuxedo made a man look taller, younger, thinner, and smarter. She was used to seeing Bags in worn out boat shoes, water shorts, and a Hawaiian shirt and wasn't prepared for the contrast. He cleaned up well. All of them did, even Father. She was pretty sure, in his head, Father pretended to be Raglan Dunne whenever he wore his tux.

"There you are, Penelope. Look at you. You are a vision."

"Aww! Thanks, Mr. Bagwell. You look very handsome."

"You have to love a girl who knows how to lie. Isn't that right, Harry?"

"Well, Bags, I think what she meant was that you look uncharacteristically well groomed." Harry joined the conversation.

"Bags is right, dear. You do look lovely tonight, not that it is possible for you to look otherwise. Oh, to be young."

"Why thank you, Mrs. Fortwater." Penelope gave a little curtsy and smiled. "I love your dress." Mildred Fortwater, tonight's designated murderer, was definitely dressed for the spotlight. "You look very handsome too, Mr. Cumberson." Penelope winked at her new friend Harry.

"I was told Mr. Bagwell was requesting my presence." Dr. Patterson said as he approached the group.

"Ahh, now the gang is all here. Good to see you, Roger." Bags grabbed his hand for a shake and pulled him into a huddle formation with the others.

"Ok, maestro, lay it on us." Harry prompted.

"Very good. For review, when the surf and turf is in front of everyone, I will take the microphone, welcome the group and launch into a few jokes, because the crowd will expect as much."

"By which you mean you can't help yourself." Roger chirped at Bags.

"Don't be jealous, Roger." Mildred defended.

"Anyway," Bags continued. "I will announce that the committee has decided the evening's program should be educational. A mix of laughter and boos will follow. I will then launch into an elaborate introduction for our distinguished guest speaker, Future Harry. In the middle of that Harry will crash through the veranda doors behind me, stagger around a bit for effect, and collapse face first on the dance floor. Harry, be theatrical. Really sell it. There is no such thing as too much."

"I will do my best. It really isn't my nature, I'm afraid."

"You will be great. I feel it." Bags continued. "The crowd will react. I will call for a doctor and Roger will come up and pronounce Harry dead with a gasp. The audience will react again. When the noise dies, I will signal to Penelope and she will kill the lights. Harry will rise like Lazarus and slip back through the doors to the veranda."

"And how long do I have to stay out there?" Harry asked.

"Just long enough to change your clothes and come back in as present-day Harry. Now, when the lights come back on, I will explain to the audience that there has been a murder and that it seems certain someone at the party is our murderer. I will ask them to work in teams by table to uncover the clues and solve the mystery of this horrible crime."

"I think we can handle all that, Bags." Roger offered.

"And Mildred, do you have your cues down?" Bags asked.

"Of course, darling, and overacting will be no problem at all."

"I have no doubt. Now the most critical thing is for you to get up and walk out of the dining room right when I begin to speak and then not reappear until the lights come back on." Bags coached her.

"I will be like the wind. This is going to be such fun!"

With that the huddle broke. Penelope left Bags to his last minute fussing and found Father, still in the bar, to escort him to their table, which was front and center at the edge of the temporary parquet dance floor that would be their stage tonight. Marika was already seated, as were Commodore Riley and his wife Lesley. She found all the nautical stuff amusing. "Commodore" meant "yacht club president."

Penelope felt a little sorry for Marika. She was used to having full attention from her date -- most every male in the room, actually -- and Bags would be distracted until the murder mystery reached the climactic reveal. Ok, she wasn't really feeling sorry for Marika. Father would no doubt pick up the slack for Bags. Hopefully he wouldn't drool too much. Boys.

Dr. Patterson and his wife Doris joined them after a few minutes to complete the table. The staff had orders to serve their table first so Bags and Penelope had time to eat before they went to work. The salad was already down before Bags sat. As predicted, he was distracted and Marika seemed confused. Also as predicted, Father was doing his best to keep her from feeling lonely.

Penelope didn't like the salad. The jumble of mixed greens, only some of which she had seen before, reminded her of the pile she would end up with after weeding the flower beds at their house in Illinois. No thank you. She asked Dr. Patterson to pass the bread and hoped the main course would be edible. Steak, she wanted steak, and some potatoes, hopefully with some kind of cheese or sauce.

When it came, the main course made her smile -- filet with a nice sauce and potatoes covered with cheese. To be fair, at this point she would have eaten her shoes. Bags insisted it needed to be dark for the show, which meant a very late dinner given how long the sun stayed up in June. She looked. It was 9:30. She definitely was about to eat her shoes. By that logic, though, she would have lapped up the scallops sitting next to her steak. Instead, she immediately slid them onto Father's plate. He assured her they were delicious and Penelope believed him. Didn't matter. She could stomach very little of what came out of the water and scallops were not on the list. There was only time for the steak anyway. She and Bags ate quickly and soon he was out of his seat with the microphone in his hand.

"Good evening everyone. Such a fantastic turnout tonight. Give yourselves a hand." He began. Penelope was not quite sure why they deserved self-applause -- maybe for staying alive so long. He continued. "Ladies, you all look radiant tonight, every one of you. Fellas, don't they look radiant tonight?" More applause -- just the boys. "And fellas, don't you look . . . well, I guess there is only so much a tuxedo can do." Laughter. "Ladies, let's give your men a hand for providing such wonderful contrast to your beauty." Laughter and applause.

"Seriously, the entertainment committee has put a great deal of thought into tonight's program and I know you were expecting some elaborate theme or over the top production. Although this is not the Commodore's Ball, we were determined to honor our fine new Commodore. Robert, raise your hand so everyone knows where you are." The Commodore turned in his chair and waived to the room. "So thinking about Robert and how best we could support him in his new role, we decided an educational program might be best." Big laughs, and a mock fist waive from the Commodore.

Penelope listened intently, while standing in the little opening leading from dining room to kitchen, hand poised on the bank of switches that would kill the lights. The staff knew it was coming and had discretely retreated to the kitchen to avoid knocking into guests during the blackout. It was the cheesiest stuff imaginable and the crowd was eating it up. Bags knew his audience and knew how to play to a crowd. It was adorable, not really her thing, but adorable, nonetheless.

"We conducted a vast search for just the right speaker. But in the end we concluded one of our very own would be the perfect fit for tonight's event -- with just one minor modification, that is." Polite laughter. Anticipatory, maybe? "You all know our good friend Harry Cumberson and I know we all ask ourselves the same question about Harry . . . 'what will he be up to next?'" Laughter. Nodding heads. "To answer that question and many others for you, please allow me to introduce Future Harry, who comes to visit us from his active post-retirement retirement community far far away at the modest age of 120 years old!"

"So this is Harry two years from now?" Someone at the back of the room yelled out. Laughter.

"Now, Walt, you know the rules, I have the microphone so I get to do the jokes." More laughs, interrupted by the doors behind Bags flying open.

"Arrgghhh," Harry stumbled through, one hand raised in front of him pleadingly, the other reaching desperately over his shoulder. "Arrgghhh."

34

Two stumbling steps to the middle of the parquet. "I've been . . . I've . . .." Theatrically. "Murdered!" He gasps and collapses face down.

The audience gasps with him. A mix of more gasps, nervous laughter, and murmuring follows. "The drama gets them every time," Bags murmurs before bringing the mic to his mouth. "Ladies, gentlemen, please, I beg you, remain calm. Doctor, so glad you are so close." Bags winks at the audience. "Please, do something!"

On cue Dr. Patterson rises from his chair and kneels by Harry's side. The crowd falls silent, waiting, watching as Doctor Patterson leans in close, pretending to listen for breathing, prodding Harry's very still body in exaggerated fashion, and trying desperately to get Harry to break character. "Bags, this is horrible. Horrible."

"What is it, Roger?"

"He's . . . Future Harry, that is . . . is, well he's deceased!" Gasps and groans follow.

"Roger, do you have any idea what the cause of death might be?" Bags asked with vaudevillian flair.

"Well, Bags, I'm not an expert on this kind of thing." Giggles from those close enough to see the body. "But I have to believe that big knife sticking out his back could have something to do with it." Raucous laughter.

"Roger, I think you might be on to something!" More laughs. "Wow! That's a big knife! Something like that has to sting a little." More laughs, more subdued.

That was her cue, "sting a little." Penelope flipped the switches and the whole dining room went dark. The murmuring that followed masked the shuffling noise of Bags and Roger helping Harry to his feet and back out the veranda doors. She counted slowly, as instructed, and also as instructed, flipped the lights back on when she reached ten.

"Oh my," Bags mock exclaimed. "The body seems to have disappeared." The continuing laughter signaled his command of the room, as if that had been in doubt. "Oh well, I suppose that's for the best. Seeing Future Harry dead might upset present-day Harry. He will already be upset enough. He was really looking forward to hearing himself speak." Laughter.

"Kinda like you, Bags." Someone shouted.

"I have no idea what you're talking about."

Penelope returned to the table as Bags spelled out how the mystery game would work. Father and the others gushed to her and Roger about how clever the opening scene was. She wondered when Harry might reappear. He was missing out on a good steak. She thought he would eat steak. Maybe not. She knew he was very picky -- OCD picky -- but he had to eat something.

Bags had begun to overstay his welcome; at least Penelope was done listening to him. Of course, she had heard it all before in the rehearsals so it was probably just her. Rather than fidget, she excused herself and headed to the bar for a drink -- which sounded more sophisticated than going to get a refill on her diet soda. Navigating the transaction with creepy boy bartender was not ideal but she would be waiting forever if she relied on the servers to bring it to her. Bobby was around 22, she imagined, and by far the most age appropriate boy on the premises. He was cute and he knew it. He never said anything overtly icky to her. And the few times she had seen him around, inside the club or doing odd jobs out on the dock, he was nice. Trouble was, he was still a boy and she could see in his eyes the same eagerness -- hunger even -- she saw in men whenever Marika was around. She was pretty sure he knew she was only 15. Eww!

"Penelope Hazard. You look like you just came from a photo shoot. Cover of Elle or Vogue?"

"Ha ha ha, Bobby. You get that I'm not the one in my family who does the tipping, right?" Sweet and yet creepy, she thought.

"I'm hurt, Ms. Hazard. Deeply hurt."

"Whatever. Refill please." She plopped her glass on the bar. "Speaking of tips, did you know Bud stuck you with this shift because the members tend not to tip much at these events?"

"Really, maybe he's used to raking it in but I'm pretty happy with the night so far." He pointed to a big glass on the counter stuffed with bills.

"Wow, that looks pretty good to me too. Maybe you're just better at this than Bud."

He grinned. "Diet?"

"Yes, please." Very cute. Still a little creepy, but cute.

"How is the Gala going? It should be rocking by now. I've poured enough drinks to lubricate a frat house."

"I know, right? Do all old people drink like this?" Penelope really hadn't been around people older than her parents until they moved to St. Georges.

"Not sure. All I know is this crowd can hold its own with anyone."

"Hey, what was that?" Penelope heard a noise. It sounded like something rustling around out on the veranda.

"Not sure. Raccoon maybe." Bobby said, hardly paying attention.

"Raccoon, really?"

"Oh yeah, or a possum, or maybe even a bobcat. Lots of wildlife around here."

"Who knew?" Penelope was about to move on when she heard something louder, like something falling. "Ok, that was not a raccoon."

Penelope was already at the door before Bobby had a chance to suggest she shouldn't go alone. From the corner of her eye she could see him follow.

"Eeeeeeehhh!" She heard herself scream. Bobby pulled open the door between the bar and veranda.

"Holy crap!" Bobby exclaimed, his voice going uncontrollably falsetto.

"Oh my god, oh my god, oh my god!" Penelope yelled as she knelt beside Harry, who was definitely not acting.

"Is this part of the program?" Bobby quizzed, clearly thinking he may have just sounded girly for no reason.

"What do you think?" Penelope turned and he could see she was now sobbing.

"Help! Help! Out on the veranda. We need help!" Bobby ran to the dining room doors as he yelled.

Bags was first out the door with Roger right behind. "What's this?" Roger uttered mostly to himself. Just as before, he knelt beside Harry. This time he was doing his real doctor thing.

A crowd was gathering and Bags was trying, in the calmest way, to convey that this was not part of the show. He was swimming upstream with an audience so used to his tricks and so filled with liquid cheer. "Please everyone. Quiet. This is the real thing. Give Roger some room."

After what seemed like a long time but was not, Roger looked up at Bags and the crowd. Even in the dim of the moonlight, they could read his face. The gasps began as he spoke. "I'm afraid he's dead. Harry really is dead this time."

Penelope didn't move from his side. All she could do was kneel there beside him, ruining her fabulous dress, sobbing uncontrollably. Then she felt herself being lifted. The next thing she knew, Penelope was sitting in one of the club chairs in the bar with Bags and her dad standing over her. There was a loud noise pulsing in frantic rhythm in her ears. Through the fog and the noise she could hear her dad saying something over and over. Eventually the noise weakened enough for Penelope to realize it was her breath sucking and blowing in absolute panic.

"Here have this, Penelope." Bags offered her a glass.

"Go on Sweet Pea, it will help." Her dad added.

"What is it?"

"Medicine." Her dad said, grinning a little at Bags.

"Seriously?"

"It will help, Pea. Just have a big slog."

Penelope took the tumbler of amber liquid, steadied her breathing, and took the biggest gulp she dared. "Holy crap! That's awful. My throat is on fire."

"Hey, that's 20-year old single malt you're cursing." Bags tried for a touch of levity.

"He's really gone?"

"I'm afraid so, Pea. I'm so sorry you had to see that."

"What happened?"

"We're not quite sure, Penelope." Bags took over. Dr. Patterson has called the Sheriff. It looks like he might have fallen and hit his head.

"Or maybe a heart attack or stroke or something like that." Penelope half asked.

"Maybe. He was very fit, of course, so that seems less likely."

"I guess. I just hope he wasn't in pain. I feel so bad for him." Penelope began to cry again.

"Maybe we should get you home and to bed, Pea." Her dad directed more than asked.

"Ok."

"Keep an eye on her tonight, Axel. Call Roger if you need anything. You have his number, correct?" Bags asked.

"I will. And, yes, I have the doctor's number. Are you sure he wouldn't mind?" Axel was a little dazed himself.

"My dear boy, Penelope is one of us. Of course he wouldn't mind."

"Thank you. Thank you so much. Let's get you home now, Pea."

And that is all Penelope remembered of the evening.

Chapter 8

"Where am I? Who are you?" Penelope asked, startling herself awake.

"You are safe. Don't worry."

"Where's my dad? I want my dad?" Penelope could barely remember her name, had no idea where she was, and did not know the woman looking down at her. She was vaguely aware of a pain in her shoulder.

"Soon. We just need to ask you some questions about last night."

"Why? What happened last night?"

"You don't remember? You had quite a scare."

"I feel drugged. Did you drug me? I don't mean to be rude but who are you?"

"We gave you something to make you calm. Like I said, you had a scare last night."

"My head is buzzing. It's not good when my head starts buzzing. I feel woozy too." Penelope looked down at her toes poking out from the blanket and wondered how she ended up on this little cot in this little room with pale gray walls.

"Do you remember anything about what happened last night?"

"No, not anything, really. What happened? Do I know you? Should I know this place?" Whatever happened, this woman really wanted to hear about it, which frightened Penelope.

"Still foggy, I guess. Don't worry. I'm sure it will come back to you soon. And, no, you should not know me or this place. You're not going crazy, I promise."

"Whoever you are, you need to give me something to call you, don't you think?"

"You can call me Agent K."

"Seriously? And what about your friend standing by the door? Should I call her Agent J or is she Zed?"

"I hadn't thought of that. Good for you. A sense of humor is a very good sign. They told me you were clever. That is Agent M at the door." Agent K said. Agent M stood expressionless in the doorway hiding behind tinted glasses.

"If you say so. Since I don't remember anything, maybe you should just let me go."

"I think if you rest a little more, maybe have a nap, your memory will return. The medicine we gave you should help." Agent K persisted.

"I guess I don't really have a choice." Somehow Penelope was sure they would not let her leave.

"Good. We will leave you. If you need anything, just call or waive your arms. We won't be far."

With that, Agents M and K departed, closing the thick gray door behind them with a solid clank. Penelope looked under the blanket. She was wearing long, pink pajama bottoms and a silky, white t-shirt. Whatever happened last night, these were not likely the clothes she was wearing. Penelope knew she should be terrified but somehow she wasn't. Her brain was telling her she was trapped in an undisclosed location being held against her will and at the same time saying "and everything will be fine." Most troubling of all, Penelope was not restrained in the bed and could move her arms easily but had no sensation of being able to sit up or even roll over. Whatever they were, she was not a fan of the drugs Agent K had given her.

Penelope contemplated what "scare" she had had the night before and what the women with hokey fake names wanted. Her memories were somewhere tucked away in her head. She knew that from the Science Channel and also from experience. Things frequently went missing in the jumble inside her brain but were never gone. Usually they didn't stay hidden long and, so far, things had come back when she really needed them. Penelope decided the best thing might be to sleep off the drugs and so she forced herself to let go.

Chapter 9

"Morning Sweet Pea. Time to wake up!" No response.

"Seriously, Penelope, it's kind of late."

"Dad, stop. Go away." Penelope snarled from under several layers of comfort.

"Five minutes and I'll be back with the ice water alarm." Father was using his annoyingly singsong morning voice. She hated that voice. What she hated more was the ice water alarm. No way she could risk more snuggling. Father never bluffed about the ice water.

Penelope sat up and plopped her legs over the edge of the bed. She was exhausted, and sore all over, and agitated. There was something from a dream . . . oh yeah, the crazy Men in Black chicks and the room with gray walls. But there was something else too.

"Counting down, Penelope. You don't want to keep your guest waiting? Do you need me to come help you get dressed?"

"No, I'm good." Any other day and she might have called that bluff. She and Father had reached the awkward, "can't see each other except fully clothed" stage. Guest? She didn't think she was expecting anyone. There was something lingering out there, though, something she should remember.

"Two minute warning."

"Stop!" Penelope pulled on shorts, slipped on a bikini top, and grabbed a t-shirt. Oh crap! Harry! That's what it was. That's why she was so tired and agitated. Suddenly the whole evening rushed back to the front of her brain. Penelope felt sick. She bent over and put her hand on the bed to steady herself.

"Hey, Penelope," Father poked his head in the door. "Seriously, are you feeling ok?" This time his voice was soft.

"Yeah, I'm good, sort of . . . maybe . . . I don't know." She could hear herself begin to babble. "Who's here?"

"Bags stopped by to check on you. Very sweet. He also wants to ask you some questions."

"Poor Bags. All that work on the Gala and it turned into . . .." She trailed off.

"I know. It's a horrible thing for everyone."

"Poor Harry. So sweet and silly." Penelope could feel the tears coming.

"I can send him away, if you're not ready, Pea. He won't mind."

"No. I want to see him. Be down in a minute."

Penelope was dressed and only needed a quick trip to the bathroom before she faced the day. The mirror check was hardly reassuring. She washed some leftover makeup from her face and pulled her hair into a tight ponytail to disguise the tangled mess that developed overnight. Good enough. It's not like there would be paparazzi.

"Good morning, Sunshine." Bags called to her before she hit the bottom stair.

"Morning, Bags. Is it actually still morning?"

"Barely," Father interjected.

"I hear you have some questions about last night."

"Sadly, yes. Maybe we should sit." He pointed to the club chairs in the living room.

"I'll bring some drinks." Father offered.

Penelope followed Bags and plopped into the chair facing his.

"First things first. How are you feeling this morning, Penelope? Last night was a horrible thing for anyone to see and particularly someone so young and sweet." Bags began.

"I don't really know how I feel. It's just all so weird. I mean I didn't really know Harry that well, but still . . .. It's so sad to think he's just gone." Penelope could feel the tears welling.

"I think that's how we all feel, my dear. 'Weird' is as good a word as any. We do not have to talk right now if you're not up to it."

"That's sweet, but I don't see it getting better any time soon. You want to talk to me because I'm the one who found him, right?"

"Yes, and I'm afraid it's more than idle curiosity. You see I am the designated liaison between St. Georges and the County. We take turns so we aren't all complaining to them separately about speeding cars, hooligans, potholes, and the like."

"And crimes too."

"Yes, we've had a few attempted break-ins and the occasional suspicious stranger lurking around, but never a homicide. This is new territory, I'm afraid."

"So you don't think it was an accident?"

"It may have been. The Sheriff likes that explanation because it means less work for him. I'm not convinced."

"Does the Sheriff want to talk to me too?"

"He does. I told him I would pop over this morning and make sure you were feeling up to it. What do you say?"

"As long as I can have you and my dad here when he's asking questions."

"Absolutely, my dear. I'll send him a text. He was shocked I knew how. That's age discrimination is what that is."

"Umm, to be fair, Bags, I just showed you how a couple of weeks ago."

"Hush, child. Clearly last night's events have you confused." Bags grinned as he pawed at his phone. "Ok, I think he will be here shortly. While we wait, what can you tell me about last night?"

"It's still hazy. Everything was going perfectly. I was at the light switches and killed the lights on cue. Harry was face down when the lights went out. While it was dark I heard shuffling noises I thought were you and Dr. Patterson helping him up and out the doors. I flipped the lights back on. Harry was gone and you started explaining the game to everyone. We had been over that so much in rehearsal I got bored. No offense."

"I understand, my dear. Please continue."

"I didn't really want to go to the bar because the new bartender sometimes seems like he's flirting with me."

"Bobby?"

"Yeah, I know it's probably just my imagination but anyway, I was thirsty so I sucked it up and went to the bar."

"Who else was in the bar with you?" Bags asked.

"It was just Bobby and me. We talked and he refilled my soda."

"Did he do anything inappropriate?" Father asked.

"No, dad. Geez. He was very polite."

"How is it that you came to be on the veranda, then?"

"Bobby and I were talking and I heard a noise. He thought it was a raccoon or something but it sounded like something bigger. I couldn't put my finger on it."

"So you just went right outside to see? What were you thinking?" Father interrupted.

"I don't know. I didn't really think about it."

"And what did you see when you opened the door?" Bags redirected her.

"Nothing at first. It was dark. My eyes didn't adjust right away."

"Fair enough. Did you hear anything?"

Penelope closed her eyes and tried to recreate those first moments out on the veranda. "Behind me Bobby was saying something like 'wait for me.' To my right, I could hear voices from the dining room. Straight ahead was the harbor and I could hear the water lapping up against the boats or the sea wall maybe."

"Anything else?"

"To my left there was some rustling -- a breeze through the palms maybe -- something like that."

"Are you sure that's what you heard? Rustling?"

"I'm not sure. I hadn't seen Harry yet so I wasn't exactly on high alert."

"And then?" Bags kept her moving.

Penelope stuttered. "My eyes. It went from black to shades of dark and I could see a blob on the tile about halfway between the door to the bar and the doors back into the dining room. I was confused. Something looked wrong. I stared at the blob until I could see better. The next thing I remember I was on my knees next to Harry and I could hear myself screaming. I don't remember deciding to scream or opening my mouth. I just remember thinking 'that squealing noise is coming from me.' Then you were there and then everyone was there." Penelope took a deep breath.

"Did you see or hear anything else that struck you as unusual?"

"I don't think so. Once I saw him there on the ground everything was kind of a blur."

"I under-"

"Oh wait. There was one thing. Probably nothing, but you said 'anything unusual.'"

"I did, indeed."

"I could see Harry pretty clearly by the time you came through those dining room doors, so when they opened it was like this flash of light coming from behind your head." Penelope waited for a reaction from Bags.

"That seems natural on many levels, my dear." He smiled. Predictable. "Was that the unusual part?"

"No . . . it's probably nothing . . . it's just that the light seemed like, I don't know . . . like it flashed in stereo, just right at that first moment."

"Stereo? I'm not sure I understand." Bags tilted his head and Penelope could see his forehead crinkle.

"I know, right? It doesn't really make sense to me either. It was like there was an echo of the light coming from exactly the other direction and maybe even a little brighter. I don't know. If you didn't notice it, I'm sure it was nothing."

"Well, we will file that one away. You never know. What else do you remember?"

"After that you were with me in the bar. I remember you made me drink something very nasty. Is that why I feel so crappy today?"

"Possibly. Remember that feeling. Last night the whiskey was medicinal. You do not need to have it just for fun. It will always make you sick the next day. Trust me."

"Yes, Bags, thank you for the public service announcement. Maybe I'll tell the Sheriff about you contributing to my delinquency."

"There is my Penelope. Good, you must be feeling a little better to be such a pill." Bags grinned widely.

"So what do I do when the Sheriff gets here?"

Bags looked at her dad, who spoke. "Tell the truth, like you just told us. And don't be afraid. He's not going to try to make you afraid."

"Ok."

The doorbell rang almost on cue. Father answered and showed the Sheriff to the living room. Sheriff Phillips, he called himself. He asked most of the same questions as Bags. It seemed to go faster the second time through, although Penelope had the distinct feeling Sheriff Phillips was less invested in listening to the details. He was a big man with wide shoulders, a square jaw, short brown hair, bushy eyebrows and a very tidy uniform. Aviator sunglasses tucked in his shirt pocket completed the look. He was a cop from head to toe. He also had a very big smile and gentle voice, which told Penelope he was definitely a dad, too.

"Sheriff Phillips, if you don't mind me asking, what exactly did Harry, I mean Mr. Cumberson . . . umm, what did he die from?" Penelope asked without thinking.

"Well, young lady, I really can't say for sure until the autopsy results come back, but it looks like he took a very nasty blow to the right temple. I take it you couldn't see that when you were bent down next to him." The Sheriff replied.

"No. What do you think happened?"

"Again, nothing but speculation at this point. If I had to guess, I would say he somehow fell and hit his head. We may find that he had a stroke or heart attack, something like that, which made him lose control and fall."

Penelope looked at Bags. She could tell he wasn't buying the slip and fall theory. "So you don't think it was foul play?"

Sheriff Phillips smiled. "Miss, I think maybe you watch too much television. Can't rule it out until we've done some investigation, of course. But honestly, most of the violent crime around here is pretty straightforward. It's either drugs or a domestic situation of some kind -- crime of passion kind of thing -- and there usually isn't a lot of mystery involved."

"Ok."

"Don't you worry about it. You live in a nice, quiet neighborhood. What happened last night doesn't change that."

"Thank you, Sheriff. That helps." Penelope wanted to make him feel better. It was a harmless fib.

Father escorted the Sheriff out. On the way he promised to call Bags as soon as the autopsy results were available. It sounded like not much investigating was going to happen in the interim.

"That wasn't so hard was it, my dear?" Bags suggested.

"Not so bad."

"And how are you holding up after two cross-examinations?"

"I'm fine. Hey, what do you think of the Sheriff's accidental death theory?" Penelope quizzed.

"Hmmm, how should I put this? What most often makes people good at what they do is handling the things that happen frequently with great skill. Sheriff Phillips is no doubt very good at those things. This, however, seems like something that happens infrequently in his world." Bags danced.

"Yeah, he pretty much said that."

"He did. So his speculation may be no better than yours or mine."

"Except that we live here and know all the people." Penelope observed.

"And undoubtedly have more time to devote to the matter," Bags agreed, "Which has given me an idea."

She could see a little sparkle in his eye. It was only slightly different than the sparkle he had around Marika.

"Bags, I thought we talked about this." Father said firmly as he returned from the front door.

"Axel, my friend, I am only talking about a little harmless nosing around; a few harmless questions here and there and maybe a little bit of research online. I could use the help." Bags pleaded.

"What kind of parent would I be, letting my teenage daughter poke around behind the Sheriff's back in a potential murder investigation?" Father persisted.

"Dad, don't be so dramatic. Look at us. How much trouble could Bags and I possibly stir up riding around the neighborhood in the gold cart chatting with old people -- no offense, Bags."

"None taken, counselor."

"I promise . . . we promise . . . if we find anything at all worth talking about, we will call the Sheriff right away. Right Bags?" Penelope shot him a look.

"It goes without saying." He answered correctly.

"Pea, why would you even want to be involved with something like this? Aren't you shaken up enough after last night?"

"Of course. I'm totally freaked out. But if someone did something bad to Harry, that means there may be a murderer right here in St. Georges. I won't be able to sleep until I know for sure."

"I hadn't really thought about it that way. Could it have been someone from St. Georges?" Father looked at Bags. She had him on his heels.

"I'm afraid so, Axel. It's a gated community after all. We don't have strangers wandering around."

Father sighed. "Just like your mother. I don't know why I bother arguing with either of you."

"Thanks, dad. Thank you, thank you, thank you." Penelope wasn't exactly sure why she was excited. It was nothing to be happy about, poking around the details of a sweet old man's death. Somehow Bags just had a way of making everything he talked about sound like fun.

"Bags, seriously, I'm trusting you to keep her out of trouble." Father admonished the much senior Mr. Bagwell. "Actually, you two keep each other out of trouble."

"You have my word, Axel." Bags shifted his attention. "So, Penelope, we're off to a late start. I think you should grab something to eat, put your shoes on, and meet me in the driveway. You can drive."

Penelope looked expectantly at her dad. "Well, you heard him -- better grab something from the fridge and get going." Father shook his head and went back up the stairs.

Chapter 10

Bags was waiting in his golf cart when Penelope walked out with a bagel clenched between her teeth. She slid into the driver's seat and looked at Bags expectantly.

"Back to the club, if you don't mind." He directed.

Penelope put the cart in gear and drove up the long straightaway to the gates of St. Georges. At the guardhouse she steered the cart left. To the extent St. Georges had a stately promenade they were now on it. Tall palms lined both sides and the landscaped median. On their right were tennis courts and a parking lot. On the left were several houses and the clubhouse. Penelope wheeled past the end of the median and parked in the circular driveway under the club's portico. It was just enough of a drive for her to finish her bagel.

"Here we are. You wanna tell me why?" Penelope asked.

"We've missed the lunch hour so we will have the place to ourselves. Also, it is the crime scene."

"Ok, but what are we going to do?" Bags was leading her to a table out by the pool.

They sat before he answered. "I think first we should go over what we know and what we don't know."

"Sounds good." A waiter appeared before she could say more. Bags must have seen the look in her eyes.

"Tyler gave the regular staff the day off. They were all here last night."

"I guess that makes sense."

"Hello there. How are you today?" Bags addressed the server Penelope hadn't recognized.

"Very good, sir. I'm Todd. Can I bring you something to drink? And will you be having lunch with us today? I can bring menus."

"I'll have unsweetened tea. The lady will have lemonade."

"Very good. Would you like menus?"

"You know, I think we will have something to eat. We don't need menus. The lady will have a steak sandwich with french fries and I will have the Cobb Salad."

Bags ordering for her caught Penelope by surprise. How very 1950 of him. Before she could think of a clever objection, it occurred to her that a steak sandwich sounded good. "Thanks, Bags. Do you always order for your dates?"

"I used to do it all the time. I usually ask what my companion would like, though. I could tell you wanted a steak sandwich but you didn't know you wanted one until just now. Am I right?"

"Yep. Guess I'm easy to read." Penelope hated to admit that Bags had nailed it.

"If that were true, you would be the first such woman in history, Penelope."

"You should watch that ordering for women thing. Not all women will appreciate it these days."

"You see what I mean. Women remain a mystery even at my advanced age."

"Whatever, Bags. Let's get started. What do we know for sure? I told you what I saw. What happened after you brought me home?"

"As you wish. After bringing you home, I came back to the club. It took the sheriff some time to arrive so Roger guarded the body while I brought everyone back into the dining room."

"Including the staff?"

"Yes. My purpose was to see who was definitely in the dining room and accounted for during the critical period, which leads us to one thing that we know for sure. Harry died at some point between the time Roger and I ushered him back to the veranda and the time you found him. That gives us a narrow window. No more than 15 minutes beginning a little before ten."

"That should help."

"Exactly. And the number of people who might have seen or heard something relevant, or who might have done something heinous, should logically be limited to those in attendance."

"Small window. Limited number of people. Got it."

"So I began taking people one by one into the bar to ask where they were and who could vouch for them. I continued to do that even after the Sheriff arrived. It took him some time to look at the body and I let Roger handle that with him. As a result of comparing everyone's recollections, including my own, I was able to compile quite a list of people unlikely to have seen or heard anything relevant, and certainly unable to have had a direct hand in Harry's demise."

"Members and guests at the Gala plus the staff working the event, right?"

"Yes, the whole staff, in fact. Tyler brought in everyone for last night."

"Except Bud, you mean."

"Ahh, excellent point. Bobby was at the bar rather than Bud. Do we know for sure he was not in the kitchen or working as a server?"

"I think so. About a week ago I talked to him. It was the night we came for dinner with Marika. He joked that I would have to tell him about the Gala because he had the night off."

"Good, good. We can check with Tyler just to be sure."

"Ok, so we have a list of people who are not suspects. By the way, we can't rule out an accidental slip or a sudden health thing yet, can we?"

"Rule it out completely? No. Presume for now it was foul play? Let's list what we know about Harry."

"Well, he was a fitness fanatic, and not just with a 'for his age' asterisk. He was buff."

"Yes, very fit and very active. He did tai chi and yoga every day so I think it fair to say his balance was quite good."

"Exactly. Oh, and he was always bragging about how his diet, meditation, exercise, blah, blah, blah, gave him perfect blood pressure and cholesterol."

"Which would seem to make stroke and heart attack very unlikely." Bags finished her thought, which she found kind of cool.

"What about a low blood sugar thing? I had a friend pass out on me one time from that. It happened really fast. Harry was pretty fussy about his eating."

"Very good, Penelope. I think you have a knack for this. But I think we can rule that. I was a little worried the excitement of being on stage might have that very effect so I made sure he had one of his meal replacement drinks just before we got things rolling last night."

"I can't really think of anything else. Can you?"

"No, and based on what we both knew of him, I am confident it was not poor balance or a weak constitution which killed Harry."

"Works for me."

"I think we also must assume it wasn't random." Bags offered.

"Right. It's not like he was wandering through a city park or down a dark alley."

"You realize, of course, what that means?"

Penelope hadn't really thought about the implications. Not random meant someone he knew was involved -- likely someone she knew. The little hairs below her ponytail stood straight up. "Yeah, let's not dwell on that part."

"Except that we must, don't you see? To identify the 'who' we must understand 'why'? The list of individuals on the property that night will help us narrow our list of suspects but we will need to connect someone on that list to Harry through motive."

"But who would want to kill Harry, or anyone else here, for that matter?"

"Ahh, Penelope, to be young again and see the world with innocent eyes. No one would want to kill you so it's hard for you to imagine. When you have lived longer, you will see things. You may even do things that give you a sense for how people come to have enemies with enough hate to kill."

"Bags that is very dark, and a little creepy."

"Yet still true, I'm sorry to say. Sheriff Phillips actually gave us a good list of motives."

"Sorry?"

"Remember when he said most of his cases involved drugs or what he called 'domestic situations?' The list is that short, I think. The things people are willing to kill for are passion and money. And most of the time money is worth killing over only when people mistake greed for a passion."

"Hmmm. I never really thought about it that way. So that means his wife has to be a suspect. Do we know anything about his financial dealings?"

"I think we start with the wife, but after lunch. She may be the key to both."

The conversation continued after their food came. Bags did most of the talking as Penelope inhaled her sandwich and most everything else on the plate.

He went through the list of guests who were not on the veranda during the critical window, like the Commodore and his wife, her father, Dr. Patterson and his wife, all but one of the kitchen staff, and Tyler, the manager. Actually, most of the rest of the guests were confirmed by multiple others to be sitting at their tables eating and watching Bags do his thing at the front of the room. So unless they were dealing with a whole table of co-conspirators, most of St. Georges had an alibi.

"Did you talk to the cook who went missing?" Penelope asked between bites.

"No, Sheriff Phillips cut my interviews short once he was done looking at the body."

"Well we definitely need to follow up with him."

"I will talk to Tyler and make sure he gets called for a shift tomorrow."

"By the way, if the regular staff is out today, who is cooking?"

"Tyler, I believe. That was his first job here." Bags responded.

"Has he been at St. Georges long?"

"Several years. I take it you think we should talk to him in some detail."

"That night he told me he wasn't working the Gala, Bud gave me this little speech about how bartenders hear everyone's secrets. I'm guessing the club manager hears or overhears a lot of things too."

"You really do have a knack for this, Penelope. Now finish those french fries so we can go talk to Harry's wife."

"Ok. Hey, doesn't it seem weird that she wasn't there to see his acting debut?"

Bags nodded. "That seems like something we should cover when we make our condolence call."

"Do we even know her name, I mean besides Mrs. Cumberson?"

"Yelena, and we must be very careful with her. She is a suspect, yes, but also a grieving widow."

"Understood, I'll let you do the talking."

"I saw her last night, you know. She was at home while he was at the Gala. I took the Sheriff over so we could break the news about Harry. She was distraught, as you might imagine."

As Penelope finished her last few bites, she pondered the weirdness of Yelena being in her house a hundred yards across the water from the club while her husband was there at the Gala. That would be a little weird by itself. The fact that she was missing his big performance just didn't compute. In a way he was the star attraction and she apparently wanted nothing to do with it. Very weird.

Chapter 11

The door opened slowly. Penelope was a little surprised it was Yelena who answered. At first glance she looked completely together, more put together, in fact, than Penelope usually looked when she was ready to go out for the evening.

She wore a plain sundress with white sandals showing off brightly colored toenails. She was about Penelope's height with blond hair in a tight little bun, milky blue eyes, and perfect cheekbones. Penelope could see her as a total hottie in younger days. She still was in a relative sense. Penelope guessed she was a few years older than Mother, which made her considerably younger than Harry. Boys. It was only her eyes that betrayed her today. They were red around the blue with deep gray circles beneath. There was no way to disguise the amount of crying she had clearly done.

"Yelena, my dear, how are you holding up?"

"Oh Bags, it's just horrible, isn't it? And I'm a horrible mess." She leaned over the threshold and threw her arms around his neck.

He hugged back reflexively. "Penelope and I thought we would stop by to see if you needed anything."

"Please, come in and sit. It's good you came. I think people are afraid to come see me." She released Bags and dragged him in by the hand. Penelope followed. "I have someone starting on the arrangements. I can't really believe he's gone. It hasn't sunk in. I hate to think what I'll be like when it does." Yelena began weeping as she walked them to the same room where Penelope sat the day she talked Harry into allowing a hole in his tuxedo jacket. That seemed so long ago.

As he sat, Bags broached the first subject. "Yelena, dear, have you heard from the Sheriff since last night?"

"No, not since the two of you came to tell me." She sat on the couch across from Bags and Penelope.

"Well, I expect he will be in touch soon."

"For what purpose?" Penelope startled at the voice coming from around the corner.

Yelena reacted quickly. "I'm so sorry. William is here with me today. He's been very kind to stay so long."

"Yes, Bill, very generous of you. Must have been quite a shock for you too, last night." Bags spoke as the man entered with a tray full of teacups.

"Quite so. I only found out this morning. A terrible shock."

"Bill, this is Penelope Hazard. She and her family have moved in just up the way. They've come all the way from Illinois." Bags made the introduction.

The man set his tray gently on the table in the middle of all the seating and bowed in Penelope's direction. "William Sturridge, Miss Penelope, at your service." He handed her one of the cups.

"Pleasure to meet you, Mr. Sturridge." She responded, taking the cup.

"Please, call me William." He said. Penelope smiled. She generally thought boys who insisted on being called William were pretentious. This one was obviously English, which hardly ruled out pretentious but made his insistence on "William" seem more natural. Or maybe having the coolest of all accents was what made it ok. He was tall. The accent made him seem taller. His wavy blond hair may or may not have been his own. The odd paunch hanging from his otherwise angular frame was all his, for sure. The big firm jaw was also his. It distracted from his middle and made the words sound even better as they purred out.

"Bill here has been Harry's business partner for years. Isn't that right, Bill?"

"Yes, I've known Harry -- knew Harry, I guess -- for ages. We made a lot of money together, we did." He turned to Bags. "Now what's all this business about the Sheriff needing to speak to poor Yelena?"

"Oh, you know, a routine part of his investigation, I suppose." Bags responded casually. Penelope could tell Bags didn't care for Mr. Sturridge.

"Investigation?" Bill and Yelena said, nearly in unison.

Bags reached for a cup from the tray. "I suppose it's part of the process whenever there's a suspicious death."

"Suspicious? What are you saying, man?" Bill stuttered as he sat. Yelena looked quizzically at Bags.

"I'm so sorry. That was a poor choice of words. I meant only that it was not a death from natural causes." Bags paused. Penelope could tell he was assessing their reactions. "Still, the circumstances were curious so believe I the Sheriff will need to make inquiries."

"Awfully inconsiderate if he insists on coming 'round this week." William offered, trying to appear calm.

"I suspect it will be a day or two. I believe he is waiting for the autopsy results."

"Oh dear!" Yelena exclaimed as she suddenly tipped over toward Bill on the couch.

"Bags! What's wrong with you?" William caught Yelena as he spoke, gently propping her upright.

"Again, sorry. I thought you might have expected that under the circumstances, Yelena. Very sorry to give you another shock."

"Bags, seriously, is there suspicion this was anything but an accident?" William asked.

"I wouldn't say suspicion, Bill, more like open questions. He had quite a knock on one side of his head."

Penelope knew what Bags was doing and was on alert for clues in their reactions. It was proving hard to concentrate. She didn't want to miss anything but she really had to go to the bathroom. "Excuse me, Mrs. Cumberson, could I use the restroom?"

"Of course, my dear," Yelena looked up and pointed. "The one in the hall is broken. You can use the one in the master suite. There are two in there, actually. Take your pick."

Penelope knew the basic layout and had no trouble finding her way to Harry's bathroom. On her way back she was not in such a hurry and loitered long enough to look around. The bed had been made with military precision. She looked in the walk-in closet next to his bathroom. Consistent with Harry's OCD tendencies everything was in perfect order. Yelena's closet was next to her bathroom. Penelope glanced in it not quite knowing what to expect and found it similarly perfect, as was Yelena's bathroom. Upon Penelope's return, it appeared to her the conversation had not moved forward significantly.

"Did you find the restroom, dear?" Yelena asked.

"Yes, thank you. I was a kind of afraid to touch anything in there. Everything is so perfect."

"I'm so sorry, dear. I know we are a bit much." Yelena cringed and smiled.

"I'm guessing at some point you had to make an adjustment to Mr. Cumberson's . . . ."

"Fussiness, dear. That's what most people call it, and no. I mean you would think it should be 'opposites attract' but I'm nearly as bad. That's why we ended up together, I think. We each decided no one else would be able to put up with us."

"Yelena, were you here all evening?" Bags tried to redirect the conversation.

"I was, why?"

"Simply trying to create a picture for myself of where everyone was. For the most part it is quite simple. Just about everyone else in St. Georges was at the Gala. I merely need to account for the few who were not."

"I understand. Yes, I was here in the house all evening except for a small errand. After Harry had gone to the club, I realized I was out of ibuprofen, so I popped out for some. I was not feeling well. That's why I did not go to the Gala."

"Thank you. And you, Bill, I'm guessing you were nowhere near St. Georges last night." Bags persisted.

"That's right. I was home all evening."

"Of course, no reason to expect otherwise."

"You don't think the Sheriff will need to bother me about last night, do you?"

"I think if there remains any question whether it was an accidental thing, he might want to ask some questions about Harry's business dealings, like whether you know of any reason someone might have had it in for Harry."

"I suppose that's right. Well you both know how to reach me if that becomes necessary."

"Of course. Well, I think we should probably be going now and let you have some quiet, Yelena. Please don't hesitate to call me if you need anything."

"Thank you, Bags," she said from the couch. "Would you mind showing yourselves out?"

Penelope was out of her chair and to the front door quickly, with Bags a step behind. As she opened the door, Penelope heard Yelena call out. "Bags, maybe you could be my intermediary with the Sheriff when the time comes."

"Of course, Yelena. I will take care of it." Bags replied, pausing to speak before closing the door.

Penelope had the cart at the end of the street before either of them spoke. "Perhaps we should go to my house and plot our next move over some lemonade." Bags offered.

"I think I need something stronger than lemonade, Bags."

"Diet soda it is," he raised his hand to signal the required left turn. Penelope laughed and floored the golf cart, which meant they were motoring along at slow jogging pace. Even so, it was only two minutes before they pulled into the garage at the Bagwell Villa. Penelope went to the lanai to fish a can of soda out of the mini-fridge, while Bags checked for messages on his answering machine. That was a generation gap thing she noticed at St. Georges. Her parents still had a landline but it rarely rang and they almost never answered. The good people of St. Georges called each other all the time and almost always on their landlines. It seemed old-timey. Bags was already talking when she walked back into the air conditioning.

"How interesting." He began. "That was a message from Yelena. She called in the time we were driving back."

"Weird. What did she want?"

"Harry's lawyer is coming to visit in the morning and she asked if I could be there with her."

"What about 'William?' He seemed willing to stick around as long as she needed him."

"You noticed that too?"

"Duh. What do you suppose that's all about?"

"He's a Brit so it may be no more than his attempt to be a gentlemen. You know, saving the damsel in distress."

"Hmmm. I guess I haven't met enough Brits. I do love his accent, though. Yummy."

"Anyway . . . Yelena said she doesn't think it would be appropriate for him to hear the discussion about Harry's business dealings."

"Ooh, that sounds juicy. We wouldn't want to miss that."

"I think you will have to miss it, my dear. I doubt Yelena or the lawyer will be comfortable having you there."

"I guess. So what am I going to do while you're with them?"

"We can find something productive, I'm sure."

"Like what?"

"Let me think." Bags looked quietly at some scraps of paper on the counter. Penelope drained the last drops from her soda can. "Oh, I know. Why don't you drive around St. Georges and try to figure out which houses are occupied and which ones are shut up for the summer."

"Because . . .?"

"Not everyone who lives here was at the Gala. Shocking, that they would miss a Bagwell production, I know." He smiled. "We have the list of those who did attend. Now we need to approximate a list of other residents who are still around. Start with the houses near the club, including those across the harbor, and also the ones near the front gates."

"Boring, but ok." Penelope frowned.

"No pouting, young lady. Now, is there anything we need to talk about from our visit with Yelena?"

"Just the whole William thing. Didn't you think it was weird there was no car parked out front and then, bam, there's William making himself at home."

"It did surprise me, although I think Harry tended to encourage visiting friends to park in one of the empty garage stalls."

"Ok, but you have to admit, the two of them looked a little cozy." She persisted.

"Yes, you mentioned that, and I admit he seemed very protective."

"I know, right? Seemed a little suspicious to me."

"Like I said, he's English. To him that might just be good manners."

"Maybe. I still think something is up between them." Penelope insisted.

"Another one of those things to file away for now. Anything else."

"Not really."

That was the end of their sleuthing for the day. Bags looked sleepy, which started Penelope feeling sleepy. Without saying it out loud they agreed to adjourn for a nap. She pictured Bags enjoying a nap in the sun, sprawled on his favorite piece of furniture on the lanai, while she was cocooned in her room hiding under a blanket from the industrial air conditioning.

Chapter 12

Penelope liked sleep almost as much as she liked burrowing under the covers to watch videos until all hours. The combination frequently meant she skipped morning altogether, crawling out of bed just in time for a late lunch. That's how she wanted this morning to go, so Penelope was not amused to be up well before ten. Once she saw the sun it was too late to ignore the day. She was up and crabby about it. Too much Hercule Poirot before bed combined with the real life mystery playing out at St. Georges combined to produce some disturbing but hysterical dreams. She couldn't remember details, only a collage of images and a vague feeling of unease. Penelope decided the dreams were best not shared, although the image of Bags with slicked back hair and a shiny little mustache pasted against his lip was almost too good to keep to herself.

Anyway, whether from exposure to events in her world or Agatha Christie's, her sleep was the opposite of restful. Coffee. She needed coffee. A quick stop in the bathroom revealed a hair tragedy. She could not bear the sight of it and turned away quickly, leaving her wondering why a family of squirrels built a nest on her head in the night. That would have to get sorted before anyone else saw her, except Father. He didn't count. Coffee remained her priority, or tea, or soda. At this point she would snort caffeine powder off the counter if she could find some. But coffee was her preference and there was always coffee.

After two cups, doctored with cream and copious amounts of chocolate syrup, Penelope was ready to beat back the tangles up top at least to the point she could make the pony tail and baseball cap thing work. Actually, she had a cute little pink runner's cap inherited from Mother at the conclusion of her "I'm going to run outside in Illinois" experiment. The hat was like new -- Mother -- running -- outdoors -- Illinois. Uh-huh.

With the hair monster contained more quickly than expected, Penelope had the golf cart fired up before half-past. Her pout the day before was legitimate. She really wanted to be there when Bags met with the lawyer. The eye roll accompanying his request that she canvass the neighborhood was less sincere. Penelope instantly recognized the opportunity to do something she had been putting off. Since day two in their house, Father had been on her to get around St. Georges and see if anyone needed her to do odd jobs.

Her steady Illinois racket was kid-sitting. The St. Georges demographics seemed to limit her opportunities to visiting grandkids and she figured the grandparents were the most likely kid-sitters in that scenario. She needed a new racket.

Lawn care didn't seem like a good bet either, which was fine with Penelope because that was way too much like real work. Most people seemed to use a lawn service. She knew this because of the chronic use of the pure evil called "leaf blower." In a sane world their use before noon would be punished as a hate crime. Pool services seemed the rule too, so that was probably off the table.

By process of elimination Penelope narrowed her options to miscellaneous help with unpleasant tasks. She guessed based on interactions with her own Nana that most retirees had at least a few things they disliked doing enough to outsource and she figured some of the older guys might even pay her to help with things they really didn't need help with just to get some attention. She was a delight, after all, and there was no reason not to share that with her new world.

It didn't matter that odd jobs and just being cute seemed unlikely to pay well. Father wouldn't care if everyone paid her in cookies and lemonade. He said he was just sick of hearing her say she was bored. She had no idea what he was talking about with that because she really didn't say she was bored very often, at least not consciously. Father would be happy to get her out of his hair and Penelope would be happy to have him stop nagging her about finding something to do, which she felt like he did with every breath, so she didn't care if there was any money in it either.

Her procrastination so far had not been a lack of motivation. It was the whole knocking on doors out of the blue asking people for things that put her off. It was the definition of awkward and kinda scary too. She refused to do it every time some team, or school, or club decided sending kids door to door to sell useless crap was the way to raise money. Her parents only even tried to force her that first time for fourth grade concert band, an episode that proved unpleasant for all involved.

For some reason, when Bags suggested she wander around to see who was home, Penelope's mind immediately jumped to using job-hunting as her cover. Somehow, the idea of using her sales pitch as a ruse for finding people who might know something about Harry, completely removed all the fear and ickiness from the door knocking.

Penelope casually worked her way around St. Georges, noting signs of residence on a little notepad and stopping at any house sending her mixed signals. She approached those doors not as Penelope Hazard the awkward teenager but as fabulous super sleuth Penelope Hazard working under cover as awkward Penelope. Ok, it would sound silly if she said it out loud but it was working for her.

She worked from the far end of the community back toward the club, finishing with the villas. Hopefully, Bags would be home by the time she reached the end of his street. Except when she had to roll right past Harry's house, her errand kept her mind off what interesting things Bags might be learning.

She was finishing a little loop of homes backing on to the man-made lake just beyond the tennis courts when she saw Bags turn onto the promenade on his way home. The race was on! By the way, anyone who had seen her play would never have put a lake next to tennis courts she might use.

Penelope beat Bags to his driveway. He tried to sell a vigorous fist shake at her. Silly man. She knew he was amused. It was hard for her not to blurt out what she wanted to ask. Penelope made it all the way into the garage and up the steps to the kitchen before the words spilled out. "What did the lawyer say? Anything good?"

"I can't tell you."

"What!" Penelope cried. "Not fair, mister."

"Well I can't tell you specifics . . . not all the specifics, anyway."

"What can you tell me? I mean seriously, who else would I tell?" Bags was quiet for a moment. Penelope knew he was dying to tell her everything. She tried to make her eyes bigger, more innocent. It kinda hurt.

"Let's see. Well, one thing is for sure, Yelena knew little about Harry's business dealings. We went over a number of things that seemed new to her."

"Interesting, I guess. What else?"

"She also did not know all of the details of his will but did know enough to understand how it would work for her."

"And do we think that matters?"

Bags paused and pursed his lips. "This stays in the room. You never speak of it except in this room. Agreed?"

"Cross my heart."

"Good. As you would expect, Harry's will provides for Yelena's continued support. There's more than enough money for that and she gets the house. However, a lot of his money will go to charities. When they moved here, Harry updated his will to change the address of his primary residence, as you would expect. But this house is worth several million more than their old house. For the last several months Harry has been talking about changing some of the other money around to account for the large amount now has tied up in this house. Yelena was going to be the big loser in that shuffle."

"How did that come up?"

"It was almost like the lawyer wanted to make sure I heard it. He went out of his way to preface it with 'as you know, Yelena . . .' to make sure I heard that she knew about Harry's plans."

"Sounds like he waited too long."

"Exactly. Apparently, he had an appointment with the lawyer next week." Bags raised an eyebrow.

"So the will gives Yelena the mall-sized house and all the money she was expecting. Do we think that would be enough to kill for?"

"Hard to say. The difference was a lot of money even for someone like Yelena. On the other hand, she was hardly going to be left to starve. Harry was a very successful man. His estate is quite large."

"Also, they were married. That's supposed to mean she loved him." Penelope added.

"And yet you had questions about her coziness with Bill." Bags reminded Penelope.

"True. Even so, cheating on your husband and killing him seem like completely different levels of bad behavior."

"I agree, and yet history tells us the spouse and the business partner are the most likely suspects. Potentially losing millions of dollars of your inheritance would be a strong motive for the right person." Bags explained.

"What about William? You don't seem to like him. Does he have a motive?"

"I'm not sure. The lawyer did mention a very large key person policy that would pay Bill as the beneficiary."

"Do what now?" Most of that sentence after "lawyer" sounded like gibberish to Penelope.

"Apologies. Sometimes when two people are partners in a business and they fear the business might struggle without one of the partners, they take out life insurance policies on each other. Usually they use money from the business to pay the premiums."

"So Prince William gets paid because Harry died."

"Yes . . . I assume the 'prince' part is because you like his accent."

"Yeah, it's dreamy." She decided to sigh for effect to annoy Bags. "But if they're still in business together, you would think Harry is more valuable to Prince Dreamy Talk alive than dead."

"Yes. Bill is a very good salesman, no question, but I believe Harry was the one who made everything else work. Also, with Harry alive, Bill could always depend on him putting enough money into the business to keep it going. The life insurance policy only pays once. Unless there is more to the story, killing Harry sounds like bad business for Bill."

"What if there is more to the story and her name is Yelena?" Penelope said, admiring her cleverness.

"Yes, if there is something between them, Bill might have feared his business dealings with Harry were at risk."

"How do we find out?"

"For now, we keep talking to people. My experience with St. Georges is that no secret remains secret from everyone forever."

"Ok, who's next?" Penelope asked.

"Why don't we go and have a drink?"

"Kind of early in the day for that, or so I'm told."

"Well, I would not want your father to think I'm a bad influence, so I will have tea and you will have something with too much sugar in it."

"I am developing a taste for sweet tea."

"It's settled. And while we enjoy our beverages we might have a word with that cook who disappeared from the kitchen. Shall we?" Bags asked, pointing to the stairs.

Chapter 13

It was only a block to the club. Penelope drove the golf cart anyway, blaming the scorching mid-afternoon heat. The novelty of tooling around on actual roads in an oversized toy car had not yet worn thin and she was determined to get full mileage out of it during her summer of epic boredom. Besides, there was something about driving Bags around that made her smile.

There was a golf cart and a big Mercedes in the marina lot and only a few boat slips empty. It was apparently too hot even to be out on the water. Inside the club the air was perfectly refrigerated. One thing they didn't mess around with in Florida was air conditioning. The hotter it got outdoors, the colder it would be indoors. Penelope welcomed the contrast.

Bags marched through the foyer, headed for the bar. The dining room was straight ahead, with the kitchen to the right and the bar to the left. Sharply to the left was a hallway leading to the bathrooms then turning right and to run to the back of the club. It provided a natural buffer between the bar and dining room with the openings to each offset several feet from each other.

Tyler called to him from the dining room before Bags could turn from the hall into the bar. Penelope was ambivalent about making it to the bar but she disliked smalltalk and Tyler was engaging Bags in smalltalk. The ambush and hijacking of Bags put the three of them in the small hallway with Penelope facing Bags and Tyler just around the corner from the first opening to the dining room. The two of them were basically standing in the doorway. While from the neck up Bags was being perfectly cordial, charming even, the rest of his body was leaning in the direction of the bar. Penelope was momentarily amused. Momentarily.

Her attention drifted to voices behind her. There was at least one table of members lingering over lunch. Her ears zeroed in when she heard her name. One thing she learned very quickly was the tendency of the good people of St. Georges to underestimate Penelope's hearing. Her parents had the same problem. With this crew it seemed more pronounced. She was already tuning out the Tyler-Bags banter so listening to the conversation behind her came easily.

"Was that the Hazard girl with Bags?" Female voice number one asked.

"Yes, Penelope. Isn't she adorable?" Penelope recognized the voice as belonging to Mrs. Riley. And yes, it was now official, everyone here found her adorable.

"She really is. I think it will be nice to have a young lady around St. Georges." More from the mystery voice.

"She's a charmer too." Mrs. Riley added.

"Then I'm sure it's a regular mutual admiration society with her and Bags." Polite laughter, including a male voice. The Commodore? Mystery voice continued. "I was in the interview with her parents before they joined. Young Penelope appears to take after her mother."

"I don't know if I completely agree." Male voice. Definitely the Commodore. "I find Axel quite a charming and agreeable fellow."

"Oh yes, he is charming, no question. Quite likable all the way around. My point is only that he is . . . 'unexceptional.'" Mystery woman emphasized the word almost like it was code for something. Her tone seemed to carry an implied "wink, wink, nudge, nudge." Aside from the curious delivery, the word seemed kind of insulting. Penelope was on her way to getting mad until it occurred to her that her dad tended to describe himself that way. Still, who did this woman think she was that she could call Penelope's dad unexceptional!

"Agreed," the Commodore conceded. "In that sense Penelope is definitely her mother's daughter."

Wait, did they all just agree Penelope was exceptional? Other than giving her mother all the credit for it, Penelope was happy to concur. Again, though, the emphasis on "in that sense" seemed like code. Weird.

"Ahem, Penelope, my dear, will you be joining me?" Bags interrupted her eavesdropping. He and Tyler were looking at her like she had two heads.

"Sorry. Sorry. Just got kinda lost for a minute."

Bags smiled as she scurried past him and into the bar. "Around here we usually call those 'senior moments.' I'm not sure you get to use that excuse."

"I know. Honestly, I was kind of eavesdropping on the Commodore's lunch table. They were bashing my dad a little. Said he was 'unexceptional,' compared to my mom. How rude, right?"

"Let me guess. They also compared you to your mother." Bags winked at her.

"How did you know?" Penelope wondered if his hearing was better than the local average.

"Personally, I think there is a great deal of your father in you, particularly the way you see the world. But your mother has a certain light in her eyes. And you, my dear, have it too."

"That kinda sounds like you're crushing on my mom, Bags." Eww! Just Eww!

"Well, she is a beautiful woman, I admit -- far out of my league, though."

"You're funny. You don't fool me. I see the way you have Marika wrapped around your little finger."

"Oh, I assure you it is the other way round, Penelope. And, for the record, she is out of my league as well. But no matter. I am an old man and have no need of that kind of adventure."

"Hmmm, color me skeptical."

"No, it is the truth. I adore the attention Marika gives me during our little dates at the club. But that is where it ends for me." He protested.

"Does she have a certain light in her eyes? What does that even mean?" Penelope rolled her apparently sparkly eyes at him.

"Marika does have it, yes. What it means, well, that is hard to describe for you without sounding silly. So I will merely suggest that you accept the compliment to your mother and to you. It is a good thing."

As Bags finished, Tyler walked from the bar with two glasses of iced tea, making sure the sweet tea landed in front of Penelope. When Tyler left, they were alone in the bar. It was mid-afternoon on a weekday during the summer so there was no bartender on duty.

Penelope continued. "Ok, have it your way. Mother and I have sparkles in our eyes. New subject. Get anything good out of Tyler?"

"That conversation will come later. I was just gauging his temperament."

"So what now?" Penelope was bored again.

"Tyler went to get Ricky, the cook." Bags answered.

Ricky walked into the bar aiming to look tough. Instead, he looked guilty of something, something other than murder, Penelope suspected. A violent nature seemed incompatible with his face, which matched his slight build and generally hunched appearance. He was pale too, which in Florida in summer would require a vampire schedule. There were no piercings, eyeliner, or dark nail polish so she concluded he was not going for the Goth look. The sideburns dipping below his earlobes had a certain hipster quality but the long scraggly hair probably ruled that out too. Besides, she wasn't sure "hipster" was really a thing in Florida. More likely Ricky was just a hot mess. Too bad. He had nice eyes.

"Ricky, sit, please." Bags motioned to a chair.

"Tyler said you wanted to talk to me?" Ricky asked nervously.

"Yes, I am Mr. Bagwell and this is the lovely Penelope Hazard. I don't believe I have seen you before, Ricky. Tyler says you started in the kitchen only recently."

"Yes, sir. Been here nearly six months, now. Am I in trouble?"

"Not at all, my boy. You were working during the Gala, yes?"

"Yes, sir. Tyler had everyone here."

"Then you know about the unfortunate situation with Harry Cumberson." Bags had not broken eye contact with the pale cook. Penelope hadn't seen this side of him.

"Yes, sir."

"We are trying to understand more about that evening so that we can tell Mrs. Cumberson how her husband died."

"Ok . . .."

"We have narrowed the time of death to a period no more than fifteen minutes long and we obviously know it happened just over there, on the veranda. We were hoping you would share with us where you were at that time."

"In the kitchen, I suppose. I was there all night. I cook and wash pots. That's all I do."

"Well, that's not quite right is it, Ricky? You see we know from several others that you were not in the kitchen during the time of Harry's death and we were hoping that if you were outside, you might be able to share with us anything you heard or saw." Bags had yet to look away from Ricky.

"I'm not sure who you talked to but . . . I mean I don't even know when you're talking about."

"Fair enough. The lights went out in the dining room -- on purpose -- for about ten seconds. The moment the lights came back on marks the beginning of our window. The window closed when everyone in the dining room heard Penelope screaming. According to the rest of the kitchen staff, anyone in the kitchen would have noticed both events. So my question, again, is where were you during that period -- and please do not say you were in the kitchen."

"Ok, ok, I was outside."

"Where, precisely?"

"I don't know. Maybe over by the dumpsters between the kitchen and the cabana."

Penelope's mind wandered as she tried to visualize the scene. The dumpsters were around the corner from the veranda on the side of the dining room by the pool. Standing by them, Ricky could not have seen the area where she found Harry. He might have heard something but she thought there were exhaust vents behind the dumpsters and, in any event, a good bit of the noise from the dining room would have been seeping through the wall of glass-paneled doors that opened onto the veranda.

The bigger issue was why he was there in the first place. It was mean of her to think he looked like the kind of boy that might hang around dumpsters, which he did, but beyond his scuzziness she couldn't think of a reason. It was a dumpster outside a restaurant on a hot summer night. It must have reeked. She snapped back into the moment right when Bags was trying to sort out the same thing.

"Tell me again why you picked that particular spot to have a smoke?" There was an edge in his voice that was new. Interesting. She pictured him more as "good cop."

"Tyler has a fit if anyone sees us smoking and sometimes people in the houses nearby complain about the smell if we go around to the parking lot. I can't afford to lose this job, you know." Ricky protested.

"And why is that, Ricky?"

Ricky went silent and looked at his feet. Penelope recognized the behavior from any number of stupid boys in school. Ricky had a secret and it was not one that reflected well on him.

"All right, crap, I guess Tyler would tell you anyway so it's not like I can hide it. I'm not really in a position to get a great job, not that this is a great job, but believe me it's way better than most of the jobs I could get right now, so it feels pretty great to me. See, I'm on probation and it isn't really a first offender kind of thing. They told me I was lucky not to get sent away this last time, so I really don't want to lose this job or mess up my probation and I don't want to get Tyler in trouble either because he really took a chance on me and we were supposed to keep my situation very quiet for a lot reasons, he said, but now you're asking me all these questions and--"

Ricky was just vomiting words. Bags had to intervene. "Ricky, please, calm yourself. Slow down. I understand. What is it exactly that you did to end up on probation?"

"Nothing really. Nothing like murder, for sure, if that's what you were thinking. No way."

"Ricky." Bags said sternly enough to straighten Penelope's posture.

"I got busted with some weed and a little meth. I was playing around with meth, just using. But I had enough weed to be dealing, they said, and I can't argue with that because I was, but then they lumped it together and said that was proof I was dealing meth and it was never meth, only weed. You wouldn't know anything about it, I'm sure but these days they take meth real serious and that's basically how I ended up on probation."

Bags paused. Penelope wondered if he knew much about this part of life. It was pretty clear he had been rich for a long, long time and even before that she doubted he spent much time around people like Ricky. Penelope was pretty far removed from that life, herself. But things had definitely changed since Bags was a teenager. Drugs were everywhere even at her country clubby school in Illinois. Weed was so common the school barely tried to police it. Kids went to the student parking lot and got high between classes and not just the Bob Marley stoner kids; honor students, athletes, and mean girls, especially mean girls.

The point was Bags might make more of this little tidbit than it merited. When everyone, even adults, stop caring about weed but it's still illegal, being a dealer starts to look like a low risk, high paying business -- Junior Achievement kind of stuff, almost. Meth, on the other hand, well she knew that was not for beginners and Ricky looked like he might not be doing so well at staying away from the meth.

"Thank you for being honest, Ricky. I'm quite certain you are not making that up. Now if we might move on, were you alone out by the dumpster while you were smoking?" Bags had moved right along from the drugs. Penelope was surprised.

"What do you mean?"

"Simple question, Ricky. Was anyone with you?"

"No sir."

"Very well. Did you see anything unusual?" Bags was being thorough. Penelope assumed he would have come to the same conclusions she had based on the position of the dumpster. If there had been someone else outside with Harry, nervous Ricky would only have seen him, or her, trying to sneak away in the direction of the cabana.

"I really didn't see anything unusual. There was no one at the docks that I could see. None of the party guests were outside where I could see them. Sometimes people come outside to smoke, which is why we have to hide by the dumpster. But that night I didn't see anyone."

"Did you hear anything unusual?"

"The screaming was pretty unusual. That's it."

"Ricky, how is it you can be so sure you saw no one and heard nothing unusual?"

"I don't know. I just am. Can I go now, sir?"

"Yes, I think we are done here. Thank you. This has been most helpful." Bags smiled for the first time since Ricky sat. Ricky rose quickly from his chair and was almost out of the bar before Bags spoke again. "Just one more thing, if you don't mind."

"Ok." Penelope saw Ricky's shoulders creep up around his neck as he turned.

"You didn't talk to the Sheriff that night, did you? Tyler said you were gone by the time he got around to talking to the kitchen staff."

"That's right. I was gone. It must have been late."

"Ricky." There was that tone again.

"Yeah, I saw him and left. I'm on probation. A rich guy dies at a party with a bunch of other rich folk. I wasn't counting on anything but trouble from Johnny Law. So I left."

"Ok. Again, thank you for being honest."

"This isn't going to get Tyler in trouble is it. I mean he really took a chance on me and I owe him everything right now. I don't want to mess anything up." Tyler pleaded.

"As long as you have been truthful and told us everything you have to tell, there is no need to worry, for you or for Tyler."

Penelope swore she saw Ricky's eyes get big with that last comment from Bags. It was also possible she was simply getting carried away. As much as she kind of wanted it to be true, she was not starring with Bags in some Agatha Christie murder mystery.

"What did you think of our friend, the cook?" Bags interrupted her thoughts.

"Kind of skeevy. Could be cute if he washed every once in a while."

"Interesting. I was hoping for something a little more substantive." Bags pursed his lips like adults sometimes did in response to Penelope, usually because they were clueless.

She ignored the slight. "Boring, but ok. How 'bout this? I think he was lying about something."

"Because?"

"Well, he walked in with that 'I'm so gangsta" swagger all stupid boys try to play when they're trying hardest not to pee themselves. And then when you asked about what happened out by the dumpster, he had that look stupid boys always have when you catch them making stuff up."

"Can you describe that look?" Bags seemed amused. Penelope didn't understand why. She was dead serious.

"Girls can just kinda feel it. I don't really know how to explain it. Their faces just go from normal stupid to extra stupid while they're lying and then they get this look like things are going well and they think they're going to get away with it."

"Well, while I don't pretend to have your keen feminine instincts about lying young men, we agree about this cook. He is lying."

"Lying about how much trouble he was in with the law seems unlikely. I mean that would all be stuff we could check. Do you think he saw something? Or maybe heard something?" Penelope was thinking out loud.

"Maybe. Maybe something else. I believe he was not in a position to see Harry directly and that makes it unlikely he would have heard something more than those of us inside at the time. No, it seems more likely he was lying about something else."

"Like what?"

"Given his background and current situation, the simplest explanation is that whatever he was doing out by the dumpsters was not consistent with the terms of his probation."

"And that would explain why he bailed before the Sheriff got to him." Penelope followed. "Maybe he was out getting high. He said he was smoking. He didn't say what."

"Possibly, although that smell is distinctive and hangs in the warm, heavy air. Smoking right outside the club would have been a silly risk."

"Umm, what part of 'stupid boys' is unclear to you? Besides, what would the members of the St. Georges Yacht Club know about how weed smells?"

Bags laughed. "Oh to be young, and believe I invented the world."

"Stop!"

"Many of the residents here are children of the sixties -- honest to god hippies. You must have heard of Woodstock, at least?"

"Maybe. Are you saying you were a hippie at Woodstock?"

"Honestly, I'm not sure. There is a month or so I can't really remember. I know I was somewhere in New York at the time."

"Weird. Ok, so the yacht club members might know that smell." Penelope interrupted the reminiscing.

Bags kept going. "On a more contemporary note, many here have at least experimented with cannabis for its medicinal qualities."

"Who knew? So when the St. Georges crowd needs to get hooked up, who do they call? I'm guessing it's not like in high school where there's always someone with an older brother or a friend with a connection."

"Not someone with an older brother, you are correct. Also not someone like Ricky."

"Ok, and there's no one else around for Ricky to sell to, which means he probably wasn't dealing that night."

"So it would seem. Still, I think the thing he was most likely to be lying about was being alone."

"Our list of things we don't know keeps getting longer every time we add something to the list of things we do know." Penelope said to no one in particular. Bags nodded.

They sat in silence momentarily and finished their tea. Penelope liked silence. Most of her friends and, actually, most adults, couldn't stand more than a few seconds of lull in any conversation. Penelope found that annoying. She also found it annoying when people looked at her like she was the weird one because she didn't have to jabber nonstop. She was comfortable sitting quietly with Bags sipping iced tea. He was less comfortable. Bags was in motion nearly every second with his mouth never wanting to be left out of the action. Honestly, Penelope found him fatiguing sometimes.

"Penelope, my dear, I think we may need to allow things to percolate a little before we do anything more. Time to go, I think." Bags could sit quietly no longer.

"What about Tyler? Shouldn't we talk to him before we go?" Penelope asked, wondering why Bags would let the opportunity slip.

"That is what he is expecting. Sometimes it works better to not do the expected thing. At the very least, it is usually more fun."

"You crack me up, Bags."

"And you, Penelope, are a constant delight."

"Of course I am." She grinned and pulled him up out of the chair.

On their way to the door, Penelope agreed to stop by the guardhouse at the front gate to pick up the guest register for the night of the Gala. Bags asked her to study it overnight so they could refresh their list of possible witnesses. Penelope would also have the list of empty and occupied houses she compiled during her door-to-door survey.

The one nagging flaw in their efforts to pinpoint who was where during the fifteen minutes that mattered was the remote controlled gate. There were two gates side by side through which you could enter St. Georges. The guest gate was right next to the guardhouse and only the guard on duty could open it. A second gate on the outside of the first could be opened by a remote signal like a garage door. The residents all had openers for the gate in their cars.

The guards might or might not look up to notice a car coming through that gate and even if they did look up, they saw the same cars all the time, so recalling a specific car on a specific evening was a lot to ask. For example, Marika's arrival would hardly be noteworthy. Technically, she shouldn't have a remote for the gate but no one would be shocked if one of the residents had given her a spare. Bags lived alone and had two cars so he probably had a spare and Father spent a whole afternoon figuring out how to program one of the little buttons in his car to open the gate, which made the actual garage door remote thingy unnecessary. If he could do it, Penelope assumed anyone could.

Anyone who knew someone at St. Georges well enough to score a remote could have slipped in and out that night without being noticed. The guest register could add to their list but not narrow it. To really be sure about everyone's comings and goings, they needed video, but Penelope hadn't noticed any security cameras on the guardhouse or on the gates. That seemed odd.

Chapter 14

Penelope gunned the golf cart down the long straightaway leading to her house, guest register in hand. Leo had it ready as she arrived. The price for his prompt service was ten minutes of chitchat. Penelope listened, nodded, and smiled at appropriate intervals, adding a comment occasionally to let him take a few deep breaths in his rambling about his seven grandchildren, the local minor league baseball team, the weather, of course, his annoyance with the yard service people, and most relevant, the comings and goings of people in the neighborhood. He was a really sweet man, exhausting, but sweet.

In between tales of peewee soccer games, dance recitals, equestrian lessons, which Penelope thought had something to do with horses, and several minutes of mutual ranting about leaf blowers, Penelope managed to squeeze two little nuggets out of Leo. It was a mix of good and bad news. To her surprise, there were no cameras to record the comings and goings of cars through the gates. Also, Leo had not been on duty the night of the Gala but was very certain both Big Mike and Connie had been. So no video to review, but at least there had been two sets of eyes that night.

Penelope's expectations for the guest register were low. She plopped it on her dresser on a pile of random papers and things. She wasn't quite sure where the pile had originated. It was like that in her room. Clutter had a way of multiplying while she was sleeping, or out of the house, or sometimes, while she was watching movies on her computer.

When Mother was around the nagging was nonstop. Father was less annoying on a day-to-day basis. He was more like a volcano. She kept her door closed most of the time so he would go for days not seeing or thinking about her room. When he was writing he might go for days without even noticing if Penelope was still living there. And then, boom, he would explode. Totally random. Mother's nagging was rude but it kept Penelope from letting the clutter goblins get the upper hand. Without her around, things could get gross. And when the Father volcano blew, it was epic. She had learned to just let him spew until it was out of his system because, for all the yelling, he was completely rational in the result. He didn't ground her or take away privileges. The punishment was always the same. Clean the room. She could hardly argue.

He also knew it was a punishment in direct proportion to the crime. You would think the combination of disgusting cleanup, effort required for the large scale decluttering, and chunk of free time taken from her schedule, might condition her to keep her room clean. He didn't understand. Mother didn't understand. It was all quite beyond Penelope's control. She had no idea how the mess got there in the first place and that seemed to be a prerequisite to taking steps to keep it from happening again.

Looking up from her bed sometime later, Penelope wasn't quite sure how the day had slipped away. It seemed like she left her room at least once to get food. Looking at the dishes stacked by the door it might have been twice. There clearly was a nap too, or maybe just an extended run of daydreams involving more mixed up plots and people from St. Georges and Poirot movies. In the middle of all that the sun had gone down.

The time slippage was nothing new for Penelope. It happened whenever she was particularly distracted. Once her brain locked on something, there was no fighting it. She might appear to be functioning normally, doing normal things like fixing dinner, watching television, doing homework, but her brain was working overtime in the background, blotting out memories as she made them.

Tonight the culprit was easy to identify. Nothing about Harry's death seemed to fit the proposed explanations. Everyone agreed he was freakishly healthy and fit. She was certain the autopsy results would confirm it. The Sheriff's big idea that Harry fell and hit his head seemed equally unlikely. Harry was no wobbly old man. He had better balance and agility than Penelope, although she was a bit of a klutz so that was not a tough standard to beat. Still, she tripped and stumbled all the time and had never once been in mortal danger as a result.

In her mind, and certainly not because she wanted it to be true because she really didn't, the only possibility that made sense was that someone hit him in the head. That explanation troubled her too. Penelope hadn't noticed the bruising on Harry's temple but she would have noticed if the side of his head had been caved in, so it didn't seem like an obviously mortal blow. She knew any head injury could possibly be deadly, of course. She had also seen lots of boys show up at school with nasty head bruises and they all survived.

Even if that thump on the head was the cause, there wasn't any great lineup of suspects. Penelope was pretty sure she had never been remotely mad enough at anyone, even the mean girls, to clump them on the head hard enough to kill them. Of course, she didn't understand gang bangers killing each other or why people started wars either. Prince William might have a reason to want to be rid of Harry, particularly if he and Yelena were a thing. Same with Yelena. But murder seemed overly harsh.

They might find other people with a beef against Harry. Bags said you couldn't be as successful in business as Harry without making enemies. Of course those people, whoever they might be, would seem more likely to get at Harry when he was not at a party with fifty potential witnesses a few feet away.

Penelope and Bags agreed Ricky was lying to them about something. He might have been doing something hinky out behind the kitchen. It might have involved someone else. That someone might have bumped into Harry on the veranda, panicked, and clocked him. Maybe he had something heavy in his hand for some reason. Ricky would definitely have a reason to lie about that. Penelope counted up the maybes in her scenario. Too many.

Bags was probably right that they needed to take a break. What they really needed were the autopsy results. Until they knew what really killed poor Harry, every scenario had too many maybes.

All of this was cycling through her head nonstop. That's how she lost track of the day. Well, that and the crazy Poirot dreams. For the last couple hours Penelope had switched to watching old episodes of Big Bang Theory, which seemed likely to produce only amusing dreams.

Her brain was still chinking away in the background when a series of shrill noises interrupted her pretend show watching and the grinding in the background inside her head. Penelope recognized the sounds immediately and stopped to think whether she had heard sirens since they had moved to St. Georges. They were pretty far from any main roads. It might be possible to hear an ambulance showing up at Sunset Point, she supposed. The only other possibility, and the more interesting one, was that something was going on in St. Georges. As she listened, the sirens grew louder and then a little softer. It was definitely coming from somewhere in St. Georges.

Penelope glanced at her phone. It was only quarter to eleven. Father wouldn't mind her going on a bit of a wander. He definitely wouldn't object if he never knew she was gone. She slipped on her sandals and out her door. Father wasn't downstairs. So far, so good. She couldn't take the golf cart. That would require opening the garage door, which would attract too much attention.

Penelope typically found that procrastination worked for and against in roughly equal amounts. Not cleaning her room until Mount Father blew never worked to her advantage, but tonight her failure to move the family bicycle back into the garage from the side of the house had mystically paid off. After a quick spritz of bug spray, she slipped out the back door and then the gate.

As soon as she was on the street, Penelope could see flashing lights down the road leading to Harry's house -- well, Yelena's house. She pumped the sluggish pedals on the family beach cruiser. Father called it "retro," which really just meant "unnecessarily heavy." Slowly she accelerated in the direction of the flashing lights. It felt surprisingly warm and humid. Maybe the effort of moving the "retro" bike had something to do with that.

Getting to the left turn took forever. She rounded the corner expecting to see a commotion in front of the Cumberson house. That didn't seem to be where the lights were. She rode past it and over a little bridge spanning one of the scary mangrove canals. The street continued around a bend and over another bridge leading to a circle of large homes backing onto either the marina or the open water of the Intracoastal Waterway. That's where the lights were.

As she approached, Penelope could see a paramedic truck in front of the house on the far edge of the circle. She could also see a light on in the Bags Villa across the harbor channel. He would probably be rolling up in his golf cart soon, because he didn't have to sneak out of his house and take a bicycle.

Penelope hopped off her bike and walked slowly toward the truck. She could see a female figure in serious conversation with one of the paramedics. As she walked closer it seemed more and more like Marika. Awkward. She was still far enough away to avoid catching Marika's eye when Bags appeared, on cue and as predicted.

"Penelope, I see you too like to chase the fire trucks around. Isn't it a little late for you to be out by yourself?"

"Well then it's a good thing you showed up, isn't it? What do you think is going on?"

"I was about to ask you." He paused and squinted. "Is that Marika?"

"Looks that way to me." Penelope responded.

"Let's go see if she can tell us." Bags motioned Penelope to join him in the golf cart.

"Really?" Penelope wasn't sure that was a good idea. The odds were stacked in favor of an embarrassing situation -- beautiful woman, married man, latish at night, 911 call.

Bags frowned a little and patted the seat next to him. She hopped in, unable to resist. They rolled the remaining few hundred feet to the Yeagle residence. From her survey that morning, Penelope knew Ander Yeagle was in Florida alone for the month while his wife, Emma, was visiting her sister in San Diego.

"Marika, my dear, what has happened here?" Bags put his hand on her shoulder from the side.

She turned and threw her arms around him. "Oh Bags, it's horrible, just horrible. I rang the bell and he didn't answer so I went round to the side and used the code to get in. I found him on the floor outside his bathroom."

"Slow down, Marika. Ander? You found Ander on the floor?"

"Yes, he was not responsive. Bags I was fifteen minutes late for our appointment. What if that is the difference? What if he dies because I was late?"

"Focus, Marika. Do you have any idea what's wrong with him?"

"Overdose. I tried to wake him up. It took forever for the ambulance to get here-"

"What kind of overdose, dear?" Bags cut her off. Now he had her one shoulder in each hand, so he could look in her eyes.

"Heroin. It was heroin."

"Heroin!" Penelope blurted, immediately regretting it.

"How?" Bags ignored her.

"I found the syringe on his vanity."

"Marika, I don't mean to be indelicate but what appointment did you have with Ander tonight?"

"Indelicate or not, that is what everyone will be asking in the morning, isn't it. Oh and it's all so innocent too . . . well at least in that regard."

"Because?" Bags pulled her a little closer for emphasis.

"Ander overheard me talking about acupuncture one afternoon while I was giving Emma a massage. He approached me the next week and asked if I thought acupuncture could help with addiction. I said I did and that led to him confiding in me about the heroin."

"I had no idea." Bags exclaimed mildly.

"No one did, not even Emma. It started with pills when he had back surgery two years ago. Eventually the doctors cut him off. He was getting his pills from a shady clinic in Miami when an acquaintance remarked that he could get heroin right here and for a much lower price, so he did."

"That part sounds like Ander. Frugal with his money and reckless with his body." Bags nodded and pursed his lips. "So I take it you were going to try to take away the craving with your acupuncture needles tonight."

"Not try, dear. It was working. This wasn't our first appointment. The others we did at a more reasonable hour. He came to my studio, usually. Tonight he said he had something he needed to take care of before I came over."

"Are you saying he was staying clean?" Bags asked. Penelope was pretty sure her jaw was now permanently on the ground. St. Georges was clearly a very different place than she thought.

"I believe he was getting there. As you know, it's a particularly strong addiction. I think he was testing to see how long the acupuncture would delay his need. I couldn't have pins sticking in him all the time so he was working on cutting back."

"And that's why you believe your tardy arrival might have made a difference."

"Bags, what if he was trying to hold out and just couldn't, and then lost control of the dose because he waited so long."

"Was he alive when the paramedics arrived?"

"He was."

"Then I am sure he will be fine. You know Ander has a very strong constitution. Have you called Roger yet?"

"Right after I dialed 911. He is meeting the ambulance at the hospital."

"Then you have done all you can. Be strong. Ander will be fine. Tomorrow, hopefully he will be awake and able to help us decide how to handle this with Emma."

"Ok, you're right, of course."

"I should drive you home, I think. You are too shaken to drive yourself."

"Oh, thank you, Bags, but I'd like to ride in the ambulance with him."

Penelope could see the paramedics bringing Ander out to the ambulance as Bags and Marika were finishing their conversation. "Maybe you can drive me home, Bags." She filled the awkward silence developing between them.

"Of course, my dear." Bags looked over and smiled. Then he hugged Marika. Penelope could see her squeezing. She let go only reluctantly. Bags turned and started toward the golf cart but then hesitated and looked over this shoulder. "Marika, dear, just one last thing. Ander doesn't strike me as one to roam the seedy parts of town to buy drugs. Did he say where he got his heroin?"

"Not specifically. Once he did joke that it was so easy it was almost like a delivery service."

"Interesting. I hope it isn't the pizza boy. I really like him." Bags mumbled in her direction. "Marika, call if you need me or when you know something about Ander."

She waived as she climbed into the ambulance.

Chapter 15

Penelope sat in the golf cart next to bags pondering what she just heard. The family bicycle rattled uneasily in the back seat. Bags played off his last question as idle curiosity. Penelope knew better. Now he was thinking what she was thinking. As they approached the turn to her house, Bags broke the silence.

"As long as you're out, how would you like to come with me to the club?"

"Didn't it just close for the night?"

"That is why we need to hurry." He turned left instead of right without waiting for her answer.

"I guess we're going to the club." She said.

Even at golf cart speed, no part of St. Georges was more than a couple of minutes from the club. She expected him to wheel into the drive under the portico. Instead, he pulled into the parking lot across the street and took a spot near the back. From it they could see the main and side entrances to the club. They were also within a few yards of the only three cars left in the lot.

"What are we doing?" Penelope asked.

"Waiting."

"For Ricky? Why don't we just knock? Tyler would let us in I bet."

"Undoubtedly. And he would immediately deduce our purpose."

"And that's a bad thing because . . .?"

"I think we may only have one chance to learn what we need to learn from Ricky. I want to talk to him away from Tyler." Bags explained.

Penelope nodded and shrugged. Truthfully, she didn't care about the tactics. She already knew most of what Ricky was going to say. Her objection to waiting in the parking lot was bug related. She knew the quick squirt of bug spray she applied on her way out the door would last only so long.

96

Fifteen minutes passed. Bags, who could not sit still or be quiet for that long, made several trips to survey the cars and surrounding parts of the parking lot. Penelope began to wonder if Ricky was planning to stay overnight at the club.

"Look." Bags whispered.

Penelope could see the distinctive gait of a sullen teenage boy. Bags waited until the figure crossed the street before stepping out of the cart. Penelope followed, strangely nervous about the encounter. Ricky was oblivious to their approach until he was nearly to his car.

"Ricky, hello there. Penelope and I wondered if you might answer just a few more questions about the other night."

"Whoa! Hey there, Mr. Bagwell. You're out kind of late aren't you?"

"Just a few questions, Ricky. Please." Penelope chimed in.

"I'm kind of in a hurry, guys. Sorry." He put the key in his car door.

"That's too bad, Ricky. I was hoping we could talk before I have a conversation with Tyler. You heard the sirens, I'm sure."

"Yeah, we saw the lights too. What happened? Someone have a heart attack?"

"Not a heart attack. Heroin overdose, actually. My friend Ander."

"Heroin overdose! You're messing with me, Mr. Bagwell. This isn't the kind of place where people use heroin."

"A week ago that would have been my reaction, but Ricky, we both know better, don't we?" Bags had his serious voice on, just like in the bar.

"Hey, just because I had a little trouble before, you can't go accusing me of something like that. I have rights."

"Yes you do, and I'm certain the Sheriff would be happy to explain them to you after I have a word with him."

"You don't have proof of anything. Why are you harassing me?" Ricky opened his car door.

"Ricky, if you leave now, I will call the Sheriff and he will jump to a conclusion just as you feared the night of the Gala. That's why you left, isn't it?"

"So how is talking to you better?"

"That depends on what you have to say. It can't really be worse to talk to us, can it?"

"Dammit." Ricky shut his car door. "So ask."

"Did you sell Ander heroin tonight?"

Silence.

"Ricky." Bags doubled up on the serious voice.

"Yeah, sure. That was me."

"Did you also sell to him the night of the Gala?"

"Not that night. I hadn't seen him in about a week. He was trying to quit, I think. Honestly, I was kinda sorry to see him tonight."

"So who did you meet out by the dumpster the night of the Gala?"

"What makes you think-"

"Ricky. I'm losing patience with you."

Wow, that was a new level of serious from Bags. Penelope wanted to say something, to be a part of the conversation somehow. It was just too good to interrupt.

"Alright . . . yeah . . . I was doing a deal that night."

"Heroin again?" Bags pressed him.

"And who?" Penelope was finally able to join the conversation, not that Bags would have forgotten to ask the question.

"Yeah, heroin. One of my regulars. She's a club member but I don't think she lives in St. Georges."

"I'm going to need a name, Ricky."

"Yeah, ok. Helen Braaten. She's a recreational user. Or at least she doesn't use much."

Bags sighed and Penelope saw his shoulders drop. His gaze wandered from Ricky to the entrance of the club and then the ground. She didn't know Helen except by name as someone who rarely showed up at club functions. Helen and her husband Stanley had one of the bigger boats in the marina. That was all she knew about Helen, except now she knew one of Helen's secrets.

"Ricky, I think we have more to talk about don't we?" Bags asked.

Ricky's eyes narrowed, producing little furrows in his forehead. He looked nervously over his shoulder in the direction of the club. "H-h-h-how? How did you know?"

"Maybe we should have the rest of this conversation indoors. I'm afraid poor Penelope may be carried away by the bugs if we don't."

Bags was right about the bugs and Penelope was thankful he noticed, or that he guessed. She understood the excuse was a convenience too. Ricky did not want anyone to see him talking to the two of them and Bags had picked up on it.

Bags pointed in the direction of his villa and motioned Ricky to get in his car and follow. Penelope found it comical to think their relocation involved Ricky driving about the length of a football field. Bags directed Ricky to park on the far side of the house and they were soon in his villa sitting around a small table usually reserved for card games.

"Now, Ricky, I think there is more you want to tell us."

"You're messing with me, right? How could you know? That's what I can't figure out."

"I need you to hear it in your own words, Ricky."

"Helen took care of her business in about thirty seconds. She acts like she's so much better than me, like it makes her ill just to be around me -- like she's such a lady sitting in her bathroom putting a needle between her toes. Stupid bitch."

"Focus, Ricky, focus."

"Right. Anyway, she was back inside having dinner way before any of the action started."

"Ok . . .." Even as he prompted Ricky to keep talking, Penelope could see that Bags was not hearing exactly what he expected. She assumed he expected what she expected, which was that Ricky was not working alone. At this point she wasn't sure they were still focused on Harry's death. Uncovering a drug ring right in St. Georges was a whole separate kind of mess.

"The main reason I was outside right then was to wait for a shipment." Ricky paused. Bags paused longer.

"Details," Bags finally broke the silence. "I need details."

"It sounds a little crazy but you have to understand, people involved with real drugs are all a little crazy and paranoid. So anyway, the way the shipment came was by water. It would all be arranged. A little boat would slip in during the night and leave the product in a bag right on the edge of dock. That night I was waiting for the signal so I could go and pick it up."

"There's a sensor at the mouth of the marina. A little siren goes off anytime a boat arrives or leaves. How did your delivery service get past that?"

"The little canals that run all through St. Georges. A kayak or raft can slip right through those."

"Of course, the one that lets out into the open water." Bags looked at Penelope. "It helps keep water flowing in and out of the marina. It's like a little back door."

"So a little boat paddles up the scary mangrove ditch in the middle of the night. Sounds kinda silly." Penelope responded.

"That does sound like a very elaborate way to get your drugs, Ricky."

"Like I said, paranoid."

"Assuming I believe your story, what does that have to do with Harry's death?" Bags persisted.

"I wasn't by the dumpster the whole time. I got itchy about the delivery so I walked out to the edge of the pool deck, over by the harbormaster's house. I couldn't see anything but I did hear something like a shuffle and then a couple of bumps or thumps over at the end of the veranda. I couldn't see anything. A little after that I heard kind of ploomp sound, like a mullet jumping and splashing in the water, except not quite like that. I froze until the door to the bar swung open. That startled me and I got right back into the kitchen as fast as I could go without making a bunch of noise."

"And you didn't want to tell the Sheriff what you heard because you think your delivery friends might have been involved." Bags put the next words in Ricky's mouth.

"You keep saying 'my' drugs and 'my' delivery service, but you know that's not true."

Bags looked at Penelope and grinned. "Penelope, we do know that isn't true, don't we?"

"Right," Penelope wished Bags wouldn't assume she was able to read his mind. She didn't like being put on the spot. "Heroin seems like a different ballgame than weed and I'm betting even a different crowd than meth. No offense, Ricky, but you're not smart enough to be connected to those kind of people. And then there's the whole marketing thing. All your time at the club is spent in the kitchen or out by the dumpsters. You would have no way of getting customers like Ander or Helen. Only someone who knew all the club members really well would be in a position to know who to approach and how. Every new conversation would have to be handled very delicately. That's way out of your league. Only Tyler could pull that off."

Penelope held her breath, waiting for a reaction. Hearing no laughter, she continued. "My only question is whether this was a fair deal for you. See, I think Tyler probably didn't have to pay you much once you got started. He had you convinced that if he went to the police, you would be the fall guy. You're the one on probation. He probably doesn't even have a police record. You were too afraid to call his bluff."

"He's not as nice as people think. He has you all fooled. My pay for all of it was keeping my job as a cook so I could meet the terms of my probation. It wouldn't have taken much for him to get my probation revoked."

Penelope noticed a curious look flash across Bags' face. She was about to ask him what was up when her phone buzzed. She only pulled it out of her pocket because of the slight chance it was her dad wanting something and being too lazy to walk to her room to talk to her. If she didn't respond, he might feel the need to check on her.

Yep, she thought to herself as she looked at the screen to see the notification, good thing I checked. It was her dad. She unlocked her phone to see the message. Uh-oh! It was a short text: "I think you should come home now." Her heart skipped.

"Bags. Bags, I have to go now." The urgency in her voice got his attention.

"What is it, my dear?"

"Got a text from my dad. I need to go home." She hoped her expression was not consistent with the feeling in the pit of her stomach.

"Oh. Well then, yes, I think you should go right away. Please tell him I'm sorry and that it is all my fault you are out so late. Take my golf cart."

Penelope was already on her way down the stairs to the garage and heard the last words trailing behind her. She glanced at her phone again. It was a little after midnight. She was in big trouble.

The worst part would be knocking on the door. More precisely it would be the few seconds after her knock and before his response. He would be in his room, sitting up in bed reading, writing, or watching TV. Noise from the door opening and closing would announce her arrival. He would hear her trudge up the stairs so her knock would in no way come as a surprise. Until she heard his voice, Penelope would be unable to assess his level of anger. It was all shades of horrific at this point.

She also knew her dad had several layers of angry within him. Penelope could predict his response to a lot of things, kid things. They were both figuring out the teenage things together and, though it was kind of a sad reflection on her social life, this was the first time she had been caught sneaking out at night. Penelope practiced her very very sorry face on the way up the stairs.

At the door she paused before knocking. She knocked and held her breath.

Chapter 16

Penelope slept in, having no desire to interact with her dad again so soon. As it turned out, the anticipation was the worst part. Somehow he knew exactly why she left the house so late and also that she would end up with Bags. He was eerily calm and the stern lecture she was forced to absorb seemed delivered more because it was the fatherly thing to do than because he was truly upset.

Even her punishment was oddly minor. She was grounded for two weeks, except when she had a paying job, was otherwise helping one of the residents, or was with Bags. Normally, that would cramp her style. These days, the exceptions perfectly described her social life, which was as tragic as it sounded.

When she finally rolled out of bed and wandered down to the kitchen, Father was nowhere to be found. The note on the counter said he was going to the gym and then to do errands. Out of spite he added "p.s., I'll be stopping for sushi while I'm out -- too bad you're grounded and couldn't come with." Mean, he was just mean.

She popped a bagel in the toaster and sent Bags a text. He was still less than proficient with his phone despite her best tutoring, so there was no telling when, or if, he would respond.

Bags responded mid-bagel with, "Well rested? You've missed a lot since you left. Bring my golf cart back and I will catch you up."

She was feeling well rested, thank you very much. Her brain decided not to swirl all night. Getting in trouble with Father was apparently enough of a distraction to push Ricky's crazy story and all the other mystery stuff far into the background for a few hours.

The text restarted her brain. Penelope decided the best way to manage it was to go see Bags so she could add a bunch of new stuff to the mix. She grabbed a bottle of water and was out the door with the last bite of bagel in her mouth.

Soon she was at Chez Bags sitting at the counter looking into the kitchen. He was trying to multitask, fixing his lunch while also wrestling with the espresso machine to make Penelope a latte. It was cute.

Penelope watched him work and listened as he explained what she missed. Ricky would be making an appearance at the Sheriff's office today. Bags worked it out with the Sheriff to spare Ricky as long as he helped them get the necessary evidence to end Tyler's misuse of his position at St. Georges. The Sheriff agreed Ricky was not the real prize. The Sheriff even viewed Tyler as a minor prize, mostly useful as a way to get to his supplier. He wanted the supplier.

This was by far the closest Penelope had ever been to the world of drug dealers or drug enforcement. It was way better than reality TV and almost as entertaining as Pretty Little Liars.

Things got even better when Bags casually dropped the real headline of the day. The autopsy results were back. The Sheriff gave Bags a preview by phone and was coming back to St. Georges to have another look at the crime scene. That's right, "crime scene." Penelope and Bags were right. Harry's death was not an accident, which meant they were officially helping to investigate a homicide -- scary and exciting.

Bags continued as he handed Penelope her drink. "The Medical Examiner believes Harry was standing or possibly kneeling when the blow was struck more or less directly from the side with something hard, heavy, and not jagged. The obvious thing would be a ball bat or a rock cradled in the killer's hand. There was only evidence of one blow to the right temple."

"So someone hit Harry one time really hard and he fell. The fall is probably what I heard. One shot to the temple killed him?" Penelope asked rhetorically.

"Sheriff Billings has the same question. He is insisting it wasn't a premeditated killing because the ME told him a blow like that could not be guaranteed to kill a healthy adult. In other words, if you were planning to kill a man, you wouldn't plan for that to be your only strike. A second blow just for certainty, would suggest intent. He thinks this was more likely an argument gone very wrong."

"But I didn't hear any arguing. I think I would have heard the kind of argument that leads to a whack on the head." Penelope objected.

"True. He also thinks it possible our drug suppliers noticed Harry watching their delivery or maybe just didn't want to take chances so they knocked him out to give themselves time to slip away."

"It does seem unlikely for the drug deal and Harry's death to be completely unrelated. I mean what are the odds of two completely different major crimes happening in St. Georges on the same night, fifty feet apart?"

"I agree, which makes it even more important to handle the Tyler situation carefully. He may be our only chance to find the men involved with that delivery."

"So what's the plan for that?"

"The Sheriff will be handling it. I think the less we know the better."

"Seriously? That's no fun." She wrinkled her nose at him.

"Yes, I'm afraid it will hamper our efforts for at least a week."

"A week!" Penelope exclaimed. "So not fair."

Bags smiled. "I see you have even less patience than me."

"Patience is overrated."

"That is not the prevailing opinion, I'm afraid."

"But it's so boring around here."

"Yes, retirement is overrated even more than patience. We will just have to make our own entertainment." Bags reassured her.

"At least I'm not grounded from hanging out with you. Hey, did you have something to do with that?"

"I don't think so. I did drop by your house this morning to speak with Axel." Bags demurred.

"Aww, thanks. How did he seem?"

"He was more calm than I anticipated. I expected him to feel obligated to shake his finger at me a little."

"Same with me last night. Weird, right?"

"I guess on the scale of all the kinds of trouble a teenage girl might find after sneaking out, chasing a fire truck with a harmless old man does not sound so bad to a father."

"Yeah, one of Mother's favorite lines is 'that's how girls end up dead in the gutter.'" Penelope added philosophically.

"I expect someday you will give your father good cause to produce some gray hairs but for right now you are wearing a little invisible halo."

"Tiara. Let's say I'm wearing an invisible tiara."

"As you wish." Bags rolled his eyes and laughed at her, which was the desired response.

Chapter 17

Penelope stared at the ceiling fan, not wanting to leave the sleepy comfort of snuggling under layers of blanket. The sun had been up for hours and the pavement would be baking by now, which only made the air inside her room colder. Father had been an easy convert to the refrigeration brand of air conditioning popular in Florida. He said it was physics in the "equal but opposite reaction" sense -- hotter outside, colder inside.

For sleep and lounging that suited Penelope perfectly. She loved to wrap up in a blanket or three. This morning -- she thought it was still morning -- she allowed her mind to dwell in that space just before sleep, contemplating how her day might unfold.

Bags had been right. The investigation had been on hold for a week while the Sheriff planned the operation to catch Tyler's heroin supplier. The more she thought about it, the more she became convinced that would end the search for Harry's killer. For a few days she had allowed herself to be caught up in an imagined Agatha Christie story. She knew most crimes, including murders, were more straightforward, just as the Sheriff said the day she met him.

The probability of the case being closed in the next few days made her happy and sad. The murder mystery sleuth fantasy she and Bags created was exciting while it lasted, but the goal, she reminded herself, was to find some justice for Harry. Penelope couldn't decide whether it seemed more tragic or less to think Harry was killed because he was in the wrong place at the wrong time rather than as the result of some more calculated plan.

There was a part of her that wanted to "solve" the case, explaining to the Sheriff exactly who and how. She didn't need to stage the big reveal with all the suspects sitting in a parlor sipping sherry as she and Bags unraveled the mystery. Still, things were shaping up to be totally anticlimactic. Sheriff Phillips acknowledged the role Bags and Penelope played in uncovering the lead that would likely bring the killer to justice. That was something. It just didn't feel like a lot. She knew Bags felt the same way, although he would probably not admit it.

The good news was that the week of waiting for the Sheriff to spring his trap had been much less boring than she feared. When Bags told her the next heroin shipment was not scheduled for a week, Penelope viewed being forced to wait so long as torture -- the kind of slow, aching torture she expected to fill her whole summer.

Since moving into the teenager free zone there had been less torture than Penelope anticipated. Staring mindlessly at streaming video hour after hour proved an underrated strategy but still one with limits. Helping Bags prepare for the Gala ended up being a good distraction at the right time. And then, of course, the few days right after the Gala had been the opposite of boring. She hated the reason, obviously. Even not knowing Harry that well, it still made her sad to think she would never see him again. But once it happened, it couldn't be undone. The best they could do for Harry was help figure out what happened. She only felt a little guilty being excited by it.

Things started looking up a little on the very first day of the investigation timeout when her mother came back early from Europe. For starters, Mother was always good for at least one coffee run a day. Coming off a ten-day trip five time zones away, one a day was a minimum. Her return also guaranteed the scheduling of some forced family fun. Penelope was usually not a huge fan of such "events" but the area was still new and unexplored for all of them, so the outings had kind of a Spring Break flavor.

They went paddle boarding one day. Highlights included Father falling off his board, repeatedly; Mother paddling frantically to shore after a legitimate shark sighting right under her board; and, of course, surfer boy Steve McDreamy's dreadlocks and washboard abs. It was a good day.

Then, a trip to Naples began slowly but ended with shopping at Coconut Point. Shopping was always a worthwhile diversion, particularly with her mom. Father was a good sport about wandering around with her at the mall. He just didn't understand the critical nature of fashion in Penelope's life the way her mom did, which was really just a way of saying it was easier to talk Mom into buying things for her.

Bags provided the entertainment the day between Surfer Steve and Coconut Point. Their trip to Boca Grande had been the subject of much planning and discussion -- all by Bags. Penelope went along with it in hope of getting in some sunbathing on the deck of a fancy boat.

As an aside, even though at least half the members of the St. Georges Yacht Club did not have boats in the marina, you couldn't be at the club long without learning about boats, sometimes by osmosis and sometimes straight up against your will. Because he talked about it endlessly -- ok not endlessly but too much for Penelope's taste -- she knew quite a bit about the Bags yacht. For starters, at only 36 feet long it wasn't really a yacht. The biggest boats in the marina were 65 feet long and 50 feet was kind of standard. Those were yachts. They usually had two full decks, meaning more than one little cubby of a stateroom "below deck," which was boat talk for "downstairs." Importantly for Penelope, most of them had at least one place where a girl could stretch out in the sun.

Bags had a picnic boat. That's actually what it was called, which Penelope found adorable, but which also meant diminished sunbathing options. This was no ordinary picnic boat, however. Bags made that very clear. This was a 1995 Hinckley picnic boat with jet drive, blah, blah, blah. Penelope kind of stopped listening to Bags at a certain point. Boats all had to have names. That was another thing she had picked up by osmosis. Bags named his Bags of Cuteness, which turned into just "Cuteness."

The big 65-foot boats seemed to be designed to impress either by being very sleek and sexy or, more pragmatically, by cramming in the maximum number of staterooms, sun decks, swim platforms, and aquatic toys. Cuteness had none of those things but it was pretty. The navy hull, soft-white deck, and polished wood trim screamed New England fishing village.

And, while most of the blah, blah, blah about the engines and radar, and sonar, blah, blah, was pointless; it turned out the jet drive really mattered. Penelope had been on a big powerboat in Illinois and the engine noise was ridiculous. Cuteness wasn't exactly the Stealth Fighter but it wasn't horrible. She and Bags could motor along and carry on a conversation.

So off they went in Cuteness. Boca Grande was fun, possibly not worth the long slog on the Intracoastal to get there, but fun. The highlight was Bags letting her drive their rented golf cart all around the little island. There wasn't that much to see. It was cute, quaint, with a street or two of little shops and places to eat -- just the kind of place her parents would eventually discover and drag her to over and over. Today, Penelope had her fill in two hours.

That might have had something to do with the scorching heat. Even with a slight island breeze it was hard not to wilt after walking half a block. After lunch they were both glad to be back on Cuteness heading onto the water where they could at least make a proper breeze for themselves.

Penelope suffered through a lot of jibber jabber about boats on the first leg of the trip. On the return leg she decided to regale Bags with equally pointless information on one of her favorite subjects. Penelope couldn't remember exactly when she had become obsessed with zombies. It was a long time ago. You would be hard pressed to find a zombie movie she hadn't seen and her knowledge was encyclopedic. The parents were split on the whole issue. Mother refused to watch with her and felt Penelope spent far too much productive time contemplating what it would take to survive the zombie apocalypse.

Father liked to watch with her most of the time and was willing to entertain a modest amount of serious discussion on the subject. He even encouraged Penelope's semi-serious attempt to write the definitive zombie survival handbook, probably because he liked the idea that she might grow up to be a writer.

She had any number of highly pragmatic ideas. For example, tube socks would be everywhere after the zombpocalypse. The number of orphaned socks in the world at any given time must be in the billions, she imagined. Food, on the other hand, would be in short supply. If you were going to survive more than a week or two, you would need to find canned goods. You would obviously have extra socks at your disposal and as long as you had one can of food, you had a weapon. Put your last can of soup in the foot of an extra long tube sock, swing that sock around by the other end and, bam, deadly zombie head smasher and tasty meal all in one. She had all kinds of good ideas like that. Maybe she did spend too much time thinking about zombies.

Bags nodded and smiled at appropriate intervals while Penelope schooled him on the finer points of fast and slow zombies, the best and worst zombie shows, and her prioritized list of things she would do when the zombies rose and civilization ended. His only comment on any of it was to agree that

Penelope had the right stuff to survive the apocalypse. His evidence was from the night of the Gala.

He said most young ladies would not have been brave enough to barge out the door to investigate the strange noise on the veranda. She hadn't thought of it like that. It was true, things that bothered other girls her age, or older, and even some boys, didn't seem like a big deal to her. Bags pointed out how calm Penelope had been hovering over a dead body. Penelope remembered it differently. She mostly remembered the part where she hyperventilated, but it was true that she freaked out only after she was there on the ground with Harry trying to help him and not when she first saw him sprawled on the ground.

Bags was a good sport to listen to her zombie ramblings. He was a better sport for listening to her rant about mean girls and stupid boys for the last fifteen minutes of the trip. She wasn't sure how she got started on the subject. It just happened that way sometimes. Penelope wondered if Bags understood the significance. She thought these thoughts all the time and ranted to herself often. Only her true friends, and occasionally, her mom or dad, got to -- had to -- hear any of it out loud.

She felt really comfortable around Bags. Her grandmothers on both sides were still alive and she even remembered a great grandmother, who lived to be 98, but Penelope never had a grandfather. Bags seemed like a grandfather, so much that she thought he must be one. Oddly, there was no evidence of grandkids at the villa and he wasn't one to talk about his past. There was no wife in the picture, currently. That much was clear. And no pictures in his house suggesting there once was a Mrs. Bags. Still, he always seemed to come up with a non-answer on the subject of his romantic history. For all the time they spent together, there were big gaps in what she knew about him.

At some point in the day, probably walking along trying to eat ice cream from their cones faster than the sun could turn it into just cream, Penelope decided Bags was the closest thing she was likely to find to a grandfather and that she was the best fake granddaughter he was ever going to meet. Once she had the thought it was more or less decided. Bags would be conferred honorary grandfather status and, whether he liked it or not, would owe her all the rights and privileges due a grandchild.

On her side of the bargain, that meant he had the privilege -- ok dubious privilege -- of listening to her ranting. Today was a particularly energetic rant. With no friends her age around Penelope had built up quite a bit of rehashed and anticipatory annoyance about stupid boys and mean girls. So far Bags was up to the challenge.

As the pent up stress ebbed, Penelope decided it was a good opportunity to segue into another attempt to unravel some of the mystery and fill some of the gaps in her Bags-related knowledge, since they were now family.

"Bags, you were a stupid boy once, you know, a long time ago. So tell me this. Why do boys struggle so much to understand the simplest things about what a girl wants?" She began.

"My dear Penelope, by that definition I'm afraid I was a stupid boy not that long ago."

"Are you telling me I will still be dealing with that nonsense even after they look like men?"

"Even when they look like old men." He smiled.

"Like the way you and all your buddies chase after Marika?"

Laughing, "A beautiful woman rarely brings out the best in men. You have deduced that correctly."

"I know, right? It's like mean girl hotness creates some airborne virus that turns boys into zombies, falling all over themselves for the privilege of being abused."

"That's not the worst part, Penelope." Bags shook his head. "You are right that a beautiful woman lowers the IQ of every man within range. But if you add love to the mix, things get much worse, for boys and girls."

"Go on . . .." Penelope urged.

"Love turns all of us into children at some point. Growing up, even growing old, offers no sure defense."

"So when was the last time love turned you into a stupid boy, Bags?"

"That is quite a question. Like any man I have been susceptible to the stupidity uniquely triggered by infatuation and you are right that had I met her at a different time, Marika would easily make me look much more the fool than she already does. But you asked about love. I have succumbed to that disease only a few times in all my years and none were recent."

"So at some point there was a great love of your life?" Penelope probed.

"Almost too long ago for me to remember and, yes, she made me act like a child. I like to think I had the same effect on her."

"You aren't giving me much hope here, Bags."

"Ignore me, my dear. Love may be the only thing truly worth living and dying for. It is just a high stakes game with the potential to create unbearable pain. It makes otherwise sane people do things you would never expect."

"Ok, good pep talk, Bags. New subject?"

"Anything but zombies, Penelope."

"Or boats. No zombies. No boats."

Having failed to get anything concrete out of Bags about his past, Penelope contented herself with recapping what they knew about Harry's death. Bags seemed happy for the change of topic and played along while they docked Cuteness and rinsed all the saltwater off of her. The post boating cleanup was an unpleasant surprise for Penelope, by the way. It was no accident Bags left that part out when he was going over the day's itinerary with her that morning. She didn't really mind. It was the kind of thing you did for your grandpa.

Chapter 18

Her day on the water with Bags had been a good day in the middle of a surprisingly good week. The week was over now. It was mildly entertaining to lounge under the covers all morning rehashing the week's highlights, particularly because her brain's annoying habit of remembering recent events in frame by frame detail made it like watching her own home videos. She was bored with that now and focused on what was supposed to be waiting at the end of the week.

Sheriff Phillips would only share general information with Bags about the planned sting. Nevertheless, Penelope and Bags had deduced it would have to happen Thursday, Friday, or Saturday night. Ricky and Tyler would have to have a reason to be at the club. The delivery the night of the Gala was not the normal drill. Ricky told Bags that much. The schedule had been adjusted to take advantage of having almost every St. Georges resident in the dining room for three hours during the party. Normally, the delivery would be made as far into the night as possible. The club stayed open latest on weekend nights. The tides would come into play because, according to Bags, the watery tunnel of terror they would use to get in and out could just about dry up in places when the tide was out. She wouldn't know personally because she was not going to go there again, ever.

When you added everything up, Friday or Saturday night during the hour after the bar closed at midnight made the most sense. It was now Sunday morning. Penelope waited up past midnight both nights in vain, hoping to hear sirens. It was beyond frustrating. The only thing she could do was whine to Bags until he called the Sheriff for an update. Bags was a morning person so he had no doubt been up for hours. Maybe he had already called the Sheriff.

Penelope was up and quickly done with the summer bathroom routine. In the summer, definitely this summer, she cut out most of the effort beyond that required for hygiene. Mother would argue she wasn't even meeting the hygiene minimum. But there was no one to impress and no mean girls looking to pounce on her tiniest hair, makeup, or fashion shortcoming. All she needed was to be minimally presentable. It was a no pictures, no paparazzi kind of day again.

Once downstairs, Penelope remembered she had the house to herself. Father was driving Mother to Miami to catch a direct flight to . . . somewhere boring in Europe. She couldn't quite remember. It wasn't London, Milan, or Paris. She kept track enough to know when her mom would be in a place where they had fashion. When Mother went to a good place, it was worth conjuring a charm offensive in the pre-departure days so there might be something cute for Penelope in her suitcase when she returned. This wasn't one of those trips. Her parents planned to go a little early and have lunch before heading to the airport so Penelope said goodbye to her mom the night before, knowing she would still be sleeping when they left.

Father would be gone most of the day. She knew her dad always asked Bags to keep an eye on her when he was going to be gone more than a couple of hours. Bags would certainly be on alert today and so Penelope was a little surprised he hadn't already showed up at her doorstep. There was nothing from him on her phone either.

It was barely still morning. Bags was clearly shirking his chaperone duties. As she cleaned out the tub of hummus with a nasty, gluten-free cracker, Penelope began to think maybe she needed to check on Bags instead of the other way around.

She liked hummus and this morning she liked it specifically because it was the easiest imaginable breakfast. Mother had started a new diet -- gluten free, dairy free, high fiber, blah, blah, blah, which pretty much meant Penelope and her dad had started the same diet. This was the last of the hummus in the house and it would stay that way until she and her dad went to the store the day before Mother returned. In her absence they would be on more of a "better eat the things you like while you can" kind of diet. It seemed fair, particularly because she was pretty sure her mom would be on the "someone else is paying for dinner and wine so let's try some of everything" diet during her trip.

Penelope finally switched mental gears as she motored past the club and to the end of the row of villas, where she wheeled into the driveway and parked. Everything seemed normal outside the Bags villa. She punched in the code on the keypad for the garage door. It opened slowly. Both cars and the golf cart were there. She paused on her way past the sleek convertible to fondle it and drool a little. Bags had taken her for a ride a couple of times but she had yet to convince him to hand over the keys.

The door was unlocked, as usual. Now that she was family Penelope didn't feel the slightest guilt wandering into his house whether Bags was there or not. Usually, he would hear her or she would be able to hear him by the time she was halfway up the stairs to the main level.

In the kitchen everything looked normal but a quick look around failed to produce any sign of Bags so Penelope started up the stairs to the third floor. This time, halfway up the stairs did make the difference. Bags was in his bedroom to the left at the top of the stairs. The door was closed. She could hear that he was in earnest conversation with someone. He was very interested in what he was hearing. It wasn't a social conversation. Bags was using his business voice. She couldn't actually hear the words so all she had to go on was the tone as it came to her muffled by something. He must be in his closet or the bathroom.

Penelope decided not to barge in. She slipped back down the stairs, found a soda in the refrigerator, and sent him a text -- "In your kitchen waiting for you to come down."

Two minutes later Bags came dancing down the stairs. "You must be psychic."

"Sorry?"

"Your timing is perfect."

"What are you so giddy about, Bags?"

"I was just on the phone with the Sheriff. It all happened last night."

"Shut up!" She exclaimed. "Don't mess with me, Bags."

"I promise. Sheriff Phillips told me the details. He is quite pleased with himself."

"Great, so now you have to tell me." Penelope ordered.

"I'll tell you in the car. Sheriff Phillips wants us to come to the station."

"Why?"

"Because he is wrong again about what happened. Come along, I'll explain in the car."

Bags was already halfway down the stairs before Penelope was out of her chair. He picked the wrong vehicle again. Bags generally preferred the easier in and out of the crossover sitting in the stall next to its sexy cousin the R8 convertible. Penelope was actually beginning to wonder why he had it. Most older guys would buy a car like that to impress much younger women. That clearly wasn't his game. The two times he had taken her for a ride in it, he drove like a little old lady, which seemed pointless. At least if he let her drive it once in a while, the poor car would have some sense of purpose. Penelope thought it must be a very sad and lonely little red car.

That was conversation topic for another time with Bags. Today would be about the investigation. Bags started the briefing even before they were past the club. He was talking faster than she had ever seen his mouth move.

The gist was that everything had happened Saturday night just like she and Bags predicted. Ricky tipped off the Sheriff earlier in the day after Tyler told him he would need to stay late and help clean up. That was the signal. The Sheriff had two boats waiting outside the St. Georges marina. One was hidden next to the private dock of a mansion on the water just past St. Georges. That one would pick up the little boat as it exited St. Georges. The other was out near the channel of deeper water that ran past St. Georges. It was the boat highway a bigger vessel would have to use to launch the smaller boat on its way to the marina. Sheriff Phillips suspected there would be such a boat.

Meanwhile, the Sheriff and two of his detectives would be lurking down the block from the club in a surveillance van. Bags had worked with the Commodore to get the Sheriff access to the club on Tyler's day off so his team could install a tiny webcam and microphone in Tyler's office, where Ricky would deliver him the brick of heroin. The Sheriff would be monitoring the webcam, prepared to burst in as soon as he saw Tyler take possession of the brick. Once Tyler had the heroin in his hands, the Sheriff would signal the boats. One would then take the delivery boat and its occupants into custody, while the other boarded the larger boat to search for more drugs.

Apparently, everything went exactly according to plan. It was all handled so quietly even Bags hadn't heard any of it. Penelope should have known there would be no lights or sirens. The whole point was to take the bad guys by surprise.

Out on the water there was only one minor surprise. The two guys on the rubber raft were right where they were supposed to be and had been taken into custody without incident. As the Sheriff suspected, there was also a forty-eight foot Sea Ray out in the deeper water. Also as the Sheriff suspected, there were more drugs on that boat, including two more bricks of heroin.

The surprise was that no one was on the Sea Ray when the Sheriff's men boarded it, which could mean one or more bad guys got away. That sounded like something the Sheriff would be interested in resolving but probably didn't have anything to do with Harry.

The two who did not get away, and Tyler too, spent a very uncomfortable night in custody. The Sheriff's detectives began to question them the previous night. The first line of questioning was about the heroin. The detectives had made clear to them they faced a slew of felony convictions and impressed on each that the only hope for leniency was to be the first to turn on the others.

The Sea Ray was registered out of Miami to a big time hedge fund manager on Wall Street. Penelope knew nothing about hedge funds, hedgehogs, or even hedges, really. Bags assured her all she needed to know was that the guy was super rich; so rich, this wasn't even the main boat at his place in Miami.

Hedge Fund Johnny -- his actual name was Jonathan something something snooty something so Penelope shortened it -- seemed mostly irrelevant to the story, except that he had a daughter who was going to school in Miami and living in the family house there. The two guys in custody were slightly less rich kids who happened to be going to school with the daughter. Apparently, they both started threatening lawsuits against the County even before they had been issued their orange jumpsuits. But all that faded pretty quickly when the detectives made clear they had Ricky, Tyler, and the Sea Ray in custody.

Their initial story was that the daughter let them use the boat in exchange for keeping her supplied with all the designer drugs she and her posse of mean girls needed for their three nights a week of clubbing. "Mean girls" was Penelope's phrasing and, yes, she was making an assumption.

The fun part was the twist. The detectives were quite successful with their divide and conquer strategy. It apparently hadn't taken long for a different story to emerge. In their individual efforts to be the most cooperative felon, both young men gave pretty much the same story about their supplier.

Once upon a time, Hedge Fund Johnny was very casual about whose money he took. You had to have a big pile of money to even know what a hedge fund was, so a lot of the fund managers figured it didn't much matter who supplied the money because it was clearly money they could afford to lose.

In his greed, Johnny went a step further. He started allowing his hedge fund to be used to launder some people's ill-gotten money, meaning Mexican drug money. When the economy tanked, a lot of hedge funds tanked harder. Some fund managers were ruined, as in "start your car and sit in it in the garage until you fall asleep," ruined. Johnny survived but lost a lot of money for some very unforgiving people. His solution was to go into business with them and work off his debt, which he did. He discovered that drug money was even easier to make than hedge fund money and only slightly more regulated in the post bank bailout landscape, so he kept going. The two meatheads in custody were part of his crew.

All of this was a much more entertaining backstory than she dared imagine. Penelope decided their capture was very bad news for the daughter and for Mrs. Hedge Fund, if there was one. The junior flunkies had happily rolled on Johnny and the Sheriff seemed convinced they were sincere in denying any knowledge about Johnny's supplier. They admitted picking up large quantities of weed and heroin from a handful of dead drops in South Florida but denied any involvement in the exchange of money and said the system was designed so they never crossed paths with anyone working for the cartel.

Penelope was pretty sure the buck would stop with Johnny. He would be a high profile arrest. That would make the Sheriff and, she assumed, the DEA happy. And Johnny only really had three choices. He could roll on the drug lords and disappear into witness protection, take his own life, or keep his mouth shut and hope his unsavory partners had continuing confidence in his loyalty.

None of that, however, really mattered to Penelope or Bags. Hedge Fund Johnny wasn't in the marina the night Harry died. What Penelope and Bags needed to know was whether the two henchmen had been and, if so, did they see, hear, or do anything relevant to Harry's death?

That's why Bags was driving with modest urgency. When the Johnny Hedge Fund story started to pour out in both interrogation rooms, Sheriff Phillips called the local DEA field office. Someone from the office would be there soon to collect the four suspects -- Ricky was arrested with Tyler to conceal his cooperation and the DEA would definitely want to talk to him. Sheriff Phillips could hold the two delivery boys only for as long as it would take to do an initial interview about their possible involvement in Harry's death. If that yielded no evidence to connect them to the homicide, the DEA would take them and that would be that.

Sheriff Phillips clearly thought one of them was the killer and he wanted to close the case. He asked Bags to come watch the interrogations from behind the two-way mirror and specifically suggested he bring Penelope since she was the one who first heard the noises and was then the first to see the victim. Bags was obviously happy to be there even if the Sheriff's motivation was a little off the mark.

"This will be our one chance to find out if either of these gentlemen have information that can help us find Harry's killer." Bags confirmed.

"So you don't believe it's either of them?"

"No," he said pointedly. "It seems too convenient and at the same time hopelessly improbable."

"Well, I don't really know what that means, but I kind of agree. All week I was unconsciously trying to convince myself they were the most likely culprits. Now that it's about to be real, something keeps yelling 'no' inside my head."

"Good, we agree. Have you ever been inside a police station or a jail?" Bags asked earnestly.

"Not that kinda girl, Bags. Sorry."

"That's what I thought. You may find it jarring. Stay close to me or to the Sheriff. It will be fine."

"Ok, what's our strategy? It's not like they're going to let us ask any questions."

"Probably not. I think we should try to split up. If they will allow it, each of us should observe one of the two interrogations. I assume they will be going on at the same time."

"That works for me as long as I have the Sheriff with me."

"Agreed."

Chapter 19

The County Jail and the Sheriff's Offices were connected. Bags and Penelope entered through the nonthreatening administrative entrance on the Sheriff's side. Sheriff Phillips soon appeared and escorted them to a conference room outside his office where Detectives Salero and Benton were waiting. Bags suggested he and Penelope should split up and each observe one of the interviews. Penelope was surprised when the Sheriff said, "I have an even better idea," and explained that they had it set up so all three of them could watch both interviews at once.

Penelope thought it funny when the detectives called them "interviews." It was a less threatening word than interrogation, for sure, which made the name seem comically insincere, almost like the detectives were hipsters trying to bring more irony into their world. The word was the only nonthreatening about the process. She was pretty sure the only people in orange jumpsuits not terrified by the experience were those who had been there so many times it felt like home.

The briefing continued. Blair Simmons and Carter Bennett "the third" were the two interviewees. Penelope couldn't wait to see them. The names were straight out of Central Casting -- "listen up people, we have a cop show in Ft. Myers that needs two hopelessly entitled blue bloods with names that would only seem normal on Martha's Vineyard."

Penelope and Bags shared what they had seen and heard that night and also what they knew from Ricky. The Sheriff went over the autopsy report to make sure everyone was on the same page. When their pre-game huddle was done, the detectives split up and went to interview rooms more or less across from each other along a hallway. When the Sheriff, Bags, and Penelope were safely behind the door of the viewing room, first Blair and then Carter were shuffled down the hall by guards from the jail part of the building and deposited in their respective rooms.

Inside the viewing room was a large two-way mirror and, centered on the wall just to the side of the glass, a large, flat panel video monitor. They had a straight shot through the glass at Detective Salero and his new friend Carter and could still see a fairly high-resolution video of Detective Benton and his pal Blair.

A few minutes into the interviews the three observers agreed the pace as well as the stories were in remarkable harmony. The trend continued through the basic description of events inside the marina.

Blair and Carter, who preferred to be called "Trip" wouldn't you know it, told the same story almost simultaneously. It was definitely the two of them making the delivery on the night in question. Dressed in all black, riding low in a black rubber raft, they moved in the shadows out of the mangrove lined canal and around the edges of the marina, being as quiet with their paddles as possible. There was a point along the dock just beyond the first row of slips where visiting boats could tie up. That was the drop point. At night it was quite dark in that area and also close enough to the kitchen for Ricky to get there quickly to pick up the package. It was a lot of money sitting there on the dock and so it was in everyone's interest to minimize the time it remained unattended.

As Blair guided them into position along the dock, Trip reached for the bag behind him and started to move it into position to lift it up onto the dock. This sounded overly cautious, they both said, but two people in a little rubber raft required a constant balancing act and any little move in the wrong direction could result in sudden adjustments and sudden noises. Neither one of them knew exactly what happened to cause it but the raft jostled and banged up into the underside of the dock. That caused Trip to scramble with the very expensive bag, which consequently made a solid thunking sound as it landed on top of the dock.

When the noise settled, they looked around. At first everything seemed cool. There was a lot of background noise coming from the dining room and neither of them could see anyone outside. Then something caught Blair's eye. There was a figure on the veranda. A fence, a couple of trees and a row of shrubs between the dock and the figure made it hard to see more than a silhouette. They kept watching, hoping the figure would go back inside so they could slip away.

After a few seconds, Blair became convinced it was a man on the veranda and that he was watching them as intently as they were watching him. It was at this point the stories diverged slightly. Blair's version suggested both young men agreed on the need for a response and he decided to take action. In

Trip's version, Blair simply hoisted himself out of the raft and onto the dock without discussion and with little regard to the noise he was making. If the mystery figure hadn't been focused in their direction before, Blair's cowboy move sealed the deal.

Trip wasn't sure what Blair had in mind. He only knew both of them would need the raft to be in the right place for them to get out of this mess, so he stayed put and held onto the dock. Meanwhile, Blair moved across the ten-foot width of the dock to the iron fence for a better view. He confirmed Trip's suspicion by admitting he wasn't quite sure what he planned to do if he saw something on the veranda. As he peered over the fence, Blair's worst fears seemed to be confirmed. The figure on the veranda appeared to be moving in his direction and he thought he could hear the man speaking.

From this point forward the stories converged. Trip observed and Blair admitted that he froze. He had no weapon and no good idea about how he might use one if he had it. The whole point of their system was stealth. Any interaction with the locals could only end badly for the operation. This was, after all, almost a weekly drop. Tyler was a good customer.

It was at this point fate intervened. What Blair initially took for a call in his direction had really been directed at a second figure. This new player was even more obscured than the first. Even without being able to see exactly what was happening, Blair recognized the opportunity. While the two figures were focused on each other, Blair slid back across the dock and into the raft. At this point neither Blair nor Trip cared much about remaining noiseless. They paddled hard until they felt safely back in the shadows on the far side of the marina, which sounded very much like it put them right outside the back door of Harry's house. They paused to catch their breath and watch for any more signs they had been compromised.

Then they heard a scream and then more noise and then there were a lot of people outside. They were glad to be at a safe distance and concluded that whatever happened on the veranda was not about them. They took the opportunity of the new distraction and got out of the marina as fast as they could paddle.

That was their story. It was consistent. It fit with Ricky's observations and the way he described the drop system. It fit with what they already knew about the immediate aftermath on the veranda. And it was grounded in logic from their perspective. All that was true and the Sheriff was having none of it. He remained convinced that after Harry saw them over by the dock, one or both of them hopped out and hit him over the head. His detectives were clearly aware of that belief and, as a result, a solid thirty minutes of repetition and cross-examination ensued in both rooms.

It eventually became clear that no matter how many times you made them tell the story, no matter how you tried to intimidate or shame them, no matter how many times you said, "I don't believe you," it was going to be the same story. Penelope could tell Bags was about to lose patience.

She was equally agitated and decided she needed to do something before one of them had a stroke from sheer frustration. Penelope motioned to Bags and then whispered in his ear. He nodded and then whispered in hers.

"Sheriff," Bags began, "I wonder if these two wouldn't benefit from a little mental distraction to shake their concentration."

"You have something in mind?" He asked.

"They keep telling the same story. Maybe that's because your men keep asking questions with the same purpose. Perhaps if they were to mix it up, take a different tack, so to speak, one of the boys might go off script. If so, then you would have them."

"Ok, but how do we do that?"

"If your detectives were asking questions of them as witnesses instead of as suspects, I think they might ask a few different questions. That might lull our young friends into thinking they have a way out, which, in turn, might make one of them slip." Bags continued.

"What kind of questions did you have in mind?"

Bags looked at Penelope and nodded. She took her cue. "Well, I was thinking, Sheriff. Both of these guys say they saw some kind of interaction between Harry -- I mean we are assuming one of the figures is Harry -- and some mystery person. If we were asking some little old lady out walking her dog that night, we would want her to describe the details of everything she saw and heard before, during, and after."

The Sheriff shook his head. "Well, I'm not sure it's going to get us anywhere but I don't have a better idea right now." He reached up to the wall and tapped a little button twice, repeating the gesture on a keyboard connected to the video monitor in the other room.

A minute later both detectives were in the viewing room listening to Bags outline some new questions. Neither detective seemed more enthusiastic than Sheriff Phillips and Penelope found herself wishing she could get into one of the rooms to take a crack at the questioning.

If they believed Blair, it was confirmation of a second person on the veranda with Harry. That was almost a given, unless you subscribed to the theory that Harry cocked his head up at just the right angle to take a falling coconut to his temple. She knew one of these two had something useful to say. Blair, in particular put himself in a front row seat for the events immediately before Harry's death.

This time the detectives were not on the same script. Their improvisation made it hard to keep up with both interviews. For Penelope it was like the normal chaos inside her brain was suddenly romping around in the world where Bags and the Sheriff could get a taste of it.

It took another twenty minutes of meandering lines of questioning and haphazard follow-up before any consensus emerged. When it did, the Sheriff was unimpressed. Penelope was happy to have something, anything, to take home from this excursion. She couldn't tell what Bags was thinking.

They would leave the building with only a few pieces of new information. First, whatever altercation led to the fatal blow was relatively short. There was no version of their story that had more than a minute or two elapsing between the emergence of the second figure and a distinct lull in the activity on the veranda.

Second, when they stopped the raft to look back, both men say they heard a sound like the splash of a mullet jumping, but with added resonance. Blair said "deeper" and Trip said "longer." That lined up with the sound Ricky said he heard. More than just confirming Ricky's observation, Trip and Blair could add that it was the only splash they heard the whole time they were paddling around the marina. Penelope found that significant because even in her limited experience, it was unusual to hear one mullet jump without then hearing another and another.

Third, and this was one Penelope hadn't thought a lot about until Blair's words matched up with something in her head, both men described the moments after Penelope screamed much the same way. They heard the high-pitched scream followed by Bobby's falsetto expletive. There was more noise and then the doors to the dining room flung open. So far that was straightforward and boring. The weird part was the word Blair used. He said it was very dark that night, which was a good thing for them, of course, and that the light coming out of the doors when they opened was so bright it seemed to bounce around, almost like an "echo." Penelope described the same moment as a flash of light in "stereo." It might not mean anything other than that Penelope hadn't imagined the phenomenon. For now it would go in the same category as other bits of information filed away because "you never know."

As the interviews fizzled, Sheriff Phillips left the room to take a call. When he returned, both detectives were looking for permission to wrap things up. The call was from the DEA field office. Two agents were on their way to collect Blair and Trip. Good timing.

Bags seized on the Sheriff's frustration and suggested follow up on one piece of information from the interviews. The strange splashing noise noted by Ricky, Blair, and Trip could point to the killer leaving something behind. The water in the marina, particularly that part, remained relatively undisturbed and was less than fifteen feet deep. It would take very little effort for a diver to nose around the bottom in that area.

As expected, the Sheriff seemed less than enthused. His problem, as it had been with the additional questions, was an utter lack of better ideas. When Salero and Benton returned to the viewing room, the Sheriff asked what they thought. They shrugged with the same "better than nothing" attitude pasted on the Sheriff's face. It felt like a modest victory. Penelope had hoped for more and told herself to be content with the entertainment value of the road trip and the notion, evident in so many of the mystery shows she watched, that even the tiniest details might prove decisive.

Chapter 20

The next few days were chaotic around St. Georges. Harry's death was a shock to the normally quiet fabric of the community both inside the gates and within the yacht club membership. It was the shock of loss, though, rather than the shock of scandal. There had been a certain amount of murmuring about the curious circumstances of Harry's death, which were encouraged by the Sheriff's involvement, but very few knew there was an active homicide investigation.

Ander's late night ambulance ride provoked a similar reaction -- discrete murmurs based more on speculation than fact. It was clear to Penelope the locals were dealing with a lot more unpleasantness than usual. The mood was more at a simmer than anything, with a vague collective sensation something unusual was in the air.

The big drug bust changed that overnight. The simmer was now about to boil over. The timing hadn't helped. Harry's funeral was scheduled for Saturday because the autopsy delayed the arrangements and also to give all the snowbirds a chance to get back to Ft. Myers if they wanted to attend. A large number of people came back. Bags accurately predicted the big turnout. It was the most tangible evidence Penelope had seen that St. Georges was like a family.

Most of those returning for the funeral decided to stay at least part of the next week and the club had been very busy Saturday night. Bags told her the bar turned into the scene of an impromptu wake for Harry. So once news of the late night excitement began to filter out on Sunday, things went a little viral, at least in a local way.

Bags and the Commodore were the only ones truly in the loop. Neither knew when the bust would happen but once they knew, there were practical matters to be handled at the club. For one thing, they were going to need a new manager. Lisa was the obvious choice. Tyler was the overall club manager. Lisa and the head chef, Carlos, divided the day-to-day running of the food and beverage service. Carlos owned the kitchen, while Lisa managed the dining room staff and the bar.

The Commodore and Bags spoke with her late in the afternoon on Sunday. The Commodore wanted Bags there to share appropriate information about the arrests. Lisa's first test would be explaining Tyler's sudden departure. Penelope was annoyed that she had to hear about all of this second hand from Bags. He treated her like his partner in the investigation but it wasn't right for her to be involved in the business of running the club. She understood why. That didn't stop it from being annoying.

On the plus side of things, Penelope found herself in the unique position of having all the scoop on something that would definitely have her dad's attention. This was, after all, a real life version of the kind of stuff he made up for his books. She even suspected the Hedge Fund Johnny character might show up in one of Raglan Dunne's future adventures.

While Bags was with the Commodore taking care of club business, Penelope was home giving her dad all the scoop on how she and Bags had pretty much handed the Sheriff and the DEA a huge drug bust, which was clearly going to result in an arrest worthy of mention in the Wall Street Journal. About halfway through her story, Penelope realized this was probably the first time in her life she and her dad were legitimately excited in the same way about the same thing. Other than her manic rambling, it felt kind of grown up.

After hearing everything, including the plan to send a diver in to look for whatever went sploosh, her dad suggested Penelope call and make dinner reservations for them that night at the club. He seemed to think there would be a big crowd. Normally he did not like crowds so she was a little confused by his eagerness. Then she saw the text from Bags inviting them to dinner. He and Father seemed to know something she didn't. She really didn't like it when adults acted like they knew best. She particularly did not like that behavior from her parents, and when they turned out to be right, well, that was the worst.

Walking through the doors at the club, Lisa was the first face they saw. She looked nervous even though greeting and seating was normal for her. Lisa reached to shake her dad's hand as he offered his congratulations. He smiled and said, "Relax, you are going to be great at this." It was very fatherly, which made sense. Lisa was a lot older than Penelope -- maybe even 30 -- but still much younger than Father.

The dining room was busier than usual and louder than Penelope could recall from prior visits. The buzz must have started well before they arrived. Even in the foyer Penelope could hear noise from the bar. It sounded packed or maybe the people there were simply more excited than usual. She predicted it would be a good tip night for Bud. Bags was already sitting when she and her dad entered the dining room. Marika was sitting next to him, which was hardly a surprise. Watching Father's eyes light up when he saw her was also not a surprise. Lesley Riley, the Commodore's wife, was at the table as well. The Commodore was still in the bar. Bags said he was surrounded by a number of members hungry for more information about the events of the last 24 hours.

While they waited for the Commodore, Bags told Penelope he and the Commodore decided there was to be a special dinner the following night. Sheriff Phillips and the DEA had a press conference scheduled for mid-morning. Bags made his best plea to the Sheriff for them to avoid referencing St. Georges but he suspected someone at the press conference would slip, which would make St. Georges a focal point of media interest. The Commodore was trying to get ahead of that with whoever would listen to him tonight but things would get even more chaotic after the story hit the news.

Penelope understood the concern. It had not taken her long to become accustomed to the benefits of a gated community. Sure St. Georges was boring sometimes -- ok chronically -- but it was also safe and predictably tranquil. She liked that. Having a bunch of reporters nosing around would not be welcome. Besides, the possibility of cameras would mean Penelope would have to spend more than five minutes in the bathroom before going out in public -- too much work for summer.

The general noise level went down once the Commodore managed to make his way to his seat. A number of other diners wandered by to chat over the course of dinner. For the most part, however, it turned into a relatively normal evening. Bags updated Penelope and the others on the planned visit from the police divers. It would be Tuesday. Everyone agreed that was best. If there were news people hanging around outside the gates on Monday, a visit from the Sheriff would fuel and prolong their interest.

Bags also took the opportunity to quietly discuss with the Commodore one of the big challenges he and Penelope were having with their unofficial investigation. The natural assumption was that in a gated community the total universe of suspects should be knowable. The Commodore and Penelope's dad were surprised that wasn't the case.

"So you can see the problem," Bags summarized. "We have a good list of members who attended the Gala. From this and the interviews completed that night, we have a number of people who could not have been in the right place at the right time to be involved; those of us at this table, for example. Unless all of us conspired, we attest to each other's location during the critical moments."

Penelope could not resist. "The guards keep a log of non-member visitors; guests, club staff, delivery people, and contractors, for example. And we have those logs for the day of the Gala. We also tried to figure out which residents were still in town that weekend."

"Yes, Penelope went door to door." Bags added. "The problem is unless they attended the Gala, we have no way to be sure which members were within the gates that evening."

"Because of the resident gate." Her dad half asked.

"Yep, and that doesn't even address the potential number of non-members who have access to a remote." Penelope added.

"She's right, Robert." Lesley chimed in. "I mean we all know it's against the rules to let anyone borrow our gate clicker but I'm quite sure everyone in the room tonight has done it at some point."

"Can you not look at the security video from the guardhouse for that night?" Father asked.

The Commodore and Bags shook their heads before Bags answered. "I'm afraid not. We had a lot of conversation about that when we upgraded the gates two years ago. It would have been a modest expense. We had a meeting with the residents and the vote was to not have cameras at the gates. The general feeling was that they would serve only to intrude on our privacy."

"And honestly, until this summer I can't think of one time we found ourselves wishing we had video to review. St. Georges is usually a quiet place." The Commodore defended. "It has been the same conversation with respect to the club itself. We have a camera covering the area outside the front doors. That's it."

"I do find the whole conversation ironic given how many security cameras have been installed around St. Georges in the last few years." Lesley offered with a chuckle.

"That's true," Penelope's dad agreed. "I suspect most people have cameras covering their driveways and front doors, at the very least. The builder put those in place at our place without us even asking."

"That sounds normal compared to what some of our friends here have done." Lesley responded. "It's always the men going crazy with their toys, of course." She added, smiling at Marika and Penelope.

Bags laughed. "Guilty, as charged. And it's not always burglars we are worried about. Say, Robert, does Brownfield still have his deer cameras up?"

"Afraid so, Bags. He is convinced there is a panther roaming St. Georges, putting all our tiny dogs in peril." The Commodore grinned. His audience obliged him with a chuckle.

"Bags, darling, all this talk of suspects makes me cringe. Do you think the Sheriff really thinks someone from St. Georges killed poor Harry? I hope this doesn't turn into some kind of witch hunt." Marika asked, pulling gently at his arm.

"Not a witch hunt, my dear. He will feel pressure to do a thorough investigation, though. I'm quite certain of that." Bags answered, patting the top of her hand. Something was going on there, Penelope decided. Actually, she had decided that the first time she saw them together.

"Thorough. I suppose that means digging into people's personal lives, doesn't it?" Marika persisted.

"The Sheriff is capable of discretion. So far he has not abused his position in dealing with us. I'm hoping to remain something of a buffer, although it will be natural for him to focus on those around Harry -- Yelena and Bill, for example, . . . anyone with close ties, business or personal." Bags offered.

His sobering words brought an awkward silence to the table, resolved only when the entrees arrived. Bags ordered a second bottle of wine for the table and another Shirley Temple for Penelope. Everyone seemed happy to have the conversation turn to the quality of the food.

As Penelope launched into her bacon-wrapped filet, the Commodore picked up from an earlier topic. "You know Bags, our discussion of cameras has me thinking. I recall Jerry making some noise a few weeks ago about installing one outside his garage."

"First I've heard of it." Bags responded between bites of his Sea Bass.

"If he did, I'm guessing you would at least be able to see any incoming cars that turned left onto Fulham and also any leaving from the Fulham gate."

Lesley saw the look on her dad's face and added. "Axel, dear, Jerry and Joan have the house just at the corner where your street begins. It looks out on the guardhouse."

"Ahh, that makes sense, then. Thank you." He responded, somehow managing to tear his gaze away from Marika. Boys. Speaking of Marika, she had been unusually quiet this evening in spite of multiple efforts by Bags to draw her into the conversation.

"They came back for the funeral, I think." Bags offered.

"Yes, I'm surprised they haven't come for dinner tonight." The Commodore responded.

"No matter. Penelope and I will pay a social call tomorrow morning." Bags said, putting the matter to rest.

Penelope decided the waiter was unlikely to show up with her drink and took advantage of another lull in conversation to excuse herself to go to the bar.

She was thinking about Marika's unusually somber mood as she made her way out of the dining room and to the bar.

"Hey Bud, I need a drink." She smiled, hopping up on one of the barstools.

"The usual, Miss Penelope." Bud played along.

"Yep, and don't skimp on the cherries."

"I hear you and Bags brought down the local drug ring single handed."

"You hear lots of things standing behind that bar, don't you, Bud?" Penelope poured it on, hoping for one of Bud's ear-to-ear grins.

"You have no idea." He flashed her only a half grin, kind of sad, almost.

"So what do you make of all this excitement, Bud?"

"It's good for business having so many people back in the middle of the summer. Beyond that, I'll be glad when things get back to normal. Can't say it will be any fun if the media starts sniffing around." Bud handed Penelope her drink.

"New subject. You think Bags and Marika are a thing? He says no." Penelope asked.

"You're wondering if I've seen something or overheard something, aren't you? Very clever, Miss Penelope."

"Well . . .?"

"Well, if I did know something, I couldn't say. You know that. But if you're asking me to guess, I would say 'not likely.'"

"But you know what I'm talking about, right."

"Of course. I think they both love the attention. Bags is safe. She can be seen with him without raising eyebrows. He's single for starters. And everyone thinks 'grandpa' when they see him."

"Attention. That's it, Bud. She craves the attention. She's not the mean girl, she's the drama girl." Penelope smiled, pleased with herself, as she took a long sip from her glass. She knew her assessment of Marika was based a lot on her own insecurity. It was actually hard to dislike Marika. Still, Penelope was happy the woman had at least one imperfection.

"Can't argue with that."

"Thanks for the drink, Bud. Good talk." She smiled and hopped off her seat.

"Anytime, Miss Penelope." Bud gave her a little two-finger salute and a wink before she turned for the door.

When Penelope sat down at the table, the conversation had turned into a rehash of the homicide investigation. She found it tiresome. Maybe it was just getting late or maybe it was that big steak rolling around in her belly making her feel tired and cranky. Her mind wandered. Penelope just wanted to know what it was that went "splash," or "sploosh," or whatever, out by the dock. Waiting an extra day for the divers was going to be torture.

"I'm sorry, I need to go." Marika said as she pushed back her chair. She was up and on her way to the door before anyone could react. The sudden motion snapped Penelope's attention back to her surroundings and she immediately wished she had been paying better attention. She knew Bags and the Commodore had done all the talking since her return from the bar, which meant that Marika's parting utterance likely marked her first words since her earlier mini-outburst.

Bags looked at Penelope with confusion and even a little panic in his eyes. He wasn't sure whether to follow or not. Penelope figured the whole stunt was calculated, which suggested she definitely wanted someone to chase after her. Bags at least recognized that he was the one Marika expected to chase her. The look in his eyes told Penelope he would have no idea what to do once he caught her. She looked at Lesley and saw absolutely no reaction. Perhaps she had seen this before and wasn't buying into the drama. The Commodore clearly knew enough to avoid even the slightest hint of motion in Marika's direction. Curiously, despite the support her dad had shown Lisa, and despite the dopey grin plastered on his face whenever Marika was in the room, or maybe because of it, he also didn't twitch.

"Why don't I go see if she needs anything?" Penelope finally broke the building tension.

"Would you? The keys are in my cart." Bags implored.

"Of course." Penelope looked at her dad and he nodded his approval.

She was fairly sure Marika was on her way to the Bags villa. Penelope headed left out the doors. Marika was out of sight. The air was hot and wet. Penelope began to sweat immediately. It would take her less than a minute to get back indoors at Chez Bags and she would still be a mess. Marika, she guessed, would look as if she had just stepped out of the makeup chair on a movie lot.

Halfway down the row of villas Penelope could finally see Marika in the soft glow of the lamps flanking the garage doors at Chez Bags. Either Marika could not remember the garage door code or did not know it. Penelope thought it odd Marika wouldn't know the number, even if Bud was right about the two of them not being a thing. It was a good thing Penelope had followed her.

Chapter 21

Penelope opened the door and led Marika up to the main floor, where she curled up in the corner of a couch facing the rarely used television in the living room. The whole transaction had been accomplished with only a few words between them. Penelope was more right than wrong. Even on the verge of a breakdown and after a hurried walk in steamy air, Marika still looked put together. Penelope, by contrast, pulled her hair back into a ponytail and decided to avoid mirrors.

"Can I get you a hot beverage? I feel like Bags would offer a hot beverage."

"Oh, thank you dear but I'm not sure it would help."

"Ok, I heard 'yes.' Plus, I'm pretty sure Bags would tell you it isn't optional. So, tea, cocoa, coffee?" Penelope looked at the rack of little plastic cups that went with the coffee maker on the counter.

Marika looked up and smiled. "Coffee, I guess. Decaf. With whiskey."

Penelope grabbed a little packet of decaf and put it in place before moving to the sink to get some water. "Does Bags even have whiskey? I thought he was more of a red wine guy."

"The liquor supply is mostly for guests." Marika explained.

"Right, always the gracious host. Where would I find it?"

"Upper cabinet next to the sink -- to your left. Use the Jameson."

"And a little whipped cream?"

"You seem too young to know that."

"My dad likes it sometimes. Actually, he liked it in the winter in Illinois. I'm not sure if he will ever drink it again now that we are in Florida."

"I find it soothing. As you said, a hot beverage."

"You expected Bags to follow you, didn't you?" Penelope asked as she typed a text telling him to come home.

"Maybe. Mostly I needed to not be there listening to more talk of Harry's death."

"I'm sure Bags will be home soon. I mean how long can he stay away from his two favorite women."

"Well, when you put it that way . . .." Marika smiled and winked. "You really are every bit the charmer Bags says."

"That's silly. He's just very sweet and easy to be around, but then you know all about that."

"I do indeed."

Penelope delivered Marika's coffee and plopped down at the other corner of the couch. They managed a version of smalltalk until both could hear the garage door opening. Penelope could tell Marika was having a hard time holding back the tears. Something was up and Bags was going to get to hear the whole story. That was fine. Penelope didn't really want to hear about Marika's problems unless they somehow related to Harry's death, which seemed unlikely.

"Marika, my dear, I was worried when you and Penelope didn't return. Are you alright?" Bags sat in one of the chairs flanking the couch.

"Oh, Bags, I'm really not and I don't know what to do. It's all just so horrible, this business with Harry and the investigation and the police."

Bags looked at Penelope. She nodded dutifully. "I should go collect Father. He may not be able to find his way home without me." Penelope joked. "Don't forget me tomorrow morning." She prompted Bags.

"Of course, dear. Do I have your permission to wake you?"

"Ok but that's not a license to be mean." She frowned.

"As you wish. Oh, and Penelope, thank you for taking care of Marika. Bad manners on my part not to come right away."

"No problem. Goodnight Marika." Penelope was down the stairs and out the door, leaving the drama girl and Bags right where they both wanted to be. She wondered if Bags would share anything the next time she saw him.

Her dad was definitely ready to go when she collected him from the club. She could see it on his face. He was not fond of smalltalk and he did not know the Rileys very well. Penelope imagined the conversation became awkward pretty much immediately after Bags left.

On their way home, her dad asked what happened to Marika. Penelope gave the summary, which seemed to be all he wanted. Back home, they said goodnight and disappeared into their respective rooms. Penelope was quickly asleep. It had been a long day.

She slept well and was happy Bags waited for a respectable hour before ringing the doorbell. He seemed content to have coffee with her dad while she showered. It was possible he noticed more than she gave him credit for when he finally made it back to his house to comfort Marika. She looked like she needed a shower then and neither the walk back to the club nor the golf cart ride home did her any favors.

She descended the stairs looking more or less ready for public viewing. Bags was in the middle of telling her dad about putting the guards on the lookout that morning for reporters trying to gain entry to St. Georges. Penelope had to wonder if they weren't all overestimating the world's potential interest in their little village on the water. She was more focused on the prospect of learning something useful in the investigation.

Bags must have been feeling the same. He was quick to end the coffee conversation and get out the door with Penelope. Her dad just smiled and waived as she dragged Bags down the stairs. On the way home the night before, her dad made a point to tell her he appreciated how she and Bags seemed to be keeping each other company and looking out for each other during the summer. Penelope hadn't thought about it quite that way. She was perfectly able to take care of herself but it was understandable for Father not to get that.

Bags jabbered about the press conference for the duration of their short trip to the house across from the front gates. Jerry, of Jerry and Joan, was puttering in his garage as they pulled into the driveway. Boy was he tall, and that smile was a killer. Even at a distance it said, "how about a hug." He was all arms and legs and smiles. Really, it was the eyes that made the smile. She couldn't imagine Jerry angry, not with those soft, kind eyes. Too bad she already picked her fake grandpa.

"Good morning, you two. Bags, you've been all over the place this morning. Could be an interesting day, I guess -- certainly been an interesting couple of days." Jerry greeted them.

"So you've heard, then. Good. The Commodore and I expected you and Joan might stop by the club last night."

"Sorry about that. I was outvoted. Joan insisted on dragging me out for dinner to that fancy place in the mall. I'm not sure it was worth having to drive all that way."

"A small price to pay for household harmony, I'm sure." Bags commiserated.

"Probably just as well, too. I hear the Commodore is having a special dinner tonight. Sounds like we won't want to miss that."

"Yes, hopefully it will help keep the murmuring down."

"I understand. Crazy story about Tyler, isn't it? Makes me wonder how many times we might have been sitting in the dining room while drugs were changing hands right outside the doors."

"Well we shouldn't have to worry about that anymore. Say, Penelope and I are out this morning tracking down some things and thought we would stop by with a question for you." Bags approached the point, finally. Like her dad, Penelope could only handle so much smalltalk.

"Sure, what's up?"

"Last night at dinner Robert and I were lamenting the lack of cameras covering the gates, thinking of the night Harry died, you know, and he suggested you might have taken care of us in that regard."

"One hundred percent correct, Bags. I have to tell you I've been a little twitchy lately. I know I'm not the only one. I hear things are well in hand but I thought, why not? So I put in a couple of little cameras. One is right outside the garage here." Jerry pointed to the corner of the eaves overhanging the garage doors. "That one covers cars coming in the gates and down Fulham, as well as cars going out the side gate over there, I suppose."

"And the other one?" Penelope couldn't go any longer without feeling like part of the conversation.

"The other one is also just under the overhang but on the other side of the house. It covers cars coming through the gates and going straight down toward the club."

"When did you put them up?"

"Before we left for the summer. Before Harry died, if that's what you're asking."

"It is, and where is the video stored? Knowing you, I don't suppose it's a VHS system." Bags asked.

"What's a VHS?" Penelope asked, just to make Bags feel old. Jerry laughed.

"It's something we used to use to show our home movies of the dinosaurs." Bags snarked back at her with a little smile.

"The video goes straight to a hard drive but anything going back more than a week gets backed up on the Cloud." Jerry winked at Penelope. "You do know what the Cloud is, right, Bags?"

"Enough to know I have no interest in it beyond having you retrieve the video for the whole day of the Gala."

"Not a problem. It might take some time. I'll put it on a memory stick for you. Will that work, Penelope?" Jerry offered, bypassing Bags just to annoy him.

"Yep. Bags has a Mac we can load it onto. How long?"

"I'm embarrassed to say, it probably depends how long it takes me to figure out that part of the system. I haven't tried to pull anything from the security company website yet. I might need some tech support. I'll see what I can do after lunch."

"I appreciate it, Jerry. Call me when you have something." Bags sounded a little disappointed.

Penelope wasn't sure why they both thought the trip to Jerry's would result in instant gratification. Of course Jerry would need time to get the video for them. After leaving Jerry's, Bags drove around St. Georges with no clear purpose. Penelope wasn't sure why but she had nothing better to do and didn't say anything. She refrained from asking about Marika. If Bags had something worth sharing and thought it appropriate, he would bring it up. It's not like he was the strong silent type. The more they drove around, the more obvious his distraction was. She became convinced they would ride in circles until the battery ran down unless something or someone snapped him back to reality.

"Hey Bags, I'm hungry. Why don't you take me out for lunch? I showered this morning so we could even go someplace nice if you want."

"What a good idea." Bags responded, glancing in Penelope's direction, almost.

Bags even broke out the convertible for their excursion. He did not offer her the keys, so it was only a partial victory. Penelope decided to take advantage of her date's catatonic state by suggesting they go for sushi. Bags was not a fan. His aversion was so strong even Penelope's sad puppy face usually failed to overcome his resistance, and sad puppy face almost always worked on Bags. Today, he agreed without incident. This was as close to Zombie Bags as she was likely to see.

Penelope's favorite sushi place was a little more disco than Bags was used to in his lunch destinations. It was kind of dark with glowing neon accent lights all around and even at lunch they usually had some kind of techno dance music pulsing just a little bit too loud for anyone over 30. The servers were all college age women dressed in black, including stretchy pants Bags probably thought were a size small. She decided before they arrived that he wouldn't say anything. She was right. He didn't have to say anything. The cartoon size of his eyes when the hostess walked ahead to seat them said everything.

Bags stared at the menu blankly for a few minutes before suggesting Penelope order for them both. She picked some things without any raw fish in them. Miso soup seemed safe too. And they had these things with crabmeat and rice that were deep fried in batter and served with a dark, sweet sauce. He would like those.

The noise gave Bags an excuse to drift off with his thoughts again. Penelope practiced using her chopsticks while she talked at Bags and pretended he was listening. There was still so much he needed to know about surviving the zombie apocalypse and delivering her next lecture today seemed wonderfully ironic given his vacant, unresponsive stare. He managed to nod at regular enough intervals to support Penelope's delusion of having his attention. She recognized the behavior from watching her dad and mom in conversation. They were good at doing it to each other in turns.

When the food came, Penelope became unresponsive, totally focused on her perfect plate of sushi heaven. She did manage to notice that Bags gobbled down the deep fried bits along with some of the other fake sushi she ordered. They were probably there less than an hour. It seemed longer. If she measured in diet soda, it was a long time. She definitely overdid it on the caffeine while she was talking zombies with her zombie date.

Now that she was super pumped up and agitated from the soda, Penelope was losing patience with Bags. Whatever was keeping his head out there in the ether needed to be over. She was about to say something as they pulled out of the parking lot when Bags finally looked at her and spoke. "Can we go to Sanibel and take a walk on the beach?"

"Ok. You went for sushi with me so I guess it's only fair for you to pick where we go next." Penelope smiled. She was happy he was back among the living. He was on his game too. Penelope's feelings about the beach at Sanibel were no secret. It had been the site of one of her very first installments of forced family fun, just a few days after the moving truck left. She liked wide, flat beaches with perfect white sand so fine it looked like powdered sugar. She loved a gentle sea breeze washing over her just enough to keep the bright sun from making her feel like an egg in a frying pan. Oh, and she liked the clear blue water rippling in on tiny waves, just enough to produce a soothing white noise.

The beach Bags was dragging her to had none of these things. The waves were choppy and loud, the sand was coarse and littered with seaweed, dead things, and sand fleas, and the water was a mix of pasty green and churned up brown. Then there was the wind, always wind, not breeze, wind. Bags knew she would never go willingly, so she wondered if he had allowed her to think she was pulling one over on him with the sushi ploy or did he merely wake up after the meal and realize his momentary leverage.

Sanibel was a thin barrier island just over the long causeway bridge from the road leading to St. Georges. It was a perfect drive for the speedy convertible. Bags seemed happy about the light traffic on the island and at the beach. Penelope would have been happier driving but it was still nice. They were parked and on the beach sooner than Penelope expected.

They walked in silence for the first hundred yards up the windy, noisy, stinky beach. Whatever it was, something was really taking Bags out of his game and Penelope began to feel like he wasn't going to share it with her. The silence was getting old. She at least had to try.

"So, Bags, don't get me wrong, I'm loving the beach walk thing, but why exactly are we here today."

"I needed a change of scenery, I guess. You're a good sport for coming along." He paused and looked out over the water. "Would you like to know what all of that nonsense with Marika was about?"

"It seems like I shouldn't want to know."

"Which means you do."

"Pretty much, yeah. Does it relate to our investigation?"

Bags hesitated. "I would like to say it does not . . . .. I think you may be a more objective judge."

"Ok, now you really have to tell me." Penelope said encouragingly.

"I remember you saying it was strange that Marika did not attend Harry's funeral because she seems like part of the St. Georges family. I thought it strange as well but wrote it off to her tendency to react very emotionally to things. Some people have a particularly hard time with funerals."

"I think the words you're searching for are 'high drama,' Bags." Penelope said with an eye roll he couldn't see.

"I suppose that is a fair description. In any event, I was only partly correct in my assessment. It turns out the more important factor was that she and Harry were, as you say, 'a thing.'"

"What? OMG, Bags, I am so sorry." Penelope blurted in genuine shock.

"Why sorry?" Bags reacted.

"Oh come on, Bags, you can't fool me. You are puppy dog in love with that one."

"My dear, it has been a very long time since I have been 'puppy dog' anything, although these days I do sometimes wet myself a little when I get very excited." Bags smiled. Penelope ignored his effort to distract her.

"Whatever. How else do you explain the sudden appearance of Mr. Mopey Bags?"

"I admit, the whole situation has me distracted, which is why I said you might be the better judge of things."

Penelope leaned into Bags, grabbed the hand closest to her with her opposite hand, and wrapped her other around his arm like he was walking her down the aisle. "Ok, so do I need any other details?"

He looked out over the water again. "Apparently, it began about six months ago. She loved him. She thought he loved her. But you must understand. For those of us who have seen so much-"

"You mean because you're old." Penelope interjected.

"Yes, thank you for the reminder." Penelope thought she could hear a little smile creep in his voice. "My point is, as you live, you discover there are many kinds of love. 'Puppy dog' is only one of them. In this case Marika was under no illusions about her place in Harry's life. Theirs was a limited relationship."

"Did Yelena know? I mean you're kind of Marika's St. Georges husband and you didn't know. So did Yelena know?"

"This is where I think Marika believes what she chooses. She says Yelena knew Harry might be seeing someone else but never suspected it was her." Bags explained.

"Ok, I don't really understand that. Did Yelena know Harry was a big fat cheater or not? By the way, this all sounds very high school."

"I wish I could tell you the dealings between boys and girls change after high school. I fear you will see the same drama at every age." Bags squeezed her hand. This time Penelope smiled. She could feel him struggling and the whole thing had her close to welling up. "The answer to your question is Marika is under the impression that Harry and Yelena had a more open relationship than most married couples."

"Well isn't that a convenient story. She isn't really that stupid, is she?" Penelope said, incredulous.

"She is quite convinced. It is not outside the realm of possibility." Bags tried to sound convincing.

"Whatever. Does that mean Yelena is getting a little action on the side, you know, some action with a dreamy accent?"

"I think we have to revisit that possibility, yes. And it may be there was no explicit agreement between Harry and Yelena. Perhaps they both were content to not ask questions so long as they were not asked any questions."

"Kinda weird either way but ok, let's assume they both knew and for whatever reason it worked for them. Why did Marika decide to blab all of a sudden? Was she feeling guilty about cheating on you?" Marika and Bags were definitely some kind of couple. Penelope wasn't about to let go of that.

"Maybe she did feel a little guilty keeping something like that from me. However, she made very clear, convincingly so, that her primary motivation was fear about the details of her relationship becoming public in the investigation."

"Yeah, that would be awkward." Penelope agreed.

"It could ruin her among the members here. You see Marika relies on the goodwill of this community for many things. We are more than just her social circle. We are her main source of income."

"So why would she risk so much just to have an affair with a guy who it sounds like wasn't giving her much hope of a future?"

"Puppy dog in love is not the only kind of love that makes people act like stupid teenagers. No offense."

"No worries. I totally get the stupid teenager thing. Bags, can you save me from that? Please."

"Not a chance, my dear, and I wouldn't want to."

"So Harry made Marika a little crazy and now she's afraid everyone is going to find out and she will be done at St. Georges. Do you really think Marika would have trouble landing on her feet, Bags?"

"Not really, no, but you have to understand how important it is to her to be accepted in our little enclave. I can't really explain it. You must take my word. And it is not just her own reputation Marika wants to protect. Yelena would also suffer. Even for the victims, scandal has a cost."

"Seems like the sheriff is going to find out once he starts digging into Harry's life."

"I told her that. She knows it is inevitable and merely asked me to try to keep it as a part of the investigation not revealed to the public."

"And you promised to try." Penelope finished his thought.

"Of course."

"You still haven't asked me the real question, you know."

Bags smiled and sighed. "Alright then, you know the question. What is your answer?"

"Marika being with Harry is definitely relevant. If Yelena knew Harry was cheating on her and was not ok with it, that seems like as good a motive for murder as any we've heard so far. That means we definitely need to dig into that subject with Yelena." Penelope began.

"And by 'we' you mean the Sheriff, I'm sure."

"Not if you want to keep Marika's name quiet. I think we need to go see her right now, in fact." Penelope said as sternly as she could manage.

"Hmmm, I'll take that under advisement. Anything else?" Bags smirked.

"What if we uncover something to suggest Harry had or was about to do Marika wrong. That could make her a suspect." Penelope offered tentatively.

"That is true but we don't have any evidence to suggest Marika was upset with Harry and, anyway, she has the two of us for an alibi."

"I can only be part of her alibi, actually. After I flipped the lights back on I returned to the table for a bit. Then I got bored listening to you explaining the rules and went to the bar." Penelope reminded Bags.

"Right, and that is how you came to hear the noise that led you to find Harry's body. Now that I really think about it, I saw you get up and Marika was still at the table. Then I saw her get up to go to the bathroom. The next time I remember noticing her was when we were all outside hovering over Harry."

"I'm sure someone saw her in the bathroom and in the dining room on her way back. Anyway, that's not much time."

"Time enough, perhaps. I will need to look over my notes from that night. We may need to ask a few more questions." Bags admitted.

"Do we think Marika could hit Harry hard enough to kill him?"

"We need to find the weapon used to be sure. I know she is very athletic."

"I bet you do." Penelope teased.

"That is not what I meant, young lady. In any event, a lover's spat could explain the knock to poor Harry's head."

"Right, like maybe she just snuck out to give him a kiss or whatever and they started fighting. She gets mad and hits him with something without meaning to kill him but he drops like a stone. She panics and runs away." Penelope played out the theme. "I guess that could have happened. Seems like kind of a stretch."

"Nevertheless, I'd be happier if we could keep the Sheriff from going down that path. We need to make sure someone inside the building saw her when she was out of my sight." Bags concluded.

Penelope nodded before asking delicately, "Bags, do you think she told you everything."

"Hard to say. She seemed eager to unburden herself. It all seemed quite sincere but I confess I was a little overwhelmed by the whole discussion. I will want to have another conversation with her on this subject."

"Ok, I'll leave that to you. And you need to go talk to Yelena too. Don't forget that."

"We will see. I think we are done here. Let's go home."

"Yes, please." Penelope looked up to see the convertible not far away. At some point in the conversation Bags had turned them back toward the car without her noticing, which did not speak well of her powers of observation.

"And, Penelope . . . thank you."

"Aww! Anything for you, Bags."

Chapter 22

As they zipped along the little ribbon of concrete connecting Sanibel to Ft. Myers, Penelope concluded that Zombie Bags was mostly gone. Hopefully the time they spent on the beach was worth all the bug bites on her legs. She was sure she could feel hundreds of them.

The convertible was through the front gate before either of them remembered to look for reporters and TV vans. Apparently, St. Georges had been spared. The stretch of road outside the gates and the turnaround in front of them were completely quiet, as usual. Bags was passing the club when he remembered the video. He wheeled the little Audi around and accelerated just enough to squeal the tires. Penelope through up her hands and cheered like she was on a roller coaster. Bags smiled.

He slowed around the corner and wheeled neatly into Jerry's driveway, where he instructed Penelope to ring the bell and inquire about the video. She did and Jerry quickly produced an envelope with a flash drive inside. He seemed in a hurry so Penelope thanked him and was on her way.

As they rolled past the club for the second time in five minutes, Penelope understood why Jerry was less chatty than usual. The parking lot was filling up and the portico driveway was already lined with golf carts, including hers.

"Bags, what time is that dinner tonight?"

"What's that, my dear?" He said, still a bit in a fog.

"Dinner?"

"Oh, right." He looked at his watch. "Hmmm, where did the afternoon go? The Commodore will not be happy. I'm already late for drinks."

"I thought so. We better hurry and get you ready." Penelope directed.

"Does that mean you don't plan on joining us?"

"Two nights at the club? Not gonna happen, my friend."

"It would make me feel better. Please?"

"But Bags," she whined, objecting to the obvious guilt trip.

"Just for dinner. You have to eat and Axel will be at the club, so that's your best chance for food. It really would make me feel better to have you next to me. Please."

"That's low, Bags. You know I can't say no to that face."

"Good. It's settled then -- just for moral support during dinner. You can take my cart and go get ready. I'll walk."

Penelope took her time in the shower washing off all the beach nastiness. No matter how Bags denied it, she knew finding out about Marika and Harry hurt his feelings. Still, as much as she wanted to be there for him tonight, the whole scene at the club, particularly tonight, would be a bit much. Penelope had to manage her exposure.

She was still messing with her hair when Bags sent the text asking where she was and what her dad should order her for dinner. He was thinking about the fish and Bags knew that wouldn't go over well. Her mom would know what to order. Bags would probably be able to guess and it wouldn't be a train wreck. The fact that he sent the text instead proved how well he understood his fake granddaughter. She opted for a caesar salad and some pasta. Then she pronounced her hair good enough, knowing it probably wouldn't survive the two-minute rainforest drive to the club anyway.

Her salad and a glass of lemonade were waiting when she found her dad and Bags at, surprise surprise, the Commodore's table. Penelope looked around -- no Marika and no Yelena. No surprise. Her dad told her the bar had been full and noisy an hour before someone began the migration to the dining room.

The Commodore looked tired. Bags missed some of the Commodore's unhappy hour and while the food service was keeping the dining room relatively quiet, the Riley's were filling him in on what he had missed.

Even though Penelope had been right in the middle of the action creating the hum of excitement and anxiety tonight, the subject matter was one she predicted most of the members would find too unsavory to speak of in front of her, or any other young woman. What she had discovered, however, was that through silence and feigned indifference, she could virtually disappear to adults even as she sat among them.

What little notice they took of her presence as she attacked her crunchy lettuce and croutons induced only mild discretion and not the kind likely to misdirect her. For example, speaking in hushed tones was the preferred tactic for the women. Of course, what they considered hushed still registered comfortably above Penelope's hearing threshold. The men seemed more inclined to try talking in nearly comic code -- wink wink, nudge nudge, know what I mean -- except they weren't being funny on purpose. Bags and her dad were the only ones that seemed to understand. They knew she would be listening to the parts she cared to hear and that she would understand the parts she found interesting.

In this case, she found little of it interesting. The two themes of the evening were, "how exciting it is to have something like this happen right here in our little marina," and, "so how many junkies do you think there are in St. Georges?" Those who knew most about the situation continued to be concerned about press coverage. People who did not trudge up and down the beach all afternoon had seen the local news. Their little drug bust was the big story but, thankfully, the Johnny Hedge Fund angle was, at least on day one, the sexier focal point. It explained why the press corps had not laid siege to their gates.

Talk of the continuing investigation into Harry's death appeared to be on the back burner, although Bags and the Commodore agreed to let everyone know it remained an open investigation and that there would be Sheriff's Department divers in the marina the next morning.

Between her salad and entree, Penelope slipped out to the veranda. The table conversation began to sound too much like blah, blah, blah, blah. She needed the noise to stop for a few minutes. When she excused herself, she could see from her dad's face how much he wanted to go with her. Mother would have been right in there with the blah, blah, blah. Her dad suffered in situations like this when Mother wasn't around.

Besides simply needing to escape, Penelope wanted to see the crime scene at night, as Trip and Blair would have seen it and as Harry and his killer would have seen it. She stared across the marina at the lights on in different houses and wondered what Yelena was doing. She might be sitting at home, looking across the marina at the lights behind Penelope, wondering about the dinner conversation. Perhaps she wasn't alone, which would probably mean she wasn't thinking about the club at all. Or maybe the lights were on to make it look like she was home. Maybe she wanted to be far away from the club. The only lights on in the whole place were on the opposite side from the master suite. Maybe Yelena was sitting in the dark in her bedroom not even aware of those lights. Or maybe she was just asleep. It was early but who could blame her for wanting to sleep away as much of her nightmare as possible.

Before going back inside, Penelope paused at the spot where she found Harry. Based on what they knew so far, the killer could not have made a getaway in the direction of the pool. He would have gone the other way -- back in the direction of Jerry's house and the front gates. It looked like there was a little path behind the row of houses facing the promenade. Jerry and Joan's house would be at the end of that path. Maybe one of their cameras caught something. It was hard to tell if you could make it that far without hitting a dead end. Even in the partial light of the summer evening, the vegetation behind and around those houses made it look like the deepest darkest jungle. Whether it was planned or lucky, taking off in that direction was a good way to be invisible.

Back inside, Penelope assessed the effectiveness of her coating of bug spray. She wasn't carried away by giant mosquitoes and her ankles had not been reduced to hamburger. She would claim victory. Her pasta was waiting at the table. Judging from the emptiness of her dad's plate, her food had been there awhile. Bags had barely touched his food. She sat and was almost immediately bored again with the blah, blah, blah.

The pasta wasn't any more exciting than the table conversation so Penelope once again used her cloak of invisibility to wander to the bar for some ginger ale. It was empty. Bud was on duty again, still wiping down the tables and tidying the bar after happy hour.

"Do you ever go home?" She asked.

"I could ask you the same question, Miss Penelope. Am I missing anything out there in the dining room?" Bud responded.

"Just blah, blah, blah, blah. Why do you think I came in here?"

"Should I make you a Shirley Temple to keep your excuse legit?"

"How about a ginger ale instead?" Penelope hopped onto the barstool. "And take your time pouring it. It should be perfect."

"Yes, ma'am. Feel free to chat while I pour."

"Seriously, Bud, are you in here every night?"

"Naw, you and I are just on the same schedule these days. I have other jobs besides St. Georges. I'm like the superhero of booze, casting my gaze over Ft. Myers, and swooping down to make sure no citizen goes thirsty."

"Ha ha. We'll call you Captain Morgan, no wait, that's taken. Speaking of superpowers, did you use that bartender hearing tonight during happy hour?"

"It was crazy busy, Miss Penelope. Everyone was very worked up about the drug bust, mostly. A few people were talking smack about who they thought might be junkies. Sometimes the snootiness really gets to me. Sorry if that sounds bad."

"No worries. It's funny, the kids I went to school with in Illinois seemed snootier than anyone at St. Georges. I guess it's all relative."

"Yeah, snooty isn't the right word. It's just that when they get together and talk, it sounds like they have no idea what it means to really work and struggle. Maybe some of them never had to fight for anything. Sometimes they just seem greedy. I don't have much and I don't need much, but what I have, I worked for and I get pissed when I see people take whatever they want just because they can."

"Hmmm, can't really say I've had to struggle with anything in life, you know, except how to survive bitchy cheerleaders and stupid boys." Penelope admitted.

"I hope you never do struggle. You're a good kid. I'm sorry. You don't need to listen to me sounding bitchy."

"No worries. You're more fun than all those people in there even when you're in a bad mood. See ya around sometime, Bud." She took her glass and wandered back to the dining room.

After only a little more blah, blah, blah, Bags gave Penelope permission to bail. He said he thought the after dinner meeting would go on for at least an hour. That was not going to fit into Penelope's plan. As she left, he handed her the flash drive and suggested she substitute viewing Jerry's camera footage for her usual late night video binge. It felt a little like blackmail. She expected that kind of thing from her parents but grandparents were supposed to be kinder and gentler, particularly unofficial ones like Bags. She decided she would let him get away with it this time because he was having a rough couple of days.

Chapter 23

Looking at security camera video proved exactly as boring as Penelope expected. Even with liberal use of fast forward, she made it only part way through the full day of footage. It was video white noise, better than any lullaby, and she faded before she made it very far.

For some reason Penelope's eyes popped open early the next morning. Well, it was early for her. It was probably because she knew the divers were coming. A quick text to Bags confirmed they were on their way. Thanks to her training, Bags was very good at responding to her texts. Penelope was quite pleased with his progress.

Bags told her he would text again when the divers were getting ready to go in the water. He seemed to think it would take them a long time to get ready. Penelope knew he would ask about the video as soon as he saw her, so she decided to power through as much of what was left as she could.

Without Bags, the review was inefficient. She hadn't thought about that when she agreed to do it. He would recognize most of the cars by sight. Penelope could match a few cars to their owners and she could identify most as belonging to a St. Georges resident, but she still had to slow the video down so she could see license plate numbers.

In the interest of time and because she needed some kind of story to placate Bags, Penelope skipped through the afternoon hours and picked up her review as the cars began to stream in for the Gala. She ignored the ones headed down the promenade to the club parking lot, focusing instead on the ones that turned left. For starters she could see the license plates of those more easily. More important was her feeling that the killer would not have rolled straight up to the club's front doors. If the getaway plan involved slipping down the little path leading to Jerry and Joan's, the getaway car would have been parked on one of the streets in that direction.

One of the cars Penelope did recognize by sight was Yelena's. Actually, Harry and Yelena had multiple cars and Penelope recognized all of them, or at least what she believed to be all of them. Yelena's favorite was a silver Range Rover. It had tinted windows except for the windshield, which Harry insisted stay clear as a safety measure. Yelena was apparently not the best driver and needed a clear field of vision. Penelope would have picked the red Mini Cooper, which looked like the Range Rover's bug-eyed daughter. Yelena said she had gone out to get ibuprofen after Harry left for the Gala and, sure enough, the Range Rover rolled past Jerry's camera and out of the gate right on schedule.

Penelope made notes on a few more cars coming from the same direction. All but one turned left, presumably on the way to the Gala. A large, white pickup went out the same gate as Yelena's Range Rover. She made note of the part of the license she could read but decided it didn't interest her. It was going in the wrong direction. She wanted to see who was arriving.

After the white pickup there were no other cars until Yelena's Range Rover reappeared, which was also consistent with her story. Penelope was feeling pressed for time and was about to fast-forward when something odd caught her eye. She hit rewind. "Rewind." She used the term without thinking and because she didn't have a better one. There was no tape to rewind, of course, and really there hadn't been at any time in her life. It was her parents' word, an artifact of the VHS days.

That was the kind of thing her brain did sometimes. She was in a hurry and it was wandering around in tangent land, thinking about why people still said, "rewind." Anyway, she wanted to see the snippet of returning Range Rover footage. There was another outdated word, "footage." Ugh, she really needed to focus.

She stared at the inside of the vehicle. It was dark and the resolution was not great. She could definitely see Yelena in the driver's seat. That wasn't what originally caught her eye. What did was something odd between the front seats. It was probably a shadow or a reflection so her expectations were low. Still, something hadn't looked quite right.

This time she played it at reduced speed. There was definitely something just behind the font seats. Her heart began to race as she cued it up for one more view. And there he was! The image wasn't clear enough to be sure it was William the with the dreamy accent, but there was definitely a man in the middle of that second seat leaning forward like he was talking to Yelena.

160

The passenger seat was empty, which left only a couple of possibilities. Maybe there was something back there needing careful attention, like a wedding cake or a small dog, maybe. Perhaps the man could not fit in the passenger seat because his leg was in a big cast. Or, more likely, he was a man not wanting to be seen by the guards at the front gate. The slightly reflective tint on the side windows would make it very hard to see into the back seat as the daylight was fading.

It had to be William. At a minimum, he was sneaking in because, as Penelope originally suspected, he and Yelena were a thing. Marika's description of Harry and Yelena's relationship suddenly felt a whole lot more believable. Penelope had her story for Bags. The rest of the video could wait. She printed off two stills of the man in the Range Rover and hit the shower. She wouldn't have time to dry her hair so it would be another ponytail and ball cap day.

As Penelope toweled off and applied moisturizer -- her skin was chronically dry even in Florida's steamy climate -- her brain was off to the races. The Sheriff was already primed to focus on Yelena and William individually as suspects. Knowing they were sleeping together, presumably behind Harry's back, would send him into a frenzy. That would be good news for Marika, as the Sheriff's interest in her connection with Harry would move to the back burner. Oh, and William had already lied about that night. He claimed to be nowhere near St. Georges.

Penelope could understand why he would want to lie about being on a booty call at Yelena's while her husband was lying dead just across the water. He might even be able to make it sound like he only wanted to protect Yelena from the scorn she would face if the world found out she was with another man that night. That would be his backup position, after the Sheriff's detectives tricked him into lying about his whereabouts. There was another, darker, reason for him to be there, of course. Sheriff Phillips would race to that conclusion.

Penelope's brain continued in overdrive all the way to the club. She parked her cart outside the front doors and walked past the pool cabana to the little marina parking lot. The Sheriff's big, white SUV was blocking the entrance. Beyond it she could see another SUV and a white pickup with lots of gear in the bed. Walking around to the pool, Penelope saw a huddle of uniformed men on the dock and two more in a small powerboat floating ten yards out. It looked like she might have missed the action.

She walked past the pool and could see a younger guy in uniform with shiny sunglasses and a Sheriff's Department ball cap. He moved to block her path as she approached. She could finally see Bags standing with the crowd of uniforms and waived to him. He saw her and tapped the Sheriff on the shoulder, who then nodded to Mr. Sunglasses to let her pass. As she walked by, she could tell by his frown that he found her presence not at all by the book.

Bags and the Commodore were trying to stand in the shade and yet still see what was happening. When Penelope walked up, she could see the two divers lowering themselves into the water. There was a lot of very official talk going on between the men in the boat and one on the dock, who was then signaling to the divers.

It was an environment intimidating enough to the three civilians that they watched in silence until the divers disappeared. At that point Bags asked the Sheriff in a whisper how the divers would know if they had found something. The officer on the other side of the Sheriff, Bob, responded for him.

"The water is calm today. The divers and the boat will try not to stir up the water. The divers will go slowly and the boat -- well you can see the boat is keeping its distance. The first step will be taking pictures if the conditions allow. That helps document any evidence they might find. I have to tell you though, this could be a tough one." Bob added.

Great, Penelope thought. All this waiting for the divers to show up and find the murder weapon and it might be a total fail. The three of them stood in silence again, waiting for something other than air bubbles to emerge from the water. She thought about taking the opportunity to share her news with Bags but the Sheriff was too close and, anyway, it would be a distraction. It wasn't that Penelope was trying to hide anything from the Sheriff. She just wanted Bags to hear it first. Ok, she wanted a little more than that. What she really wanted was to go with Bags to visit Yelena and talk to her about her supposedly open relationship with Harry. And she wanted that to happen before the Sheriff charged over there with accusations about William.

Bob looked surprised when the divers surfaced. It seemed to be ages to Penelope. The first one popped his head up and gave the man on the dock a signal. He dutifully turned and bent down over a footlocker shaped thing, returning with what looked like an extra large freezer bag. He knelt down at the edge of the water and held the bag open. The second diver appeared a few seconds later and lifted one arm as far out of the water as he could.

The man on the dock leaned down and scooped whatever the diver was holding into the bag like he was bringing a fish in with a net. The divers waited for further instruction while the man on the dock walked the bag over to the Sheriff. Bags and the Commodore leaned in as the Sheriff stepped forward to look at the bag. Penelope couldn't see through them but she did see the look on the Sheriff's face.

The Sheriff motioned her forward. "You're the reason we're out here today, young lady, so I think you should see."

Penelope stepped forward, unsure what to expect. It took a few seconds for her brain to decide what her eyes were seeing. In the bag was a big lump of something. It was covered in a layer of muck colored goo. Under the muck it was dark and there was a rounded part.

"Can you tell what it is?" The Sheriff asked.

"It looks like something stuffed inside a dark sock. A man's sock, I think. A rock, maybe?"

"That would be my guess, young lady. We need to get it to the lab and let the ME look at it but I'd say you're looking at a murder weapon."

Penelope paused to absorb the Sheriff's words. "Rocks don't just spontaneously jump into men's dress socks, do they?"

"Not in my experience, no." The Sheriff chuckled.

"So someone put it in there and used it to hit Harry."

"I think that is a fair conclusion . . . which means . . .." The Sheriff prompted her.

"It was planned. Someone planned it. That makes it murder, for sure, right?"

"The technical term is 'premeditated murder.'"

Penelope felt the blood begin to drain from her head. She didn't know why. She and Bags had been sure of this from the start. Somehow, seeing the actual murder weapon made it too real. She grabbed Bags by the arm to steady herself. "I don't feel so good."

He wrapped an arm around her. "Sheriff, I think this has been a bit much for Penelope. I'm going to take her home, if you don't mind."

"No, of course not, Mr. Bagwell. We're going to wrap this little party up and get out of here anyway. I'll be in touch when we know more." The Sheriff responded. "You take care of yourself, Penelope."

By the time Bags had Penelope around the pool, through the parking lot, and in front of the pool cabana, she had regained her composure. "Sorry about that, Bags. I'm ok now."

"I think I should take you home anyway." He responded.

"I agree. I have something to show you."

"From the security cameras?"

"Yep. It's big."

"And you didn't say anything earlier because the Sheriff was there." He raised an eyebrow.

"I wanted you to see first." She confirmed.

"And you're not going to tell me now, are you?"

"I want your unbiased reaction, just in case I'm seeing things." She lied. Really, she was just being theatrical.

At her house, she planted Bags at the kitchen counter. There was a note from her dad. He was out running errands. Penelope ran up the stairs to her room to get her laptop, being careful not to run on the way back. She occasionally had problems with stairs and with dropping things.

She cued up the appropriate section of video and turned the screen so Bags could see. "I'm going to show you at regular speed first. Then we can slow it down if you want." She pushed the button.

"Yelena's Range Rover." Bags identified the vehicle.

"Yep, watch when she turns." Penelope instructed.

Bags leaned in. "Yes, I think I do see something. Can we slow it down?"

Penelope cued up the beginning and started it again, this time in very slow motion. She watched Bags as it played.

"Oh my!" He blurted. "Can you freeze it?"

"Way ahead of you." Penelope handed him the two frames she had printed.

"I can't tell who it is in the back seat -- definitely a man and definitely not wanting to be seen." Bags stared at the pictures.

"I'm willing to bet it's William." Penelope offered confidently.

"I tend to agree."

"And I think we need to go see Yelena right now, while the Sheriff is otherwise occupied."

"Penelope, we can't reveal to her that we have this evidence. That could jeopardize the Sheriff's investigation."

"I know. We don't have to reveal how much we know but how much we know will definitely help us ask smarter questions." Penelope pressed him.

"You are very clever and more than a little devious."

"Why thank you." She smiled.

"I don't suppose I can keep you from coming along."

"Not a chance."

"Yelena may not want to discuss these things in front of you. What if she asks you to leave?"

"I will, but she won't ask. I'm practically invisible to adults when serious talk is going on."

"Hmmm. Well, we will see."

Chapter 24

Penelope hoped Yelena was home and alone. They needed to talk to her alone. Bags rang the doorbell a second time after waiting patiently for the first ring to produce a reaction. This time the ring was followed quickly by the sound of footsteps. The door opened and there was Yelena.

She welcomed Penelope and Bags, ushering them to the same seating area where Penelope watched Yelena and William do everything but cuddle as they both talked about Harry's death. This time it was just Yelena. Penelope thought she looked too good for a woman still in the early stages of grieving the loss of a husband. She could feel her perception of Yelena now being tainted by what she knew -- ok, what she thought she knew -- about William and Yelena.

Bags moved past the polite greetings and necessary chit chat before pouncing. "Yelena, dear, you are no doubt aware the Sheriff is treating Harry's death as a homicide."

"Yes. The very thought makes me ill. Who would do such a thing?"

"At this point, we really have little idea. The Sheriff has little idea. He was convinced at first that Harry stumbled into the middle of a drug deal and paid the price. That scenario now seems unlikely."

"What does the Sheriff think now?"

"I'm not sure he has any solid ideas just yet. I do think it is fair to say the people closest to Harry will come under scrutiny. That is standard in such investigations."

"Me, you mean."

"And Bill. Harry's spouse and his business partner are really the only two places the Sheriff has to look. He will have his detectives dig into Harry's life, his dealings, his acquaintances, as well as yours and Bill's. I say this to you now so it will not be such a shock when it begins."

"I appreciate it, Bags. What do you think he will hope to find?"

"Someone with motive. Anyone who had reason to think they would be better off with Harry gone." Bags explained.

"Is that the only reason for your visit?"

"I do have a question. I have heard from someone that your relationship with Harry was not exactly as it seemed, outwardly."

"What do you mean? I loved Harry and he loved me."

"And I did not mean to suggest otherwise, only that the terms of that loving relationship might have been different than what we typically assume in a marriage." Bags danced around the obvious.

"I have no idea what you are getting at." She responded curtly.

"I understand. And we do not have to speak of it further. My apologies. However, I suggest that you work on your response on this issue before you next speak with the Sheriff. As I said, he will dig into every detail of Harry's life and yours."

"And William's. Yes, I heard you say that." Yelena's words trailed and her head dropped slightly.

"His detectives may not be the brightest but they are thorough and he has nowhere else to look right now, Yelena." Bags paused and looked at Penelope, as if to confirm her prediction of invisibility. "So, we will be off now. Again, very sorry to upset you." He stood and motioned to Penelope to do the same.

"Wait, don't go." Yelena said quietly, without looking up. "Ask again. Ask what you really want to ask."

Bags sat. "You and Harry were not exclusive, were you?"

"No." Yelena said in the tiniest voice Penelope could imagine.

"You knew Harry was seeing someone."

"I assumed. I didn't know. If he was, I have no idea who."

"And you?"

"Yes."

"Did Harry know or just assume?"

"He knew. He knew because he wanted to know. I didn't know because I didn't want to know. We tried to honor each other's preferences."

"Was the marriage just for appearances, then?"

"That is a horribly unfair way to explain what was between us."

"Will you explain it to me. I don't want to offend you. It's just a hard thing to understand from the outside."

"And that is exactly the reason we decided no one at St. Georges could know. We did not begin this way. At first we were drawn to each other because we saw the world in the same way and had the same needs. There was physical attraction, of course, but the real force between us was our absolute certainty we were not fit companions for anyone else. We were good for each other. Being together allowed both of us to cope more easily with the world. That comfort gave me the confidence to think there might be something more out in the world for me. Harry experienced the same thing but it happened to me first. Other men began to notice me and I liked that.

"I gave in to the temptation. I was a poor cheat and Harry found out. We fought. I moved out. It was terrible for a few months. During that time Harry met someone. And then one day he showed up at my door and asked me to come home. We talked all night and concluded, once again, that we needed each other. Being apart amplified our obsessive-compulsive tendencies to a degree no one else could be expected to tolerate.

"We recognized the cycle would repeat. Together we would give each other confidence, which in turn would lead to temptation and a desire to experience something new. We would not be able to keep the secrets and we would be torn apart, only to realize we needed to be together. We decided that if we changed the rules of our relationship, there would be no need for the ugly part of the cycle. The only question was whether what worked in our heads would work in our hearts. I will tell you it has not always been smooth sailing but, for us, it worked more than not. What marriage have you seen that could claim more?"

"Thank you for sharing, Yelena. I have no doubt you loved each other very much."

"And now you understand why we chose to keep our secrets. Most people here would have a hard time understanding and, even if they accepted us, we would always be that strange couple who plays around on each other. We would always be the 'swingers' of St. Georges. We did not want that."

"I do understand, Yelena. No one else had any business knowing. Of course, under the circumstances, the Sheriff will see it differently."

"I know. Bags, what am I to do?"

"I think telling the Sheriff the truth is a good start. I doubt he has any interest in exposing the details of your life to the public."

Yelena dropped her head to her hands and began to sob. Penelope hesitated, not sure she wanted to give up her invisibility. Bags seemed stuck in his chair. Yelena sobbed harder. Penelope couldn't stand the awkwardness and moved to Yelena's side, putting her arm around the sobbing woman's shoulders.

"Yelena, my dear, I know this will be difficult but you will get through it."

Yelena picked her head from her hands and wiped her eyes. "You don't understand. I can't tell the Sheriff. It will ruin lives."

"What will?" Bags pressed.

"He knew but who will believe that now?"

"Yelena, what are you talking about?"

"I told you already, Harry knew who I was seeing. He always knew. He thought it was a bad idea. He told me that. But he never told me to break it off."

Penelope could see that Bags wanted to press her again. Instead, he let the silence work for him.

"It was William. He was with me that night." Yelena said to end the awkward pause.

"I see . . . and you worry the Sheriff will find that suspicious." Bags offered.

"He will believe William and I conspired to be rid of Harry."

"And your alibi is that the two of you were having a clandestine liaison while Harry was at a party a hundred yards away."

"Bags, please don't make it sound so torrid."

"But that is how you expect the Sheriff to see it?"

"Why would he see it any other way? Why would he look beyond the surface?" Yelena offered, struggling to control her tears.

"You are right that it will be unpleasant with the Sheriff but you must tell him the truth. The truth always comes out eventually. You cannot afford for the Sheriff to think you a liar."

"I know you're right. I do." She gathered herself, still oddly unaware of Penelope's presence. "I suppose he will want to speak with the two of us separately."

"I believe he will. And he will ask what conversation you have had with each other about the investigation. He will assume that two lovers have talked about their stories before talking to the police." Bags warned her.

"What are you suggesting?"

"More of an observation. If I were investigating this case, I would assume the two of you would only need to coordinate your story if you had something to hide."

"So I shouldn't speak with William about this until after we talk to the Sheriff. Is that what you are saying?"

"That seems impractical under the circumstances, I know. I guess I would only say you should be very careful how much you discuss." Bags shifted in his chair, waiting for the words to sink in with Yelena. "Out of curiosity, have you and William had any conversation concerning what you might say to the Sheriff, if asked about that night?"

Yelena hesitated, "William said he thought it best that we continue to keep our relationship private and, particularly, that we not reveal his presence at St. Georges that night."

"I see." Bags shot a glance at Penelope. She could tell by his reaction that her poker face was letting her down. It was a good thing she was still sitting beside Yelena and out of her line of vision. "What will you tell the Sheriff when he asks you if you were alone at your house that night?"

"What can I say? You are right, lying now will only make matters worse."

"And what would you say if he asks whether the two of you can account for each other for the whole night?"

"Well, of course he stayed the night."

"I'm sorry, that's not really what I meant. I think you will have to account for every minute of each other's time during the Gala."

"We obviously weren't in each other's view every minute." Yelena sounded confused.

"Yes, but were there any significant gaps? Did either of you go for a walk, for example? Or did you take a long bath -- that kind of thing?" Bags kept probing.

Yelena thought for a moment. "At one point I went down to the kitchen to get a snack for us. I suppose we were out of each other's sight for five or maybe ten minutes. As far as I know he was upstairs in the bedroom that whole time."

"You do not mean the master suite, I take it." Bags clarified. Penelope already knew the answer. The lights she saw in the guest wing the night before were Yelena and William. That was part of the arrangement, she suspected.

"That's right. The master was only for when Harry and I were together -- another one of our silly rules. William and I were in one of the guest suites that night."

"Were there any other times that evening when you were apart for more than a few minutes? By the way, when did William arrive? I don't recall seeing his car out front that night or in the morning."

"I told you the truth. I did leave St. Georges on an errand just after Harry went to the party. William was the errand, I'm afraid. I went to pick him up -- another attempt to keep a low profile."

"And then?"

"I opened wine and we had a drink standing around the island in the kitchen, while I made a salad for us. We ate and had a little more wine. I'm not sure how much time passed. We were not watching the clock. And then, how can I say it without being crude . . . I suggested we go upstairs."

"I think that says it." Bags smiled slightly. "And so you were occupied upstairs for sometime, yes?"

"Yes . . . oh wait, no, not right away." Yelena stopped. Penelope could see the color drain from her face slightly. She leaned into Yelena, anticipating a faint. "William said he was tense." She paused again and looked in Penelope's direction before continuing. "I . . . offered a solution." Penelope could see Bags blush just a little at the top of his cheeks. Penelope rolled her eyes -- like the "solution" she meant was really going to be lost on Penelope. Yelena continued. "William suggested we go in the hot tub in the back. He knew I would not go in that filthy thing. I told him not to become too relaxed and that I would see him upstairs when he was done."

"How long was he in the hot tub?"

"I can't be certain. It seemed a long time. I was a little annoyed, to tell you the truth, but I know how he likes to sit and soak among the bubbles. I took a shower and picked up a romance novel. I'm not sure how long I had been reading when William returned. He knew to go straight to the shower to wash off the hot tub slime. After that we were occupied for quite awhile."

Holy crap! Penelope poker face surely didn't survive that last bit. She could tell Yelena understood the importance of what she was saying too. Bags was the only one still composed.

"Well, I think that is something the Sheriff will want to hear."

"But how can I do that to William? It sounds like I am selling him down the river."

"It only says the two of you were apart for longer than a few minutes at some point in the evening. William will describe what he did during that time just as you have described what you did."

"I hope you are right. Oh Bags, it's all just so horrible! And now no one will understand how much Harry and I loved each other. I miss him so much."

"I believe you, Yelena and I'm sorry to have upset you. I think maybe we should leave you now, unless there is something you need from us." Bags stood.

"No, and thank you. It is hardly your fault I am in this awful mess. And it really has helped to talk through it with you before the Sheriff comes to see me." Yelena stood and moved toward Bags. Penelope followed.

"I'm sure it will all work out, Yelena. Try not to let it get to you."

"Thank you, Bags." She hugged him. "And thank you, young lady. You were very sweet today." She put her arm around Penelope for a squeeze as they walked to the door.

In the golf cart on the way to Penelope's house, she and Bags went over what they just heard. It seemed certain William would become the focus of the investigation. Neither of them could tell how much of Yelena's story was true. Parts of it had to be true. They knew William was with her that night. She wouldn't say they were having an affair unless that was true, although in her story, it wasn't really an affair. And she definitely would not have made up the part about William being outside for so long unless she was looking to frame him, which didn't seem like her.

Bags said the next steps belonged to the Sheriff. The murder weapon would be analyzed and William and Yelena would both have an appointment with the detectives in one of the Sheriff's interview rooms. It was hard to say how long all that would take.

Penelope could tell that Bags was still getting over the initial hurt of finding out about Marika and Harry. She suspected that would take time. As he pulled out of her driveway, Penelope decided she might need to invent some excuses to see Bags over the next few days.

Chapter 25

For the two days after the divers visited St. Georges, Sheriff Phillips worked on the investigation like a man possessed. Bags shared the images from the video camera with him, which predictably heightened his interest in Yelena and William. The detectives then found a bank record indicating almost $200,000 had been withdrawn, in cash, from one of Harry and Yelena's accounts. The timing seemed suspicious to Sheriff Phillips though he struggled to say why. While waiting for the medical examiner and the other forensics people to look over the sock, he invited them William and Yelena in for questioning. Both brought lawyers, which probably made the Sheriff more suspicious.

According to Bags, who had a couple of calls with the Sheriff, Yelena told much the same story to the detectives as she shared with Penelope and Bags. William reluctantly admitted the relationship, more reluctantly admitted his presence at St. Georges the night Harry was killed, and had a very fuzzy memory of the whole hot tub situation. When the detectives started pressing him on the details of the large insurance policy, William's lawyer abruptly ended the interview.

Before he walked out, William suggested that the detectives look as diligently into Harry's love life as they had into Yelena's. The fact that the Sheriff mentioned it to Bags suggested he planned to follow up. It was going to get messy, Penelope feared.

Most of the residents back for the funeral stayed in town for a while. It was Friday and many of them would be leaving the next day. Expecting a big turnout, Bags planned to eat at the club that night and invited Penelope and her dad to join him. Penelope wondered whether Marika would be there too.

As it turned out, her dad was leaving in the afternoon to pick Mother up from the airport in Miami. They would be staying the night there so it would be just Penelope for dinner. She knew Father and Bags cooked the whole dinner thing up so Penelope would have a babysitter. He should have just told her. Penelope didn't love being alone at night in her house anyway and she always had fun with Bags.

As usual, Penelope was up late the night before watching movies and had been happy to sleep through most of the morning. She was ultimately lured downstairs by the smell of breakfast. Her dad was making bacon and eggs. That was sweet, even if his motivation was guilt about leaving her alone overnight. She ate a lot, which seemed to make him happy. They talked about what he had planned for Mother in Miami. It sounded a little boring but very sweet. He also gave her the weekly progress report on his latest book. Father liked to joke that her college fund was made up exclusively of book royalties so she had a vested interest in helping him. She played along.

After breakfast Penelope decided to put on her swimsuit and take the golf cart to the club for a little poolside lounging. Father suggested she do something productive instead, to which she replied, "Summers aren't supposed to be productive." Then she kissed him on the cheek, told him not to do anything in Miami she wouldn't do, and went upstairs to change.

As she pulled on her swimsuit, Penelope made a mental note. Sometime later in the day, or maybe the next morning, she would need to clean her room. It was probably kind of clean when her mom left. Family harmony would be enhanced if it was close to that condition upon Mother's return.

Ponytail and ball cap looking perfect and sunglasses in hand, Penelope skipped down the stairs, only stumbling once, and grabbed her swim bag and from the cupboard. The convection wave slapped her in the face before the garage door was fully up. She wouldn't need to bake by the pool for long to take her tan to the next shade.

She pulled the golf cart out of the garage and launched up the long straightaway to the front gate without paying much attention. That was the danger. She been there about a month and everything in St. Georges was so familiar she barely noticed anything as she drove around. Today, she made a conscious effort to look down Yelena's street as she passed. She wondered how Yelena was coping. It had been a rough week.

Penelope turned her head back to the road just in time to swerve right. Her heart jumped. She had strayed too near the middle of Fulham Road just as a white SUV was barreling at her from the direction of the main gate. Her heart went from regular to pounding in less than a second. The shock of seeing the big truck bumper coming at her disoriented Penelope and it took a few seconds for the second and third vehicles to register in her brain. It was a whole parade from the Sheriff's Department -- two SUVs and a squad car.

They turned right just after passing her. Penelope had now stopped by the side of the road and it took a few seconds to register that they turned down Yelena's street. She fumbled in her swim bag for her phone and sent a quick text to Bags. He definitely would want to know about this.

Penelope wheeled the golf cart around and headed for Yelena's. By the time she arrived, the Sheriff and several of his officers were marching on Yelena's front door. She stopped across the street in a driveway one house up to she could see. The front door opened, the Sheriff held up a piece of paper, and the other officers filed into the house.

The Sheriff lingered at the door with Yelena, who appeared distraught. Penelope pulled her phone out again and sent Bags another text -- "You really need to get over here!" No immediate response.

A minute later the Sheriff and Yelena disappeared into the house, leaving the door open. Two officers were left to loiter outside. One of them kept a watchful eye on Penelope. It was uncomfortable and she was glad when Bags drove past and pulled up at Yelena's. He motioned Penelope to join him. There was a brief conversation with the two men in uniform as she approached. The result was Bags walking past them to the front door. Penelope slid by quickly and joined him.

Just inside the front door was another officer. Bags spoke briefly to him about the Sheriff, causing the officer to jabber into the radio thing pinned to his chest. The Sheriff appeared shortly.

"Is Yelena here?" Bags asked.

"Yep, I told her you were here. She wants to keep an eye on my men while they search." He responded.

"Do you think she's in the right frame of mind to do that?"

"She was borderline hysterical for a few minutes, which is not unusual. I suggested she call her attorney, which she did. Now she seems better."

"Can you tell me what it is you are looking for in Yelena's house?" Bags asked, hopefully.

"Not just her house. I have another team at the business partner's house."

"Looking for?" Bags persisted.

"Why don't we step outside?" Sheriff Phillips walked to the door and waited while Bags and Penelope walked past. "Normally, that isn't the kind of thing we share with a community liaison. But since you two get a good chunk of the credit for what we've found so far, I'm going to bend the rules."

"I appreciate that, Sheriff."

"I think I told you already about the big cash withdrawal from one of Mr. Cumberson's accounts right before he was killed. We have since learned that Mr. Sturridge had a side business with some very unsavory characters. His partners did their best to run it into the ground, which forced him to borrow money from some even shadier types. He was into a loan shark for over a hundred grand and he was at the point where he was going to start losing body parts if he didn't pay the debt. He claims the cash withdrawal was a gift from Mr. Cumberson to pay his loan shark debt but that seems too convenient."

"I had no idea." Bags exclaimed.

"Seemed like none of his fancier friends did, including the wife."

"So you think maybe he had Yelena made the withdrawal and then killed Harry before he discovered the missing money." Bags ignored the insult and pressed the Sheriff.

"Possibly. Definitely doesn't make him look less guilty. But that's not why we're here. Our background check also revealed that Mr. Sturridge was a competitive swimmer in his youth."

"I don't understand." Bags wrinkled his forehead.

"The way I see it, fifteen minutes would be cutting it close if he had to slink around the neighborhood from here over to the club and back. But from the back of this house, the scene of the crime is no more than a hundred yards away. We know the water was calm that night. A strong swimmer could be there in a few minutes. That would leave plenty of time to kill Mr. Cumberson and swim back. We know Sturridge took a shower after his supposed hot tub soak, which was a very convenient way to wash off the salty muck before hopping in the sack with the wife."

Penelope could tell the Sheriff was pleased with his theory, which Penelope found a comic departure from his original "the simplest story is almost always the right one" approach.

"So you are looking for swim trunks?" Bags asked.

"Actually, that would be helpful but what we are really hoping to find is a sock." The Sheriff replied, knowing his answer would not be understood.

"I'm sorry. Socks?" Bags cocked his head.

"The matching sock, right?" Penelope blurted.

"Very good, young lady." The Sheriff smiled at Bags. "The forensics folks tell me the sock is made of wool from something called a vicuna, which I guess is like a fancy llama. Very expensive socks -- the kind of expensive socks only someone like Mr. Cumberson would keep in his closet."

"And if that is indeed his preferred brand, you will conclude the murder weapon came from this house." Bags followed the Sheriff's logic.

"More importantly, I think we will be able to say the murderer came from this house. If I'm Sturridge, I don't want to lug a big rock along on my swim. So I take the sock with me and find a rock on the other side. He knew the club well enough to know there would be big rocks in the landscaping by the patio."

"And if you don't find the mate to your murderous sock?" Bags asked. Penelope could tell he was becoming frustrated.

"If the socks are that rare, it doesn't matter." Penelope observed.

"That's the way I see it. At six hundred bucks a pop, you aren't going to find them in many closets even around here." The Sheriff confirmed.

"So you think the sploosh sound wasn't the rock at all. It was William?" Penelope quizzed.

"Probably. Or he could have tossed the sock in and then lowered himself carefully from the dock. Either way, same result."

"I admit it is an elegant solution to the problem of William's partial alibi and the vicuna sock element is intriguing. What doesn't make sense to me is why William would risk using a sock so easily traced back to Harry's house." Bags questioned.

"Arrogance. Wouldn't be the first time a criminal underestimated law enforcement. Sturridge wasn't planning on us finding the murder weapon. He might even have thought he could keep us from finding out about him and the wife."

Bags frowned. Penelope could tell he was unconvinced. The problem was he didn't have a better suspect to offer.

"Mr. Bagwell, as long as you're here, I want to let you know we will be talking to your friend Marika."

"Any particular reason?"

"I'm pretty sure you know why, but ok, I'll play along. Harry was more discrete than his wife. Even when we started digging into his life, there was nothing pointing directly to her, except his phone records, that is. The wife was pretty sure there was someone. She said she thought it had been going on for about six months. Harry didn't have a lot of friends and not much contact with people outside St. Georges, with one notable exception. About six months ago one number started showing up more regularly than any other. We tracked that number to Marika."

"I see." Bags pursed his lips.

"Then we looked at her phone records for the same time to get the complete picture. She's kind of a social butterfly around here, isn't she?"

"Actually, Sheriff, I think a lot of St. Georges people are customers. She teaches yoga and does massage, and other stuff, I think." Penelope said, trying to help.

"Ok, that explains a lot." The Sheriff nodded. "By the way, Mr. Bagwell, are you one of Marika's customers?"

"Not really. More like good friends, I would say."

"Very good friends, I would guess. See the thing I found most interesting about her phone records is that your number shows up even more than Mr. Cumberson's. Mr. Bagwell, is there anything you want to tell me before I talk to your friend Marika?"

"I think people around the club sometimes jumped to conclusions about the two of us but I assure you we are just friends. Perhaps her attention to me was meant to distract from her relationship with Harry." Bags responded.

Penelope could hear the sadness creeping into his voice. "I don't think so, Bags; not the way she looks at you." She offered. The two men exchanged looks. She recognized the face. It was the one Father used when he wanted to say, "you'll understand when you're older."

"In any event," Bags added, "We are certainly no more than friends."

"Ok. I had to ask. It is possible, of course, that I will need to talk to you as a witness at some point." Sheriff Phillips warned.

"I understand completely."

Penelope was wondering how this awkward conversation was going to end when the front door swung open to reveal a small uniformed woman holding two large plastic bags, each containing a piece of clothing.

"Sheriff, we have it!" The deputy said, holding up the bags. "A large surf shirt and compression shorts."

"Where did you find them?"

"Tossed into the back of a cabinet in the garage with some other beach gear."

"Tossed?" Penelope asked.

The deputy looked to the Sheriff, who nodded his permission for her to respond. "Yes, they were wadded up in a ball. Mrs. Cumberson says she doesn't recognize them."

"Ok, good work, Deputy Ranson. Young lady, what was it about the word 'tossed' that caught your ear?"

"Well, it's just that Harry, I mean Mr. Cumberson, wouldn't toss his clothes around. He was super OCD."

"She's right, Sheriff. You should see his closet." The deputy added.

"Good to know. Thanks. Make sure you get that logged in and secured in the locker." The Sheriff motioned to one of the vehicles before continuing. "Find anything else?"

"You were right about the fancy socks. He has a drawer full of them. So far we've only found matching pairs. Still looking for that extra black sock."

"Ok, keep looking, and take one pair from the sock drawer so we can test the fibers and confirm we have a match."

"Yes, sir." The deputy brushed past Bags on her way to one of the vehicles.

"Sheriff, it appears you may be winding up here. If you have nothing else for me, I think we will get out of your way."

"Sounds good, Mr. Bagwell. I will be in touch when we know more."

"Thank you, Sheriff." Bags flashed a half-smile before turning away. Penelope took the cue and followed. She was a little in shock and wondered how Bags was feeling. You wouldn't know from looking at him. Other than a little wobble when Marika's name came up, he had been cool like the other side of the pillow. He couldn't fool her, though. Bags was worried about Marika. "Just friends." Whatever, Bags.

Chapter 26

Driving to the Sheriff's Office with her dad made Penelope nervous in the same way she felt being called to the principal's office, not that that happened a lot. Poor Father. He was barely out of the car after driving home from Miami when Penelope hit him with the urgent request for a ride downtown. Penelope wasn't sure why she had been summoned. Well, that wasn't true, exactly. She knew what she was supposed to do there but she couldn't quite figure out why. All her dad knew was that he got to play chauffeur for another few hours. Lucky him.

The request for Penelope's presence came from the Sheriff, through her dad, of course. Hardly a day passed without a little jab in the ribs reminding Penelope she was "just a kid." The Sheriff couldn't deal directly with a minor. Anyway, the version of the story she heard wasn't straight from the source. Based on what her dad told her, Marika was the one who wanted her there. She could kind of see how that might happen. What was impossible to divine from her dad's version was whether Marika or the Sheriff was behind the request that Bags not be there.

Penelope felt a little guilty not telling him what she was doing but she didn't want to get in trouble with the Sheriff, a sentiment Father emphasized as very important. Just as important to Penelope, she didn't want Bags to sit and fret, knowing Marika's interview was happening. She was definitely going to tell him after -- even if the Sheriff instructed her otherwise. She had to have his back. Hopefully, it would all be a non-event.

Even on her second visit, Penelope found the Sheriff's office intimidating. If anything, it was a little worse this time. Her dad seemed oddly at ease. Maybe that's how she looked the first time. Maybe it was all so foreign the first time that your brain really didn't know how freaked out you should be. Or maybe he was distracted, like he usually was, with thoughts of his next book. Sometimes she could literally see him sizing up a location, or person, or conversation, trying to imagine how he might use it in one of his stories.

Sheriff Phillips came to collect them, just like the first time. They ended up in the same viewing room where she and Bags watched the detectives grill Trip and Blair. The difference this time, the Sheriff pointed out, was that Marika knew Penelope and her dad were watching.

Apparently, everything had been arranged very cordially. The Sheriff asked Marika to come in for an interview and she scheduled a time. The request for Penelope's presence was a part of that. The Sheriff told Penelope it would be off limits for her to sit in the interview room, which seemed reasonable and also completely unrelated to her age. He suggested they make an appearance in the room before things started so Marika could see that Penelope was there. He warned that she might have a change of heart at the last minute and not want Penelope to observe. Again, it all sounded reasonable and maybe even a little too civilized.

Being inside the interview room was super intimidating. The view from the other side of the glass did not do it justice. Penelope could tell Marika was nervous. She stood, gave Penelope a hug, and thanked her for coming. "Why me?" Penelope asked, unable to keep it in.

"You will see." Came her cryptic response, as Marika stroked Penelope's cheek with her hand. Penelope nodded, not knowing how else to react.

A minute later she was back in the viewing room with her dad and the Sheriff. Detective Benton wasted no time. The interview began with several minutes of what must have been required questions and disclaimers. The interview was being recorded and also observed. It was voluntary. Marika could exercise her right to have an attorney present at any time.

To the Sheriff it probably sounded like a lot of blah, blah, blah. It was the kind of talk Penelope usually found pointless and boring. Instead, it sounded terrifyingly serious and she could not think about anything else while it was happening. Marika must have had a similar reaction, though she didn't let the detective see any sign of nerves. Penelope was glad for both of them when the preliminaries were done.

"Ms. Jones," the detective began with the real part of the interview. "You knew the deceased, Harry Cumberson, correct?"

"Yes."

"Ok, can you describe for me the nature of your relationship with him at the time of his death."

"At the time of his death Harry and I were lovers."

"For what period of time were you lovers? When did that start?"

"Around the holidays, so around six months ago."

"During that time did Mr. Cumberson ever indicate to you or say anything that led you to believe he had any enemies?"

"Nothing like that, no."

"Did he ever say anything about any arguments he might have had with the people?"

"Not that I recall."

"Anything like that with respect to his business partner, Mr. Sturridge?"

"No."

"His wife."

"No, we tried not to talk about Yelena."

"I imagine you did. And did Mrs. Cumberson know about your relationship with her husband?"

"Harry told me she suspected Harry was seeing someone but did not know it was me." Penelope thought Marika seemed very comfortable with this topic.

"Did it bother you to sleep with another woman's husband?"

"I believe Harry and Yelena had a more open relationship than most married couples. I was not the first woman Harry had been with while he was married and the same is true for Yelena. Harry was aware of her relationship with William."

"So you're saying they were swingers." The detective editorialized.

"No, it was their version of polyamory. I believe that's what they call it. You might say 'open marriage.'" Marika refused to be drawn in by the detective's trick. Good for her. Penelope made a mental note to look up the word of the day, "polyamory."

"Uh-huh. How did Mr. Cumberson feel about his wife carrying on with his business partner?"

"He thought it was a bad idea, of course. I know he told Yelena that. I don't believe he did more than point out that it was a bad idea. Again, though, we did not talk about Yelena much."

"Fair enough. Let me ask you this. Do you have any thoughts about who might have killed Mr. Cumberson?"

"Him, no. I can't imagine it was anyone who knew him. He was a very sweet man."

"Ms. Jones, you seemed to hesitate just at the beginning there. Is there something you were thinking about? Something else you wanted to say?"

"I'm afraid you will laugh or be cross with me."

"I promise I won't."

"Well, you asked about Harry and the answer for him is what I said. I was thinking about the two of us and then about me. It's just that for the last few months I have had this feeling like someone is watching me. It sounds crazy, I know. Who would be interested in me? But sometimes I am convinced I see the same car pass my house over and over and sometimes I think I can see a car following me while I am driving. I even convince myself I can hear someone lurking outside my house at night."

"Have you ever seen someone specific, someone you could describe for us?"

"No, I'm sorry. Most of the time it is just a feeling."

"And it has crossed your mind that this person you can feel stalking you might be involved with Mr. Cumberson's death?"

"You asked. It came to my mind. That's all. Like I said. I know it sounds crazy. Even to me it does." Marika shook her head, slightly embarrassed. Penelope wondered if Bags new about Marika's phantom stalker and then she wondered if that was the thing Marika wanted Penelope to hear.

"I'm glad you shared it. Every little bit of information helps. You never know. And, Ms. Jones, if you do see someone specific, you call me or 911 right away, ok?"

"Yes, of course. Thank you."

"Ok, where were we?" Detective Benton looked at some papers in front of him. "Oh yes, were you aware of any medical condition Mr. Cumberson might have that would make him more susceptible than most to a blow to the head?" He asked.

"I know he was very concerned about his testosterone levels. That was the main reason for his exaggerated fitness routine. I think he used a testosterone cream."

"Did you have any reason to believe he had soft or brittle bones?"

"He thought he had low bone density. Before we became intimate, he came to me several times for massages. I asked why his muscles were so knotted. He said he liked to lift heavy weights to keep his bones strong. That is really the only time we talked about the subject."

"Thank you. Very helpful. Ok, new subject. Did you entertain Mr. Cumberson in your house at times?"

"Yes."

"And did you ever sleep over at the Cumberson's home?"

"Yes."

"Sometimes when people are dating, they leave various things at each other's place, like a toothbrush, makeup, or maybe some spare clothes. Did Harry have a stash of things at your place?"

"Toiletries, as you said. No clothing though. Not that I can remember, at least."

"Ok, and how about you? Did you leave anything at his place?"

"No. Never."

"Very good. Let's talk about the night Mr. Cumberson was killed. My understanding is that you were at the party. A guest of Mr. Bagwell, is that right?"

"Yes."

"By the way, did he know about your affair with Mr. Cumberson?"

"It wasn't an affair and no, he did not."

"What should we call it, then?"

"You said 'relationship' before."

"Fine." Detective Benson paused.

So far Marika was holding up well. Penelope continued to wonder why Marika wanted her there listening, though.

"Ms. Jones, I want to ask you some very specific questions about that night so please listen carefully." Benton paused waiting for Marika to nod. "Let's call the area outside and behind the dining room of the club the 'patio.' Were you on that patio at any time the night Mr. Cumberson was killed?"

"Yes. When we heard Penelope screaming, Bags and Doctor Patterson rushed through the doors to the veranda. A number of us followed. A little crowd gathered around poor Harry. I couldn't really see him but I knew he was there. I fainted. Someone caught me. I don't remember who it was."

"And you're saying that is the only time that night you were on the patio where Mr. Cumberson was killed?"

"Yes."

"Now let me ask you about the time just before you heard the screams. My understanding is that Mr. Cumberson was in the dining room on the ground pretending to be dead until the dining room lights went off. When they went on again, he was gone. My question is, where were you between the time the lights came back on and the moment you heard the screams?"

"When the lights came back on I was sitting at a table with the Rileys, the Pattersons. Penelope came back to her seat just after the light came on."

"And is that where you were until the screaming started?"

"No. Penelope excused herself to go to the bar. Shortly after that, I excused myself to go to the restroom. I was walking back to the table when I heard Penelope scream."

"Was anyone in the ladies' room with you?"

"There was a woman in the other stall when I entered. She left before I did. We did not see each other."

"And how long would you say you were gone from the dining room?"

"Not long -- five minutes, maybe."

"Now about those fancy socks Mr. Cumberson left in your bedroom-"

"I think I said he left only toiletries." Marika corrected. Penelope was suddenly very angry with Detective Benton.

"My apologies. But you did know about his fancy socks, right?"

"Yes, vicuna, I think. They were the only dress socks he wore. They are very soft."

"And there is not chance we would find a pair of those socks at your house?"

"That is a different question. Harry did give me a pair of his socks. I wear them to bed sometimes or around the house. They are very soft and warm."

"What color are those socks?"

"Black I think. Harry was very traditional. He only wore black, navy, or brown."

"And you still have that pair of socks?"

"Yes, I think so. I haven't worn them since Harry died. Anything that reminds me of him is too much for me." Marika's voice trembled slightly. Penelope expected her to start crying.

"I don't mean to upset you but it would be very helpful to us if you could find those socks -- the sooner the better. If you do, you can call and I will send someone to pick them up." Penelope could tell the detective was trying to sound nonchalant. Marika had no idea he was baiting a trap.

"Ok, would I get them back at some point. I know it sounds silly but they do mean a lot to me." Marika responded innocently.

"I think so, but we would need to keep them for a while."

"I suppose I have little choice." She sighed.

"It would be very helpful." Benton smiled. Penelope thought it a kind smile, although it might have been a devious one.

"Ok. Ms. Jones, did Mr. Cumberson ever give you other gifts?" The detective started, baiting another trap. Penelope was not liking where this interview was going.

"Yes."

"He bought you a number of very nice things, I bet. Any jewelry?"

"This ring." Marika held her right hand up for the detective. It was the biggest, greenest emerald Penelope had ever seen.

"Did he ever give you money?"

Marika hesitated. Penelope could tell this line of questions was making her feel cheap. "Yes, but never directly."

"Can you explain what you mean by that?"

"A few months ago my car needed a new transmission. He wanted to buy me a new car. I refused. So he paid for the repairs, instead. And a few times he took me clothes shopping and paid."

"Is it fair to say he had a desire to take care of you?"

"He said that to me sometimes, yes."

"You were involved with someone, romantically, I mean, right before your relationship with Mr. Cumberson started. Is that correct?"

"Yes."

"And is it true that you ended things with that man so you could be exclusive with Mr. Cumberson? That was one of his rules, wasn't it?"

"Yes."

"And the first fella, he wasn't rich was he?"

"No."

"Pretty smart, trading up like that?"

"The 'trade up,' as you say, had nothing to do with money. Harry was kind and smart and funny and we understood each other." Marika started to well up.

"Did you love him?"

"I did. And he loved me?"

"Did you ever fight?"

"I honestly can't recall either of us ever saying a cross word to the other, detective."

"If you don't mind my asking, what was the end game for the two of you? I mean you say he loved his wife and there were rules about your relationship. Did you expect it to go on forever?"

"I didn't really think about that. I suppose I would have got around to thinking about it eventually. But six months -- it was still very new between us."

"Did he ever talk about ending things with you?"

"Just once, a few weeks before the Gala. I was at the club having dinner with Bags. Harry and Yelena walked in. They didn't sit with us. Bags asked but Harry begged off. The four of us chatted just long enough to be polite. I was with Harry the next night. He asked if he looked at me the way Bags looked at me. I told him I didn't understand. He said he knew he could never look at me that way. Then he said he saw the way I looked at Bags too. He got a little emotional and said maybe it would be for the best if we broke it off. He said Bags would always have more to offer."

"And how did you respond?"

"I told him he was being paranoid and silly and that he was stuck with me. That was the end of it."

"Were you being honest?"

"What does that have to do with finding Harry's killer, detective? I object to these questions."

"Fair enough."

"Ok," Penelope said under her breath. That was definitely why Marika wanted Penelope at the interview and it was pretty clear she didn't want Bags to hear it, at least not directly. It made Penelope feel good to know she wasn't the only one who noticed the way those two looked at each other. Kind of sad that Harry saw it.

"Well I think that is my last question for right now. I appreciate your cooperation. Oh, and please don't forget about the socks."

"I can go now?"

"Yes, Ms. Jones, you are free to go. Just don't leave the area without letting me know."

"Ok."

Penelope looked at the Sheriff for some indication of what she should do next. Her dad didn't wait. "I guess we can leave now, as well." He prompted.

"Absolutely, Mr. Hazard, and thank you for coming in on short notice on a Saturday. It obviously meant a lot to Ms. Jones and that helped the interview go smoothly." Sheriff Phillips responded.

Chapter 27

Father was suddenly very interested in the investigation. He peppered her with questions on the drive back. Penelope couldn't tell if it was genuine interest or more book research. She decided it didn't matter. It was the first conversation with him she could remember that didn't have a tinge of parental condescension. It made her feel grown up.

They agreed the interview was an indication the Sheriff considered Marika a potential suspect. Her dad thought William must still be the prime suspect. It was hard for either of them to see Marika running out to the back of the club, stuffing a big rock into one of Harry's socks, and then hitting him in the head with it.

They also agreed that the Sheriff's theory about William swimming across the marina to kill Harry was too much like a movie of the week. Her dad suspected Sheriff Phillips was under some pressure to close the case, which made him more inclined to force fit a theory to the facts. At the same time, like Bags, they didn't have any better theories.

Speaking of Bags, what was she going to tell him about the interview? She had to say something and once he knew she had been there, he would want details. He would also wonder why. That was a question better directed to Marika. Penelope was sure she knew what Marika wanted her to hear. Why it was important that she hear it remained a mystery. Her dad's take on it was the super helpful "women remain largely a mystery to me."

Penelope spent the rest of the day intentionally distracted. She conned her dad into taking her shopping on the way back from the Sheriff's Office. That helped. They stopped for coffee, which was also good. By the time they got home, most of the day was gone. Penelope's primary goal at this point was to avoid Bags. Her hope was that Marika would talk to him, which would take most of the pressure off Penelope.

All she really had to do was avoid blurting out "even Harry could see that you two are in love." It sounded easy enough but simple things like that had a way of becoming such a focal point that your brain only had room for the thing you most wanted to ignore. It was like the tremendous, hairy mole perched on her fourth grade teacher's cheek. There was a whole face to look at all around the mole and never a reason to reference it -- ever. And yet it was all Penelope could see when she looked at poor Mrs. Miller. Every time she went to the teacher's desk it seemed inevitable Penelope would open with "excuse me Mrs. Mole." Marika's confession to Detective Benton was beautiful and sweet -- definitely not a hairy mole -- and yet she needed to not focus on it. Good luck with that, she told herself.

Tonight would not be a problem. Her mom would want to stay in and have family time. Pizza would probably be involved. Mother was allowed one cheat meal a week on her diet. After pizza it would be an early night for her parents. They almost certainly stayed up way later than usual during their reunion in Miami. She didn't really want to think about what that involved. The result was all that mattered to Penelope. It would be a measured dose of forced family fun tonight, after which she could disappear into her room, her nearly immaculate room, to watch movies.

The evening went exactly as Penelope predicted. The morning did not. She woke up to banging on her door. It couldn't even be ten yet. Why was Father beating on her door? It was definitely Father. She could tell by the rounded quality of the thump the side of his fist made on the door. By the time she was upright, still sitting in her bed, Penelope could feel the effects of her vampire movie hangover. It was a double feature hangover. Ugh.

Apparently, Bags was on the phone convinced he had a problem only Penelope could solve, or at least that was the impression she had from the parts of Father's urgent little rant that actually filtered into her brain for processing. She took the phone from her dad, still in a haze. "Hey Bags, I thought we had an understanding about mornings."

"Circumstances beyond my control, I'm afraid. Marika called in a panic this morning -- something about not being able to find her socks. About the only coherent thought she managed was to direct me to you. She seems to think you can explain it to me."

"So she told you about the interview?"

"I deduced there had been an interview based on some of the thought fragments streaming from her mouth. She's very upset."

"Yeah, about the interview. I'm sorry Bags. I kinda thought it should be her thing to tell you."

"That is a very mature conclusion. In this instance I would have preferred a more childish approach. The problem we have is that Marika is unable to tell me much of anything in her current state."

"Ok, yeah the socks." Penelope hopped off her bed, hoping the movement would help her focus. "Detective Benton asked if she knew about Harry's vicuna socks. Then he asked if there might be any at Marika's house. She said Harry gave her a pair and Benton told her it was really important for her to find them."

"Ahh, now I see. The woman is hysterical. She kept yammering about only having one sock and asking if that mattered. Did the detective say why he wanted her to produce the socks?"

"No, he was cagey. She didn't know about the sock they pulled from the water. I think she should have had her lawyer there."

"I told her that too. Anyway, after we resolve the sock crisis maybe you and I can talk about why she wanted you there for her interview."

Penelope decided to use selective hearing. "Bags, if she can only find one sock, that's going to look suspicious."

"Yes, I realize that. I think she must have the same instinct. It sounds like she has been up all night looking."

"So you are on your way to help her find the sock, I hope."

"Yes, Penelope. I have to tell you how refreshing it is to have someone in my life again who likes to tell me what to do."

"Ha ha. All part of the service, Bags."

"Getting in the car now. I will text you when I have an update. I won't forget our unfinished business, young lady."

"I know, I know. Good luck." Penelope ended the call.

She expected Marika to call Bags -- was counting on it, actually. She also expected Marika to go home, dig the pair of black socks out of her dresser and give them to the Sheriff's people without thinking much more about it. Detective Benton asked about the socks to be thorough and almost certainly expected the same result. If Marika could only produce one sock, she would be a suspect, which was exactly what Marika had hoped to avoid.

Thanks to Bags and her dad, Penelope was, awake, up, and thinking obsessively about the case. Her dad made breakfast for her out of mock pity. It didn't help. She sat at the counter eating her omelet like a zombie. Her mom, who had clearly been up for hours because she was now on Europe time, tried to start a mother-daughter conversation, which also didn't work, and eventually led her to drag Father out to do grocery shopping.

This was Penelope's first murder investigation so maybe it was supposed to feel like something was missing. Her frame of reference was a combination of Agatha Christie books and TV police dramas. Her brain had become conditioned to expect everything to fall neatly into place, including the inevitable dramatic confession in the final few minutes or pages.

Rationally, she knew life didn't work that way, just like high school didn't work the way all her favorite shows promised it would. She wasn't a hot 25 year old model turned actress playing a high school junior dating a gorgeously dangerous 30 year old model turned actor playing a high school senior. Her parents didn't go out of town once a week seemingly for the express purpose of allowing her to have said hunky boyfriend stay over or so she could have the epic, booze soaked, drug filled rave in her backyard that the neighbors and police mysteriously were cool with for several hours until something dramatic happened to move the plot forward. Also, there were no vampires, werewolves, witches, demons, or demon hunters in her high school. In short, TV high school allowed teenagers to have cool lives and do cool things. Real life didn't, just like it didn't necessarily bring murder investigations to a tidy conclusion.

Still, it seemed like something needed to start making sense. Maybe they weren't even looking at the right list of people. Penelope's brain continued to swirl around the same set of facts -- the hidden relationships, the sock, the business troubles -- until it was like Groundhog Day inside her head. She needed to break things up. A golf cart ride, maybe. No that would be too passive. A run would be better. Too hot. It would have to be a walk.

She was gone over an hour. The walking helped. It was a good distraction and healthier than sitting in her room watching shows on her computer. By the time she was done with the full circuit of streets, Penelope was wringing wet. The big bottle of water she took with her was gone. She drained another as soon as she stepped in the door. A shower was definitely in order. Normally a midday shower seemed like work. This one, with the water mostly on the cold side of the dial, was heaven.

Once she cooled down, Penelope realized she was hungry. A full bag of white cheddar popcorn later, the hunger was mostly gone. As she lounged in the family room watching whatever DIY show was recording for Father, it became clear the next step for her was sleep, which came quickly. Sleep on the couch tended not to be deep sleep for Penelope and when her phone buzzed with a text from Bags, it was just enough to bring her back to consciousness. He wanted to talk to her. She agreed to go to him. It seemed like the thing a fake granddaughter would do.

Somehow the heat seemed more oppressive even under the canopy of the golf cart than it had during her walk. The two-minute ride felt extra long. Bags had the garage door open and she was able to park in a little patch of shade.

"Hey Bags. How's Marika?"

"Not that good, I'm afraid. Together we exhausted all possible hiding places for that blessed sock. We never found it. I told her to call Detective Benton and explain the situation. What more can she do?" Bags replied, clearly agitated.

"Did you at least calm her down a little?"

"She is more calm but it seems like she simply ran out of the energy required to be hysterical more than because I calmed her."

"I'm sure you didn't do any harm, Bags. She needed you and you came. Just showing up must have helped."

"Maybe. At some point while we were digging around for the sock, her hysteria became less about the sock itself and more about why the sock mattered."

"Bags, you didn't?" Penelope shook her head.

"I know, I know. But what else could I do. It didn't feel right knowing something so important and keeping it from her. At the time, I didn't think she could get more hysterical."

"So you told her about the sock the divers found and that made things worse." Penelope sighed. She also wondered whether that crack about feeling too guilty to hide something from Marika was really aimed at Penelope and what she might be keeping from him. He was just about that clever.

"Considerably worse, yes. So now she believes the Sheriff might be at her doorstep at any moment to arrest her."

"He won't, will he?"

"I hardly think so. Based on what I have seen and heard, I doubt he has enough evidence to arrest anyone and William surely would be first in line if the Sheriff needed to make an arrest."

"So time will pass and she will see. It's just gonna suck to be her for a few days, which probably means it's gonna suck to be you too." Penelope grinned across the counter at him.

"I suspect you are right on both counts. Now, let's talk about you for a few minutes."

"It's about time. That was way too long for the conversation not to be all about me." She said mockingly.

"Why do you suppose Marika wanted you there for her interview?"

"Gee Bags, I was hoping she told you. I'm kinda fuzzy on that."

"So there were no clues in the interview itself?"

"Maybe she just wanted to know there was a friendly face in the building with her. They let me say hello before it started. She seemed happy to see me."

"Did she tell you why you were there? I wager you asked when you had the chance."

"You don't know everything, Bags. And 'no,' she didn't say why." So far, so good. Penelope was managing to deflect his questions.

"She tried to tell me a little about the interview. The details are clearly jumbled in her head right now. How did she do?"

"She was a superstar, Bags. I was impressed. And the detective was kind of a jerk. He was fishing around pretty good."

"For example?"

"For example, he implied that Marika was only with Harry for his money. Apparently her last boyfriend was not rich. Do you know anything about that?"

"Not really. I know she is rarely without a man for long, at least not since I've known her. She is beautiful and funny and kind so that is not hard to explain."

"She said she was with Harry about six months before he was killed. Does that sound right?" Penelope asked.

"Six months -- so sometime before the holidays. Interesting. Harry and Yelena kept to themselves when they first moved to St. Georges. Always very cordial, of course, but they did not embrace the neighborhood or the club's social scene."

"So?"

"For Harry that changed about six months ago. I foolishly thought I was the one responsible for bringing him out of his shell. Clearly, it was Marika."

"So did they start mysteriously showing up at the same events?"

"Not exactly. Marika rarely misses the opportunity to be part of life at the club. That has been true more than just the last few months. So, yes, when Harry began to show up, they found themselves together. If you mean to imply they used those opportunities to flirt, it was the opposite, to the point that we began to wonder what was wrong with Harry. He seemed the only man in the club immune to her charms."

"Too funny. So they had everyone fooled, even you. Pretty impressive, although I have to say it sounds a little too much like high school."

"As I have said before, when it comes to love, we are all made to feel like children at some point, and sometimes like fools, as well."

"That's just depressing, Bags. But since you brought it up, tell me again why there's never been anything between you and Marika?"

"You are a determined matchmaker, I'll give you that. I can't speak for her directly. I can say that for as long as I have known her, she has never been without a boyfriend for more than a few days. So even if I wanted to court her, the door slams shut very quickly, sometimes before I would have reason to suspect it had opened. From her perspective, it seems she has never had trouble finding someone more to her liking."

"But if that door stayed open?" She smiled as she asked.

"I think it would be too complicated. I think I have been alone too long to have the energy required to be otherwise."

"Chicken."

"I'm sorry?" He wrinkled his forehead.

"It just sounds like you're afraid or lazy. Those are both super lame excuses." Penelope scolded her fake grandfather.

"Hmm, no riddle about why the two of you get along. She has the same feistiness. Promise you won't get together and gang up on me." Bags smiled and pretended to laugh a little. Penelope could tell the conversation made him sad and interpreted that as a good thing. He should not underestimate her matchmaking ability.

Chapter 28

When Penelope opened her eyes the next morning, she found herself, yet again, obsessing about the investigation, going over and over the same facts. There had to be something she could do to get a different perspective. It was like she was inside an endless loop. Seeing things from a different perspective so she could add something, anything, new to the equation required adding something new to the loop.

Unfortunately, all she could think of was to go back and look through all of Jerry's video. Ugh. When she found the images of William things spun out of control, with the Sheriff at least, and she never bothered to go back and finish the job. Luckily, Penelope anticipated having to turn over the flash drive to the Sheriff and had copied all the files onto her computer. So now she could dive into 18 hours of video times two cameras. Penelope was pretty sure her two detective friends were not going to put in the time necessary to do that, so maybe she would be able to find something fresh.

And so she huddled in her room cave looking at the comings and goings of a typically quiet day in a super quiet neighborhood. It was slow and dull even at double speed. She dutifully logged a description and plate number for every car that came into view. She also logged every golf cart appearance. It was mind numbing. She fell asleep at least twice, once for a couple of hours. In between naps she kept at it. Her persistence was driven more by a need to tame the swirl in her head than the more noble desire to find the truth. It was working. A seemingly endless mind-numbing task was apparently just the thing for tranquilizing her brain.

By the time Penelope was getting around to the potentially interesting part of the video, she heard noise downstairs. It was her parents returning from somewhere. She didn't even know they were gone. Of course they could have been in and out several times without her hearing them. Her dad called up to announce dinner. This time it was Thai food. Until she was in the kitchen and could smell panang curry, Penelope had no idea she was hungry. Suddenly, she was ravenous.

It was the best Thai food she ever had, or so it seemed. That's how hungry she was. Such was her complete focus on food, even the obligatory dinner conversation was less annoying than usual. The one non-food thought she had over the next half hour was mild surprise at not hearing a peep from Bags all day, which was probably not a good sign. He was either mad at her or events at Marika's turned out to be less straightforward than expected. She sent him a text, a really adorable text.

Back in her room the video was waiting. In a post-meal burst of focus she was able to slog through all the video from the camera facing the promenade. If there was anything useful in the parade of cars and carts going to and from the Gala, it would only become apparent after an even more tedious exercise in matching vehicles with the people at the club that night. For that she would need Bags.

She switched to the Fulham Road camera. There was a lot less to see. Penelope still got a little rush seeing Yelena's Range Rover with William in the back seat. After that, there were a few cars and carts coming from her side of St. Georges. She deduced they were the fashionably late crowd. The latecomers irritated Bags to no end. He wanted everyone in their seats and quiet when the curtains went up on one of his productions.

After that, the same people went home and Bags drove the Sheriff over to Yelena's to give her the bad news. That was it. All she had to show for her day was strained eyes and a list of vehicles.

Then she remembered standing out on the veranda thinking about what the killer must have thought right after Harry hit the ground. Jerry's Fulham Road camera took in a wide view. At double speed she hadn't noticed anything but cars and carts -- no sign of Mr. Brownfield's elusive panther, for example. Maybe at regular speed she would see something else.

Looking at several hours of video was out of the question. Assuming the clocks on the cameras were reasonably accurate, she could narrow the window considerably. Starting 20 minutes before Penelope flipped the lights back on in the dining room seemed reasonable. Another 20 minutes after that should cover the critical window.

Ten minutes in and Penelope's mind started to wander. This was as close to watching paint dry as she could imagine. It was worse than studying for a math test. Suddenly the profound wisdom of Mr. Brownfield's motion activated cameras became clear. The only thing keeping her going was a desire to be able to say with complete confidence there was nothing useful on the video other than her boring little list of cars, carts, and times. That was something, a sad, sad, something.

Penelope watched frame-by-frame the dim, grainy, night vision images of an empty driveway and street. She thought there would at least be a raccoon or stray cat but not even that. Five more minutes and she would be done.

And then she saw it, something at the very edge of the screen just for a second. Even in real time she barely noticed. Penelope backed up the video and inched through it at half speed, unsure if it was anything more than a moonlight shadow cast by palms moving in the breeze.

Wow! Penelope paused to make sure her eyes and brain agreed. She stopped the video and backed it up to find the best single frame. Definitely not a shadow. Definitely a person. And definitely not someone just out for a stroll. It looked like the figure of a man. He was wearing dark clothes, bulkier than would have been appropriate for the weather, she thought. The view was only from the side and back. Of course this guy wasn't going to be like one of those dumb "smile for the security camera" criminals you would see on TV sometimes. That would be way too convenient.

But wow! Her brain was swirling again. It was all she could do to print images of the best frames. She wondered how the Sheriff would react. If this was the killer, his stealth swimmer theory was wrong, which meant he would have to find a new prime suspect or at least rethink the timeline to keep William as a suspect.

Bags would want to see this right away. It was already a stretch to think Marika could be the killer. This should put an end to that conversation once and for all, despite the missing sock. She sent the text. Bags replied before she was done changing out of her lounging clothes. He was home. She would be right over, Penelope responded.

On the way, Penelope strategized how she would tell him. It was news befitting a bit of spectacle. The problem was it was so big she would likely blurt it out the second she was in the door.

As it turned out, she was able to find a little restraint, enough to at least explain what she did and why before jumping to the big reveal. Bags rewarded her with a big response. They had both been spinning around the same scenarios, always with the same unsatisfying conclusion that something was missing from the puzzle.

Penelope launched into her story practically before she reached the top of the stairs at Chez Bags. When they both managed to calm themselves, he reminded her of something he apparently said when she walked into his kitchen. It was his big news of the day, which hadn't seemed very big until he heard her big news. In a moment of synchronicity, Sheriff Phillips called Bags while he was texting with Penelope and asked if they could meet the following day for a status update. He suggested Bags invite Penelope. The Sheriff was in for more than a status update, they agreed. She had seen Bags giddy or nearly giddy only a few times. It was predictably adorable. She couldn't decide what made her happier, finding the St. Georges equivalent of Big Foot pictures or seeing Bags react when she told him.

That night Penelope had to go all out to find a distraction sufficient to give her any hope of falling asleep. It was hard to imagine any real sleep happening in the half day sandwiched between her big video discovery and the meeting with Sheriff Phillips, which was set for mid-morning in the bar at the club. This was a night for The Sound of Music. She wasn't sure why that movie had always been a guilty pleasure. It just was. It went without saying this was something the mean girls must never discover, but if anyone could calm her brain enough to allow sleep, it was a young and feisty Julie Andrews.

The alarm seemed more evil than usual when the pain of it in her ears finally registered in her brain. Few things matched the frustration caused when a half-awake teenager could not manage the mechanics necessary to stop the noise coming from her phone alarm after multiple failed attempts. Father laughed at her for using an alarm for a mid-morning wakeup, not because he thought it unnecessary, he was quick to point out, but because it was. He knew she would otherwise sleep through lunch most days and that amused him. Jealous much? He had offered the night before to come in and wake her at the requested time. She refused to give him the satisfaction.

The good news was that she had slept. Julie to the rescue. Her hair was proof she slept deeply. The way it gathered into a gravity defying, vaguely geometric shape on one side of her head reminded her of a sculpture they had in the Contemporary wing at the Art Institute in Chicago. Her reaction was the same. It wasn't art but it was worth seeing somehow. She memorialized the moment with a selfie -- one she would share with a very select audience. There would be no getting by without a shower today and, thankfully, the bottle of detangler was full. Good thing she built in extra time for emergencies.

Bags was waiting when Penelope walked in the doors at the club. "Good morning, my dear. You look lovelier than usual today."

"Hmmm, maybe because you're extra happy this morning." Penelope replied. "Or maybe because I took a shower."

He smiled. "I appreciate the effort. Waking up before eleven must be a shock to your system."

"Tell me about it. At least I slept, though. Wasn't sure I would be able to. Did you?"

"Sleep? Enough. These days I don't sleep much anyway. I don't like to give the Reaper too much time to work with on any given night." He laughed, admiring his punch line.

"Ok, kinda creepy, Bags. Am I early?"

"No, the Sheriff is late. Let's go to the bar. He will find us."

Penelope followed Bags to the bar. They sat and Lisa came in to offer drinks. Bags opted for a celebratory beer. Penelope needed diet soda, highly caffeinated diet soda. It really didn't matter which kind.

The Sheriff walked in just as Lisa was delivering their drinks. He politely declined her offer to get something for him. Bags asked that she shut the door on her way out. The three of them sat at one of three tables lined up in a row between the doors to the veranda and the bookcase lining the opposite wall of the shotgun shaped bar.

"Thank you for meeting with me this morning, Mr. Bagwell. You too, Miss Hazard. I'm hoping this is more than just a courtesy update. You two have been very involved in this investigation so I want to get your thoughts on some things because, frankly, I'm not sure where to go next."

Penelope looked at Bags. They agreed he would pick when to reveal their big news. She was practically vibrating with anticipation.

"I appreciate that, Sheriff. I think it safe to say Penelope and I have reached a similar conclusion after a considerable amount of thought. Maybe together we can find a fresh approach." Bags began.

"I hope that's the case. Anyway, shall we start with a recap? Feel free to jump in any time if you think I am missing something."

"Please, go ahead." Bags prompted. Penelope stared at him, fairly certain she was frowning.

"We know how the victim was killed. We know where. Thanks to the planning that went into the murder mystery skit, we know with a high degree of precision when it happened. We can be fairly certain we have the murder weapon. We have a witness who saw a second figure on the veranda but no other eyewitnesses to what happened there. Penelope heard some noises, which is what led her to discover the body. With me so far?"

"I am." Bags answered, looking at Penelope.

"Yep, me too." She added. Now she thought Bags was just messing with her.

"Good. With regard to suspects, we have William Sturridge, Mrs. Cumberson, and Ms. Jones. All of them have strong connections to the victim and all three have at least some potential motive. None of the motives are overwhelming, however. All three also have a connection to our most interesting piece of physical evidence. Marika has admitted the victim gave her a pair of his fancy socks. After an exhaustive search, she can produce only one and it is the same color as the one we pulled out of the marina. Mrs. Cumberson obviously had access to the victim's sock drawer, which, curiously, had four pair each of navy and brown but only three pair of the black socks. Mr. Sturridge likewise had access to the victim's sock drawer, including on the night in question."

"All true statements so far, I suppose." Bags agreed.

"I know, Mr. Bagwell. You and I differ on whether Ms. Jones had motive. Duly noted."

"What about means and opportunity?" Penelope asked.

"Very good. You have a future in law enforcement. I think we have to say all three had means. When you put a big rock at the end of a long dress sock, it doesn't take a lot of brute strength to get it swinging hard enough to inflict the wound that killed our victim. Mr. Sturridge was obviously strong enough. Ms. Jones too. She's a fitness instructor and a very fit one at that. Even Mrs. Cumberson could have whipped that rock around and smacked someone in the head with it. And, as I mentioned, they all had access to the sock. The rock came from the landscaping right there at the scene."

"And opportunity?" Bags prompted him again.

"That's where it gets tricky. All three have at least a few minutes of gap in their alibis. Mr. Sturridge is the easiest. We found his swimwear at the victim's house. Mrs. Cumberson admits he was outside and out of her view for as much as 20 minutes before he came back up to shower. That would give him enough time to slip in the water, swim over, kill Mr. Cumberson, and swim back. His shower is consistent with that scenario and we know he was more than capable of doing the required swimming. Heck he probably could have done most of it under water."

"But Yelena could not have done that." Bags interjected.

"Right. Even if she could make the swim, her own story is that Sturridge was outside where he would have seen her get into the water. His story is the same -- he was in the hot tub the whole time."

"Could she have gone out the front door and around on the streets?" Bags asked. Now Penelope understood what he was doing.

"Maybe, but that would make her very visible both going and coming and we don't have any indication she was seen. I'm guessing when my detectives finish reviewing all that video you gave us, we will find no hint of her car."

"What if she walked? Her or William?" Bags pressed.

"That's the thing. We can't rule it out but the timing would be very tight."

"What about Marika?"

"Same idea. She went off the radar for a few minutes. We've done a number of follow-up interviews from that guest list you gave me and no one can place her in the bathroom or coming and going from her table. So we can't rule her out. But again, it's hard to see how she could get out the door, kill her lover, and get back in so quickly."

"I agree, of course." Bags responded. "What else is there to consider?"

"Well, that's what I'm hoping you can help me with today. What you just heard is pretty much all I've got." The Sheriff admitted.

"So you have three suspects, identified primarily based on their respective relationships with Harry. There are enough indications to prevent ruling out any of the three and, at the same time, no compelling case against any of them."

"That's one way to put it, yes."

"Well while I don't know that we can offer a complete answer today, I think we can add an important piece of evidence." Bags pulled the three frame shots from a manila folder in front of him and pushed them across the table.

The Sheriff spread them apart and stared at each, in turn. "Ok, I think I know what I'm looking at but why don't you spell it out for me."

"Penelope." Bags said, motioning with his head for her to speak.

"Right, ok, so yesterday it occurred to me that when I was originally looking at the video files, I got so excited after I saw Mr. Sturridge in Yelena's Range

Rover that I stopped looking. Last night I went back and finished the job. I kept a copy on my hard drive when Bags took the flash drive to you. It didn't take too long because I went through it all on fast forward and only stopped when I saw something new. I have a whole list of cars and golf carts that went past either camera that day. You can have that too. Then I started thinking I should look at the file from Jerry's Fulham Road camera in real time instead of fast forward. So I watched the 40 minutes right around the time Harry was killed. I think these images would have been captured a little after I found Harry's body." Penelope stopped to breathe.

The room was suddenly very quiet, the kind of quiet that makes lulls in a conversation awkward. She looked at Bags. He smiled approvingly. They watched as Sheriff Phillips studied the images. He held one of them up to the light for a few seconds before ending the silence. "Holy Moly, young lady. I think you found a picture of our murderer."

"Which changes our thinking considerably, I think." Bags offered.

"Yes, well we will have to confirm that these images are on the video we have back at the office, of course. That's the official evidence. But, yes, it changes things."

"Would you like some time to process this new tidbit or should we keep talking?"

"Both. I'm thinking this means we can rule out Ms. Jones. I'm sure that's what you were hoping to hear this morning."

"I think you would admit she was always on the periphery as a suspect. We can now write off the missing sock to her documented inability to keep her room tidy. Some people never grow out of that." Bags smiled at Penelope.

"Wouldn't know anything about that, Bags." She responded, sticking her tongue out while the Sheriff continued to study the pictures.

"I guess you could put it like that." The Sheriff answered, still distracted.

"And Yelena?"

"I'd say it's looking more and more like she's in the clear too. I'm looking at these images and seeing a man. I think our killer has to be a man."

"So we are back to William, then?"

"Well, I hate to give up the only suspect I have left." He paused. "Darn it, I knew that swimming theory was just too cute to be right. Would have made a good story, though. You have to admit." The Sheriff shook his head.

"It would have made a good screenplay, I'd say. I mean it's not Agatha Christie but still . . .." Penelope chimed in.

"Sheriff, I think we have to accept the possibility that our killer is a man not yet on our radar."

"Mr. Bagwell you were supposed to help me simplify this investigation today not blow it up completely." He shook his head and sighed.

"I share your frustration, Sheriff. Think of it this way. Now we know there was a legitimate reason why all three of us were going in circles. We have broken the cycle."

"Yeah, by taking us back to square one." The Sheriff protested.

"Not quite. I think it would be very hard to say it is random that the murder weapon was constructed using one half of a pair of $600 socks just like the ones in Harry's closet." Bags observed.

"Good point. So our killer had to know about Mr. Cumberson's taste in socks. That will help."

"Also, if the sock wasn't random, that means the killer wanted us to make the connection back to Harry." Penelope interjected.

"That's right," Bags picked up. "There can be only two reasons for that; to throw suspicion from the killer or to frame someone close to Harry."

"Well, Mr. Sturridge is still our only suspect and we know he had some shady associates. This seems a little too cute for that kind of low life to orchestrate, but it's worth having my detectives nose around a little. Maybe this was never really about Mr. Cumberson."

"You see. Progress!" Bags said, encouragingly.

"I suppose it is. Hey, while we are on the subject of what we know, tell me what you think about this business of Mr. Cumberson being worried about brittle bones?"

"I'm not sure I'm following you." Bags looked at him quizzically.

"My fault, Bags. In her interview, Marika said before she and Harry were a thing she saw him as a client a few times and he mentioned that he worked out so much because he was worried about low bone density." Penelope tried to fill in the blanks.

"That's right." The Sheriff continued. "So I asked my medical examiner if that could happen -- you know like osteoporosis but in the skull. She didn't think so but agreed to look at Harry's x-rays again. Turns out he wasn't completely making it up. His head was just a little on the porous side -- probably not enough to matter but it certainly didn't help him survive that blow to the temple."

"Interesting." Bags wrinkled his forehead.

"So maybe more than just Marika knew about it from Harry. And someone who knew that about Harry would be more likely to use a rock to the head to kill him than someone who didn't." Penelope finished the Sheriff's story.

"That was my thinking, yes. Depending on how many people Harry told that little story, it could help us narrow our suspect list, that is, once we have built it back up again. Anyway, it's on my list of things to ask Mrs. Cumberson next time I see her."

"More progress. Your visit has not been wasted so much as you thought, Sheriff." Bags smiled.

"It definitely wasn't wasted. I always want to get to the facts in a case. Sometimes the facts make life harder, that's all. Well, it looks like I have a lot to do all of a sudden. I think I'll let you two get back to your day. Again, thank you."

Bags rose with the Sheriff. They shook hands. Penelope took the Sheriff's hand when he offered it. When he was gone, they sat.

"Wow!" Penelope exclaimed. "That was fun."

"Wow indeed."

"Should I feel guilty about how much fun that was?"

"Maybe a little." Bags answered.

"I think you enjoyed it more. And I don't think you feel even a little guilty. In fact, I'm sure of it."

"Then you hardly need me to respond. We do have a problem, however."

"You mean like all of a sudden not having a clue who killed Harry? Duh. It was still fun."

"Yes it was." Bags smiled.

Chapter 29

Penelope was once again awake far too early. It was like none of the people around her understood the importance of her summer sleep. It was the one thing she had. She had no friends her own age in Florida, which meant her social life was defined by people literally old enough to be her parents or grandparents. And this was her last summer of pure childhood. The following summer she would be driving, hopefully, which meant a job -- probably one involving a deep fat fryer and a horrible polyester uniform. This summer was supposed to be about day after day enjoying an utter lack of scheduling, work, responsibility, and expectations.

Sheriff Phillips was among those who had not received the memo about Penelope's dire need to be left alone until noon. Predictably, he called Bags late in the afternoon after yesterday's meeting at the club to ask if he could have Penelope's log of the comings and goings of cars on the video. His detectives, it seemed, were not as far along reviewing the video as he had hoped and he wanted to get them going on finding new suspects as soon as possible.

It was Detective Benton who showed up at her door to collect the four sheets of paper full of relatively neat printing she had assembled while slogging through the video. He thanked her profusely for saving him so much grunt work. Penelope was polite and only mildly friendly. She had not forgotten how rough he was on Marika. Job or not, some of his questions and comments made Penelope mad.

Since meeting with the Sheriff, and really since finding the images of the killer, Penelope's head had been remarkably calm. She found the timing odd. Despite their attempts to make the Sheriff feel better, Penelope's reaction was the same as his. They were back to square one. That should be making her head spin more not less. Perhaps the calm resulted from the removal of an irritant. Right up until their meeting with the Sheriff, Penelope found herself chafing more and more against the direction the investigation was going. Until it melted away, she was unaware of the amount of stress that was creating. Today all that stress was gone.

Part of her annoyance at having to set an alarm for this morning was the quality of sleep it interrupted. Any sleep not preceded by brain swirl was pure bliss to her and rare enough not to be messed with lightly. She remembered only one dream, which was unusual for her. It wasn't even a distressing dream, just odd. In it she woke and sat up to find herself back in the same gray room from the Men In Black dream she had the night Harry was killed. This time there was no Agent K or Agent M and as soon as she recognized her surroundings, she settled back in her bed and went back to sleep. That was the whole dream. It was actually kind of soothing.

Despite the cranky start, her day was poised to be a good one. It seemed clear her brain intended to take the whole day off, so now all she had to do was decide how to exploit her freedom. She decided to turn lemons to lemon soda with some late morning sunbathing by the pool. They had reached that part of the Southwest Florida summer characterized by rain clouds rolling through every afternoon with more consistency than an Amtrak train. It never rained much, so she was told, and it tended to cool things off for the evenings, so the clouds weren't a disaster, unless you wanted to sleep past noon and then bake in the sun. She was up. The sun was bright. The pool beckoned.

Predictably, she was the only one there. It was heavenly solitude. She plunged into the water a few times to cool down, reapplied sunscreen a few times, and listened to music from her phone. That was it. If there was anything useful going on in her brain, it was happening politely in the background.

The clouds eventually came and chased her indoors. The timing was good. Any longer in the sun might have overwhelmed her sunscreen. A leisurely shower and some leftover pizza kept her happy day going. After lunch she tried to watch movies but the darkened skies and softness of the rain on her window put Penelope right out. By the time her eyes opened, it was time to eat again, followed by more movies and sleep. Other than the wretched start, it was a day of summer the way summer was supposed to be for a teenager.

The next morning started at a more appropriate hour, which was good. What was not so good, what was, in fact, lame, was the surprise trip to Naples scheduled to begin just before noon, or in Penelope time, just after breakfast. Father swore he told her about it a week ago. She protested, insinuating he might be experiencing early senility. He laughed, which made her mad. In truth, he might have mentioned it. There was every chance her brain dropped a few things over the last few weeks. That happened when there was a lot of swirl inside her head.

It was a work trip for Father, if you could call it that. He was meeting his literary agent, who was in Miami for the week and decided to drive over to see one of her lesser clients. Father offered to meet her in Naples to save her some drive time. Normally, Penelope would petition her way out of that kind of event but she liked Kate. Kate was funny. Also, there was shopping in Naples and her dad was usually in a good mood after meeting with Kate, so Penelope might benefit from a little trickle down happiness.

The drive wasn't horrible. Father was working on a new book and he wanted to tell Kate all about it, so he practiced his pitch on Penelope. It was cute the way he thought he was a real author. He was, of course, and Penelope was proud of him. He just wasn't anyone most people had heard of, which made it odd to hear him talking so earnestly, like he was describing the next great bestseller. What she liked most about hearing about his new book was how he wasn't talking at her like he was her dad. It was almost like the other day when he wanted to talk about the investigation. She felt grownup.

Lunch was good. The restaurant was right downtown on Fifth Avenue -- fancy and casual at the same time. Kate was charming and funny, like always. After the food was gone, her dad sent her to wander the shops right around the restaurant. He gave her his credit card too. It was really a win-win. He didn't like to shop and what she really liked about having him shop with her was his credit card.

In an hour she had seen everything she wanted to see within the three-block radius of the restaurant. Her only purchase was a cute top that matched a pair of shorts she didn't wear that often because she didn't have the right top.

The ride home was quiet. Her dad only had so much social interaction in him and when he was done, he was done. Penelope understood completely. Luckily, Bags began texting her as the shopping was winding down and now she could respond properly. At first he wanted to know where she was. When she told him, he remembered right away, which meant her dad had mentioned it to Penelope and, for a time at least, she had remembered.

Now Bags was updating her in little bits about the Sheriff's progress with the investigation. It wasn't great news. So far the detectives hadn't found anything to link any of William's business associates to the murder. Also, Harry's accountant confirmed that the large cash withdrawal he made just before he was killed was for William. As William said, unbeknownst to Yelena, Harry had offered to bail him out of his trouble with the loan sharks. A gift. It was kind of romantic of Harry, Penelope concluded.

The detectives had also ruled out Marika's boyfriend just before Harry. He might have had access to her pair of the vicuna socks, so it was a lead worth pursuing, but it didn't take long to confirm his alibi. Apparently, the not rich ex was working as a waiter at an event at a nearby hotel that evening. His boss confirmed it and even offered access to the security video, which the guy swore would show his car sitting in the employee section of the lot all evening.

The Sheriff said Penelope had a knack for police work. Hearing Bags describe what Detectives Benton and Salero were doing just to confirm a bunch of dead ends made her think she would hate being a detective. The time she spent looking over all that video was a good example. In thirty hours of dark, slightly grainy images, there were two snippets worth seeing. She suspected most of the time there were no worthwhile snippets. Bags had a ready example of that. One of his texts confirmed that the list she gave Detective Benton, the list it took her a whole day to compile, yielded nothing useful. All the cars and carts matched up to people with no possible connection to Harry's death.

Kate's job seemed like much more fun, even if it did require sucking up to clients like her dad. Penelope could do that. She was delightful, after all. She didn't know much about what her mother did but even that sounded like more fun than being a detective. The more she thought about it, lots of things sounded like more fun. She could see herself growing up and running the clubhouse like Lisa, for example. Even Bud the bartender seemed to have a better job than the two detectives she knew.

They were finally turning off Highway 41 when a phone number she didn't recognize popped up on her phone. She opened it, expecting some inappropriate text spam. It was from Marika. Bags had given her Penelope's number. He had to drive up to Punta Gorda for a dinner and Marika wanted company for the evening. Reaching out to Penelope was probably something Bags suggested, which might mean he had a reason to want her to accept, so she would. The offer was a good one, anyway -- sushi at her favorite place followed by movies and manicures at Marika's.

Her dad had no problem with the plan. He was probably loving the fact that she was spending her time with the likes of Bags and Marika instead of some sketchy guy like Ricky the drug dealer with nice eyes. That dynamic was not lost on her. She would let him keep feeling grateful every time the doorbell rang and it wasn't some hormone crazed teenage boy. It would be her secret that, for this summer at least, the whole boy thing seemed like far too much work.

Father was so comfortable with Marika's plan for the evening he agreed to drop Penelope off at the restaurant. Marika was already there waiting. For the next hour or so Penelope tried to eat her weight in sushi while she and Marika had somewhat awkward girl talk. Penelope allowed herself to be grilled about high school in Illinois, including mean girls and stupid boys. They talked about what she thought her sophomore year at a new school would be like. To the extent she could do so between bites, Penelope steered the conversation toward fashion, which was her favorite subject, even more than the zombie apocalypse. When there was no more room for sushi, they settled up and headed for Marika's house.

Penelope had no idea where Marika lived. She had driven by Marika's business, which was part yoga studio and part spa, a few times with Bags or her dad, but he subject of Marika's home address had never come up. For a good part of the drive, Penelope thought maybe Marika was planning to take her back to St. Georges. They were only a mile or so from the front gates when Marika turned down a side street. Two more blocks and they were in Marika's driveway.

Her place was more like a large cabana than a small house -- one story, basically square, two bedrooms, a bathroom, and the rest was a combination of the living room and kitchen. Even as small and simple as it was, Penelope guessed it was a pricey piece of property. It was not on the water and had no direct access to water, but it was near the water and near the bridge to

Sanibel. Penelope guessed its proximity to St. Georges was what appealed to Marika.

Inside, it wasn't fancy like Harry's house or the Bags Villa but it was comfortable and elegant at the same time -- a perfect reflection of Marika. Of course she was a gracious host. Marika was going to have wine, she said, and offered Penelope a blood orange Italian soda. Bags must have told her it was Penelope's favorite. Then Marika disappeared into her bedroom. In a few minutes she called Penelope to join her. Marika had already changed into yoga pants and a t-shirt. She was holding a pair of cute sweats and matching t-shirt for Penelope. "Let's be comfortable tonight." She said. What was wrong with Bags, Penelope thought.

Marika grabbed a little caddy of nail polish and related accessories and left Penelope to change. When Penelope returned to the living room, Marika motioned her toward two shelves of DVDs. "I hope there is one you want to watch."

Penelope scanned the shelves and quickly stopped on The Princess Bride. She held it up.

"Excellent choice." Marika beamed.

"Why thank you." Penelope gave a mock curtsey.

"You know, Penelope, you should never be with a man who does not like Princess Bride. It is a sign he lacks imagination and has no sense of romance."

"Good tip. It is one of my favorites." Penelope handed it to Marika, who turned the TV on and cued up the start of the movie.

"My little home entertainment system is not up to St. Georges standards, I know." She said.

"But you can actually make yours work without a set of instructions taped to the coffee table." Penelope said, alluding to the hopelessly complicated system Bags had in his living room.

Marika laughed. "I know. I feel like I'm taking an IQ test every time I want to change the channel on that TV of his."

"You gotta love him, though. He just keeps at it." Penelope giggled.

"I know. He is adorable."

"So, speaking of loving Bags, is that why you wanted me at the interview?"

"Very clever. I was wondering how you would bring it up." Marika took a sip of her wine. "Yes, that is one of the things I wanted you to hear. I feared it would somehow come up and wanted Bags to hear it from a friend rather than the Sheriff."

"And you couldn't tell him?"

"Bags and I, . . . we are complicated. I didn't think I would be able to say what I wanted to say."

"I haven't told him anything about that yet, by the way. I will if you want."

"Maybe if it hasn't come up naturally, it is best it not come up at all." Marika said, thoughtfully.

"It seems like he's been alone a long time. I don't think I've even heard him talk about having family around."

"I have known him longer than you and I don't know a lot more about his family. I know he has children. I think they are far away. The people of St. Georges are his family now."

"Seems like that's true for you too."

"St. Georges is like a family, no doubt. Now we are both a part of that family." Marika winked at her.

"So what about you? Do you have family somewhere else, like Bags?"

"Not really. I have no children, obviously. My parents are gone."

"I'm sorry."

"Thank you. It was a long time ago, sadly. I have older brothers -- much older. I haven't seen them in a long time."

"That's kind of sad. What about their kids? Do you have any nieces or nephews?"

"Not that I know." Marika said almost in a whisper. Penelope sensed there was at least one sad story in Marika's past.

"Well now you have me. You said I was part of the family." Penelope smiled.

"No question about it." The light returned to Marika's eyes.

"So, new topic. You said the thing about Bags was one of the things you wanted me there to hear. What else did you want me to hear?"

"I also haven't told Bags anything about my paranoia. I didn't want him to know at all and I certainly didn't want him to hear from the Sheriff."

"So you don't want me to tell him? Did Harry know?"

"Harry knew. I had to talk to someone. I needed someone to tell me I wasn't going crazy."

"And now that's me?"

"Yes, lucky you. It isn't fair to burden you with any of this. I know that. But here we are."

"I don't mind. Actually, I like that you don't treat me like a kid."

"Sometimes it is hard to remember you are so young."

"Thanks, I think. I don't think you're crazy, by the way. Do you think maybe one of your old boyfriends has turned stalker? I mean, I'm guessing guys get pretty upset when you break up with them."

"I don't think so. It feels more sinister than a lovesick ex. And why do you assume I am always the one doing the breaking up?"

"Seriously? Look at you. You're gorgeous. You're sophisticated. You're kind. No boy would ever walk away from all that."

"You are very sweet. Many of the men I have known have concluded I am more crazy than kind."

"Hmm, not really buying that. But while we're kind of on that subject, did it make you mad when Benton accused you of trading up to Harry from your old boyfriend."

"It made me sad. I don't care how he wanted to make me look but those questions were disrespectful of Harry and of Bud. That's what I didn't like."

"Wait, what?" Penelope could not have heard that correctly.

"Oh, I'm sorry. I assumed Bags would tell you."

"He told me the Sheriff looked at your ex because he had access to the socks but he didn't give me a name. Come to think of it, he went out of his way to avoid using a name." Penelope paused as she thought about her earlier exchange with Bags. "So, Bud? Our Bud . . . the bartender?"

Marika smiled. "You disapprove. I can tell."

"No, no. I can totally see it. I mean you couldn't have thought he was 'the one' but he is a charmer, and very cute."

"He was good for me. The right man at the right time. They don't all have to be Mr. Right."

"I get that. Is it true that you broke it off with Bud to be with Harry?" Penelope asked.

"It suited the detective's purpose to make it sound so simple. Life is rarely simple."

"So what really happened?"

"Things with Bud began casually. That suited me. After a few months he became very possessive and jealous of any time I spent with other men." Marika explained.

"He couldn't have been the first guy to fall for you like that."

"Men are so strange. They say they don't want any commitments and then act like they own you. It always surprises me. It shouldn't, but it does."

"So what happened?"

"I could tell it upset him knowing I had a social life beyond the time we spent together. It was hard for him to be there at the club when I was there. We made it a point to stay away from each other. We were getting to the point there was more pain than joy between us. And then I got to know Harry. There was a physical spark between us and we also saw the world in much the same way. His situation with Yelena made it seem that we could manage to be together without too much attachment."

"So you were going to dump Bud anyway and then Harry shows up and seals the deal?"

"I took Harry's appearance as a sign, I guess. Because of the St. Georges connection, I made certain neither ever knew about the other, which was very tricky at one point because there was a little overlap. Bud suspected there was someone else. For a time he was convinced it was Bags. As soon as it became clear Harry wanted something exclusive, required it actually, I broke things off with Bud."

"Bud and lots of other people have thought you and Bags are a thing, FYI." Penelope confirmed.

"Yes, and that worked well for Harry and me, so I did not object too loudly." She admitted.

"So how much overlap?" Penelope asked. The more she learned about adults, the more they acted like teenagers.

"In time it was a month, maybe a little more. You have to understand though, at that point Bud and I were seeing each other infrequently, maybe once a week."

Penelope was still trying to process the notion of Marika and Buuud, the surfer bartender, and also Marika juggling Bud and Harry. Very high school. Her mind began to wander when Marika snapped her back.

"Penelope," she whispered. "Did you hear that?" She rose as she spoke.

Before Penelope could answer, the door behind them exploded into the living room. Marika stumbled backward. A huge man in a dark coat stepped into the room. Penelope froze. The man covered the distance to Marika faster than Penelope could even see. He lifted her with one hand on her neck.

"Where is he?" The overdressed hulk barked.

"Who?" Marika managed to squeeze out, gasping for breath.

The man lowered Marika and pushed her hard against the wall. "Don't play with me, bitch! Your brother. Where is your brother?" He growled it. She pawed helplessly with both hands at the massive hand pinning her in place.

"I was a girl last time I saw him." Marika answered meekly.

"Lies! Where is he?" The dark haired man persisted, growing angrier.

Penelope suddenly became aware she was a helpless spectator watching her friend being killed by an overdressed monster. Even if Marika gave him what he wanted, the man would not want either of them alive as witnesses. She looked around. His violent entrance had already made the room a mess. There was a big conch shell on the ground near her, knocked from its place on a side table. Penelope grabbed it. As her assailant yelled louder at Marika, Penelope wrapped her fingers in the mouth of the big shell and took two big steps forward to launch herself off the arm of a couch in the middle of the room. As she rose in the air, Penelope lifted her arm high, bringing it down hard on Marika's attacker.

He sensed movement and flinched at the last second, causing her to miss his head. The sharp points of the shell crunched into the monster's shoulder. His shoulder dipped under the blow and he lost his grip on Marika's throat. Penelope landed and found herself slightly behind and to the left of the hulking intruder. She hadn't planned for that. He towered over her. She raised the big shell again, hoping to land a second blow. Instead, the man twisted toward her and swung a thick arm backward. Penelope sailed across the room and landed on the floor flat on her back. Her head cracked back hard against the ground as the wind rushed from her lungs.

She looked up, dizzy and struggling to find her breath. The man turned back to Marika. Penelope's heart sank. The room began to grow dim around her. Somewhere in the twilight in her head, Penelope thought she could see another figure enter the room, also dressed in dark clothing but not the ridiculous gangster coat their monster wore. The figure flashed across her field of vision and was on the much larger man before he could react. What happened next was a blur of motion obscured by her fading consciousness and the dark clothes both men wore. It seemed like the larger man eventually fell to the ground under a decisive blow.

Penelope allowed her head to drop back to the floor. She gasped, finally able to take a breath. Her head continued to spin. A face appeared above her as if hovering in the air. It was her dad. He said, "Stay with me, Pea, help is coming." And then everything went dark.

Chapter 30

Penelope opened her eyes. She wasn't at Marika's. At first she thought it was another of her weird dreams. The room wasn't quite right, she decided. As the fog in her head lifted, Penelope sensed she wasn't alone. Also, it was a hospital room and she was hooked up to a bunch of stuff.

"Dad?"

"I'm here, Pea. How are you feeling?"

"Ok, I guess. Where am I?"

"Hospital."

"Why?"

"What's the last thing you remember?"

Penelope thought for a moment. Inside her head everything was strangely blank. That never happened. She was the girl with the high-def memory. Where did it all go? She thought about her dad's question -- the last thing she could remember.

"Marika." She blurted.

"That's right. You were at Marika's last night."

"You." Images were starting to come back to her.

"Me what?

"That's the last thing I remember; you kneeling over me telling me help was on the way." She clarified.

"At the hospital, right?"

"No, at Marika's. I was on my back on the floor about to pass out and you just kind of were there all of a sudden." She insisted.

"I wasn't at Marika's, Pea. I went straight to the hospital when she called."

"Wait, what?"

"I think your memory is playing tricks on you. The doctor said that might happen. Do you remember why you were on the floor?"

"If it wasn't you, who was it? Did I just imagine it?"

"Maybe. Or maybe it was the police officer who found you and Marika. He has short brown hair like mine and he is very handsome so . . .."

"Ha ha. Now who's imagining things?" Penelope's brain was finally beginning to cooperate. "The big guy in the coat. Where is he?"

"Good, you are starting to remember. Apparently, he was the reason you have such a headache today."

"But where is he?"

"Long gone by the time the handsome policeman arrived. You are very lucky, both of you."

"What about the other man in black?"

"Marika didn't say anything about another attacker. I thought it was just the one."

"No, no. The big one had Marika jacked against the wall. He was going to kill her. I picked up a big conch shell and clocked him with it. That's when he knocked me across the room. I barely put a dent in him."

"Don't sell yourself short. Marika says you hit him hard enough to disorient him. She grabbed a vase from the bookshelves next to her and hit him in the face. After that he ran out."

"No, there was another man. It all happened so fast. Marika didn't hit the big one, the other guy did. There was a fight. The big, mean one dropped like a stone. I leaned my head back and that's when I saw your face. Some guy in a dark track suit showed up and saved us, I swear."

"Ok, ok, try not to get worked up. You have quite the knot on the back of your head. They did some tests last night and nothing seems broken but you still need to take it easy, Pea."

"How long do I have to stay here? It kinda creeps me out."

"They wanted to keep you overnight. I think when the doctor comes this morning he will let us go home."

"Were you here all night?"

"Well, you know, I figure it's like research for me." He smiled.

"Is Marika ok?"

"Bags says she's really shaken up and also very worried about you. He took her back to his place. I came here with you."

"I'm glad she's alright. That guy was going to kill her."

"Do you remember anything else about last night?" Father asked.

"Well, it seems like I can't really trust anything I do remember so maybe I should just keep my mouth shut for now. I don't suppose Bags is coming to visit."

"I think he and Marika will come see you at the house later. For now why don't you try to rest? You had a very traumatic experience last night."

"Ok, don't go anywhere, though."

"I'll be right here. Don't worry."

Penelope closed her eyes and tried to relax. It didn't work. The short conversation with her dad kicked her brain into gear and now the whole day was playing and replaying inside her head. She slowly remembered more and more detail. Her dad was right. She did have quite the headache. If he wasn't the one with her just before she blacked out, maybe the rest of her memories were faulty too.

The more she thought about it, the more likely that seemed. It couldn't have been her dad. She could believe he might try to stalk her if she was on a date with someone like Ricky. He might delude himself into thinking he could do all the things Raglan Dunne could do. But she was with Marika and he knew that. Penelope had to have imagined she saw his face and heard his voice. The bummer was it sounded like she missed out on meeting a cute police officer, although she would have to confirm said cuteness with Marika -- unless he came to check on her in the hospital. Ha ha. More likely he would be checking on Marika.

Penelope was annoyed she had to wait for the doctor. She had a headache. No big deal. She was just about to be mad at this doctor who was clearly in no hurry to come check on her, when Roger Patterson walked in.

"And how are we feeling this morning, young lady?"

"Dr. Patterson?"

"You were expecting someone else?"

"I figured it would be whoever was on duty at the hospital today."

"Well we can't have just anyone looking after you, can we? We take care of each other in the St. Georges family."

"Good to know."

"Speaking of which, I hear you were quite the brave little hero last night protecting Marika."

"It didn't feel brave, or particularly helpful."

"Don't sell yourself short, Penelope. It was very brave."

"Ok, can my reward be that I get to leave this place now?"

"Let's see how you do on your feet first."

Penelope sat up and swung her legs over the side of the bed. It was at that point she realized she was wearing only a hospital gown. Yikes. She could feel the cool air on her backside. Slowly she slid off the edge. With one hand she grabbed her dad's arm. The other was busy trying to hold things together behind her.

"Careful. Go slowly." Doctor Patterson warned.

Penelope's head was buzzing more than spinning. Her legs felt stable under her. She leaned on her dad and took a step. The trailing arm was not only occupied with covering things up, it was also attached by tubes to an IV rig next to the bed. She took another step and let go of her dad.

"It feels pretty good, actually." She said, hoping to fool both men.

"I suppose that's good enough, Penelope. No sense keeping you here longer than necessary." He winked and added, "This place is full of sick people."

She smiled. Her dad smiled.

"Would you like the nurse to come in to get you unhooked from these machines and help you get dressed?" Doctor Patterson asked, glancing at her dad and then back to her.

"That would be perfect. Thanks." She answered.

"Got it." Her dad nodded. "I'll just wait out in the hallway."

Even after she had the green light to leave, it still took almost an hour before she was in the car pulling away from the doors of the hospital. The whole way home she stared out the window thinking about those few terrifying seconds at Marika's. The images of the second man were now clear as day in her mind. She could picture his silhouette standing over the big pile of limp monster on the floor. Funny how your mind can play tricks.

Father was cute when they got home. He helped her to the couch, insisting she stay on the first floor where he could keep an eye on her. He also forced her to start drinking water. Doctor's orders, he said. On the plus side, he let her eat ice cream straight out of the tub. She was settled now and suddenly bored. Her dad hovered in the kitchen, pretending to clean. Silly man. She finished the ice cream and asked for something other than water to drink. He brought root beer. Penelope wondered how long she would be able to milk the situation.

While she was mulling that over, she heard the garage door open and concluded it must be Bags and Marika. The number of footsteps on the stairs told her she was right.

"Oh, Penelope, I'm so happy to see you!" Marika said, practically running the last few steps to the couch.

Penelope sat up so she could be hugged properly. "Me too. Are you ok?"

"I am, thanks to you."

"Not sure about that but, whatever. Who the heck was that guy?"

"I really don't know."

"It seemed like you knew what he was talking about, though. What was that business about your brother?"

"I really don't remember very much about what he was screaming at me. I think he must have been mentally deranged. I hear you have been having some trouble remembering last night as well."

"That's what they tell me." Penelope sensed Marika was keeping something from her. It started her mind going again. Bags sat at the end of the couch and started talking. She remained vaguely aware of him and of her responses to him while her brain was going in a completely different direction. It was all she could do to hang on for the ride. Before the intruder Marika was telling her something important, or Penelope remembered it as somehow important. It wasn't about Bags or Harry . . .. Suddenly she had it. It was funny how her brain worked. Just one random thing in her conversation with Marika. That's what it took. And now everything seemed so clear -- well almost. Weird.

"Anyway I am very happy to have my two best girls safe today." Bags finished a thought that Penelope hadn't really heard.

"Marika, could you nose around in the fridge and find me something to eat? Father is hopeless in the kitchen. He would probably bring me a broccoli stalk."

"Of course, my dear." She stood and wandered into the kitchen. Her dad would appreciate that.

"Alright, she's gone. What is it?" Bags asked.

"You mean that wasn't very smooth?" Penelope frowned.

"Smooth enough but I know that look, young lady. Tell me." He leaned closer to Penelope.

"Bags, I know who did it. I know who killed Harry."

"Are you certain? You did receive a substantial blow to the head last night and you survived a very traumatic attack. Marika was hysterical most of the night."

"Yeah, I heard you had a sleepover. Good for you, by the way. And, yes, I am very sure I know who. What I don't know is how. I'm going to need your help with that."

"Then you will have it."

Chapter 31

Penelope was annoyed to be sidelined the rest of the day. She wanted to be the one doing the work to prove her theory. It was only fair after she spent all those hours looking at pointless video. Bags was on the job as soon as he left her house. Though he kept her updated by text, he was having all the fun. Not surprisingly, the Sheriff was unimpressed with her solution. She suspected he sent Detective Benton to do the requested follow-up just to keep the peace with St. Georges and also so he could say "I told you so." She didn't care. They needed his help and Bags got him to say yes.

From her couch prison things seemed to be taking forever and late in the day Penelope reached her breaking point. She talked her dad into taking her on a golf cart ride. The golf cart ride was not just about relief from boredom. She was hoping something would trigger a new thought about how the killer managed to slip in and out. To that end, she suggested they stop at the marina parking lot and walk along the dock for a few minutes. She could tell her dad viewed the request suspiciously. He was still falling all over himself to be nice, though, so all he said was, "Only a short walk, I think."

The walk proved unproductive, except for the bugs. They loved it. In her haste to hunt for clues, Penelope forgot to douse her legs with bug spray. It was a feeding frenzy. Her dad was the first to notice and immediately called time on the walking and the riding. Soon they were in the cart on the way to the safety of their garage. It was the least likely place for an epiphany she could imagine and yet there it was, the last piece of the puzzle. The text was on its way to Bags before her dad had the golf cart in the driveway.

The rest of the day was torture and not just because her head still hurt. Penelope knew she was right and waiting for the last few pieces to fall into place was agony. Her only relief was the entertainment of having her dad wait on her hand and foot, like the princess she truly was. That was fun right up until he brought her the medicine Doctor Patterson prescribed to help her relax. Her parents were not big on prescription medicine but her dad decided to go along with the doctor just for one night. Penelope knew he was thinking more about his own relaxation than hers. She took the little pill anyway.

It worked. When her eyes opened the next morning, she had no memory of going up the stairs, changing clothes, or getting into bed. It also seemed like she had been sitting on the couch taking that little pill only moments earlier. Penelope looked out the window. It was earlier than she expected. She checked her phone. There was a note from Bags. If her dad approved, she could accompany him on what they both hoped would be the last errand required to acquire the proof needed. She responded immediately. Of course she would go. Father would say yes. She had no doubt.

Penelope was out of the shower and in the kitchen before it occurred to her that her headache was barely noticeable. One bagel, one sad puppy face conversation with her dad, and she was down the stairs to the garage to be picked up by Bags. He was waiting for her. The errand took longer than Penelope expected and was not nearly as exciting as she had hoped. It began to feel like boring grunt work that one of the Sheriff's detectives should be doing. Bags let her use his phone to correspond with the Sheriff while he drove. She tried to make her texts sound like the ones Bags sent. He had a formal style, which she had fun trying to mimic.

The goal was to secure the Sheriff's help in setting up a meeting at the club with some of the interested parties. The purpose of the meeting would be to lay out the results of the investigation in hope of having the killer slip up. It was unorthodox but Bags thought it necessary. The problem was that even though they had worked out all the details of the crime, there was still no physical evidence to support an arrest. They would need a confession, or at least some kind of ill-advised admission. At this point, the investigation had been going on long enough that anyone hauled in for an interview would be on alert and likely would bring a lawyer. They needed the element of surprise.

The Sheriff didn't like unorthodox things. He liked the safety of going by the book. This investigation had already tested his resolve on that issue and Penelope knew it. I mean seriously, it is definitely not "by the book" to have an old man -- sorry Bags -- and a teenager helping with a murder investigation. Negotiation by text was not going particularly well. That changed late morning when they finally secured the last piece of the puzzle. When the Sheriff agreed, he suggested they do it that afternoon. Detective Benton had been nosing around enough the day before to possibly put their suspect on alert. Time was of the essence, he said. Bags agreed, or rather

Penelope agreed on his behalf. She was tempted to send Marika a text or two while Bags wasn't looking, you know, just to move things along. She didn't.

Bags dropped her off at home. He was taking charge of assembling all the right people. The Sheriff and Detective Benton would be at the club at four. They would use the bar, which was a pretty normal place for meetings. The other members wouldn't think twice about seeing the doors closed. They even had a little "Meeting in Progress" sign on a metal stand they could put outside. Her dad insisted on attending with her. Not only was he feeling extra protective at the moment, this was actually the kind of thing he might be able to use in his books. He insisted she put on long pants and a "proper" shirt. Silly Father.

Penelope and her dad arrived right at 4:00. Bags and the Commodore were waiting. Also on the guest list were Yelena and William, Will and Trish Wilhight, Roger Patterson, Ander Yeagle, and Marika. Some of the attendees would be there just for show, obviously.

The official start time was going to be 4:30. Bud was on duty for happy hour and was happy to make drinks for the early arrivals. It was nearly quarter to five before Yelena and William showed up. Bags invited them to order drinks before the Sheriff kicked off the meeting. It seemed to Penelope both had already had one or two before they arrived.

The Sheriff began. "I know the matter of Mr. Cumberson's death has weighed heavily on the people in this room and on the larger St. Georges community. I also am aware there are those unsatisfied with how long our investigation has taken. That is one of the reasons Mr. Bagwell thought it a good idea to hold this meeting. You see we have some updates on our progress for you and he believes this is the right cross section of interested parties to hear those updates."

"To that end, I want to thank each of you for attending on short notice." Bags interjected.

"Yes, thank you for being here." The Sheriff echoed. "As I was saying, this has been a very unusual case in many ways. One of the most unusual things about it is the extent of cooperation my department has received from your community and, in particular, through your liaison, Mr. Bagwell, and also

Miss Hazard. She is here specifically at my request in case any of you wondered about her presence. In fact, the most recent developments in our investigation have been made possible only because of Mr. Bagwell and Miss Hazard so I am going to let the two of them share what we have learned."

"Happy to do it, Sheriff. It has been a most unusual set of circumstances, not that I am any kind of expert on murder investigations, of course. What we have to share with you tonight will demonstrate just how unusual. Penelope, would you like to start us off?" Bags looked at Penelope, smiling. She was not expecting that.

Penelope looked at her dad. He gave her a "why not" shrug with his shoulders. "Sure," she said and soon found herself standing with no idea why she was standing -- and also happy her dad had insisted she dress like a grownup. "I think not everyone has been really involved in the investigation so I'm going to start at the beginning." Her brain was speeding ahead as she spoke. "I think you know I was the one who found Harry's body. At first the Sheriff thought his death was some kind of accident or maybe a heart attack or stroke. The autopsy revealed Harry was in good health and that the cause of death was a single blow to the temple. Also, the nature of the wound suggested it could not have been an accident.

"Within a day or two, Bags and I kind of stumbled onto Ricky the drug dealer, which led to Tyler the drug dealer, which slowed things down for a week while the Sheriff set things up to catch the guys one rung up the drug ladder from Tyler. I think everyone watched the news and knows how that turned out. Anyway, during that week, we all started to believe Harry stumbled into a drug deal and one of the drug guys killed him. When the Sheriff caught the two spoiled brats who were delivering heroin to Tyler right here in the marina, their stories pretty much killed that theory." Penelope stopped and turned to Bags. "Should I keep going?"

"Please. You're doing a wonderful job." He said.

"Ok, so Ricky the cook told us he heard a sploosh sound that night while he was out waiting for the drug delivery. Trip and Blair, the drug delivery guys, also said they heard a sploosh sound and one of them said he saw two men arguing on the veranda. That led to the Sheriff's divers coming out to look in the water over by the back edge of the veranda. They found a black dress sock with a big rock stuffed into the foot. The medical examiner said it was most likely the murder weapon.

"The interesting thing was the sock. It was no ordinary sock. It was vicuna -- very expensive. It turned out that was the only kind of dress sock Harry had in his closet." Penelope stopped again and looked at Bags. "Is it ok to get into the more private stuff?"

Bags looked at Yelena. She pursed her lips then nodded. He looked at Marika. She smiled at Penelope and shrugged. "I don't think we have a choice." Bags concluded.

"Right. The sock seemed like a direct link to the people closest to Harry, and after the drug deal connection started to look dubious, the Sheriff went back to basics anyway, which meant focusing on the people who knew Harry and might benefit from his death. I don't think we need to get into all the details of certain things right now, so I will just say it came to light in the investigation that both Yelena and Mr. Sturridge stood to benefit from Harry's death, particularly because of its timing."

"I don't think that's a fair statement at all." William interjected.

"Well, Mr. Sturridge, I could go more into the details and we could put it to a vote in the room if you'd like." The Sheriff said, raising his eyebrows at William.

"That would serve even less purpose. I think I've made my point." He responded, wilting.

"Uh-huh. Penelope, please continue." The Sheriff prompted.

"Like I said, at that point it seemed like both Yelena and Mr. Sturridge had motive. At first, both of them were unaccounted for that evening. With a little more looking into things it came to light that Mr. Sturridge and Yelena had been seeing each other romantically for some time and that he was with her here in St. Georges that night." Penelope stopped and looked around the room to see whose eyes got big. Like Bags once told her, nothing stays a secret at St. Georges. William and Yelena appeared to be old news already.

She continued. "That seemed to give both of them a little more motive. At that point a theory emerged. Mr. Sturridge -- William -- and Yelena decided it was in both their interests for Harry to be gone. Yelena knew she could not do the deed herself. William, in a bizarre act of chivalry, volunteered. Her part that night was to get him into St. Georges unnoticed. Once inside the perimeter, he only needed to move unseen from Harry's house to the darkness behind the club.

"Harry was excited about his role in the Gala's murder mystery production. He would have told Yelena all the details. Yelena would have only needed to share a few details with William. When the lights went out, Harry would disappear from the dining room and he would need to be gone long enough to change out of Future Harry's jacket and into Present Harry's. When the lights went back on, the show would resume and everyone inside would be focused on Bags.

"That would be William's signal. He would attack, striking Harry first in the head to disorient him or knock him unconscious and then he would beat poor, defenseless Harry to death with a weapon that could easily disappear into the water. Everything was working until something happened just before or just after that first blow. Somehow there was more noise than William expected, which caused me to appear through the door from the bar. Looking back, it seemed like a stupid move on my part." She looked at her dad, who nodded confirmation.

"Anyway, as the door opened, William panicked. He was able to hide in the darkness and then slip away in the chaos that followed my screams -- and Bobby's. At some point, he had the presence of mind to fling the murder weapon into the water. That way, even if someone struck up a conversation with him as he walked back to Yelena's, he would not be holding it and there would be nothing but time and location tying him to the crime.

"Once back at Yelena's, only a midnight search of the house would cause problems. The next morning, his presence as trusted friend of the family would attract little attention. No one would think to ask how he got there. Even the absence of his car out front would raise no suspicion because it was a running joke that Harry had more garage spaces than cars. Visitors were often invited to park in one of the empty ones." She paused again. William smirked.

"They were each other's alibi, of course, and a funny thing happened when they talked to the detectives. Both admitted there was about fifteen minutes of the evening when William was supposedly in the hot tub alone and Yelena was upstairs in the house. That would be a silly story for co-conspirators, which made it seem more likely William acted alone, except now there was a problem with the timeline. Fifteen minutes didn't seem like long enough to get from Yelena's house to the club, kill Harry, and make it back, particularly not if the goal was to do it without being seen.

"The detectives continued to dig and it came to light that William was a competitive swimmer in his youth. It seemed very possible for a strong swimmer to cover the hundred yards between Yelena's back door and the veranda outside the club in a minute or two, leaving ample time to club Harry and make the return swim in the fifteen-minute window. The hot tub story even gave William the cover he would need to take a shower before rejoining Yelena."

"Sheriff, do we really have to listen to this?" William protested.

"No, but she's going to keep talking and I strongly advise you to sit still and keep quiet." The Sheriff responded emphatically. "Please continue."

"One thing I got a little out of order is about the sock. We didn't actually know what the sock was right when it came out of the water. It didn't really look special at that point. A couple of days later the Sheriff's forensics team identified it as a fancy vicuna sock. That led to a search of Yelena and Harry's house. They found some swim gear William later admitted was his, which made the swim across the marina theory more likely. Also, there was a whole drawer of vicuna socks in Harry's closet, except it seemed like one pair of black ones was missing. The sock that came out of the water was, of course, black." Penelope took a breath.

"To complicate things, it wasn't too long after that when Marika revealed she and Harry had been romantically involved for about six months. Apparently, Harry knew about Yelena and William but Yelena did not know about Marika, although she suspected Harry was seeing someone. Harry and Yelena had a more flexible arrangement than most married couples, so it wasn't exactly cheating for either of them." Penelope could see Yelena smile nervously. This time the reaction in the rest of the room was more noticeable. It seemed that Marika and Harry had done a good job keeping their relationship a secret.

"It also came to light that Harry had given Marika a pair of his vicuna socks, black, of course, and she was only able to produce one of them to the Sheriff. They were very soft, apparently. Marika did not appear to have a strong motive to kill Harry but she did have a connection to the sock and there was a window of five to ten minutes when she said she was in the ladies' room but no one recalls seeing her. Unfortunately for her, it was the exact time when Harry was killed.

"At that point in the investigation, there were possibilities but no prime suspect. It began to look like the truth might not come out. Then, almost out of boredom, I decided to look through every frame of the hours and hours of video from Jerry's cameras from the day and night Harry was killed. Most of the time I spent was a complete waste and I'm still a little bitter about it." Penelope waited for the polite, nervous laughter. There was a little more than she expected. Good.

"I decided to watch the forty minutes of video right around the time of the murder without using fast forward. After a day of staring at grainy video, I found just a few seconds of a dark figure moving at the edge of Jerry's driveway and then disappearing in the direction of my house. The Sheriff agreed it almost had to be our escaping killer and it meant the swimming theory was a dead end." She could see the Sheriff wince a little each time she talked about his swimming assassin theory.

"It also meant Marika could not be the killer because she was back in the dining room in time to join the group that gathered on the veranda after Bobby and I started screaming.

"As the Sheriff said at the time, the investigation was back to square one, except it wasn't really. The vicuna sock still seemed important. You wouldn't just have one of those lying around. The killer chose to use that sock in order to point the finger back in the direction of people close to Harry. That was something to go on. It led to a deeper look at some of William's other business partners. They were not kind and gentle, like Harry. They were -- are -- thugs. It seemed too subtle a move for a thug to murder Harry just to cast suspicion on William but it was worth pursuing anyway.

"Similarly, Marika's most recent boyfriend before Harry might have known about the socks and, depending on timing, might have had access to her pair of them. Also, as motives go, it would not be the first time a jilted lover lashed out at his replacement. The old boyfriend quickly turned into a dead end, however, because he had a well-documented alibi. Back to square one.

"The vicuna sock had to be important and yet it was not proving helpful at all. Also, there was a nagging problem with the method of murder. A sharp blow to the temple can definitely kill a normal, healthy man, but you couldn't guarantee death with one blow to the temple the way you could with some other methods, like a knife to the base of the skull, for example.

"Marika shed some light on that problem when she talked to Detective Benton. Apparently, before they were dating, Harry told Marika the reason he lifted weights was to keep from losing bone density. It was something he was very concerned about. Yelena confirmed that later. Now, whether that was a legitimate fear or not, and whether it would affect the sturdiness of his skull, it was possible that someone who knew about Harry's professed frailty might be more optimistic that one good shot to the head would kill him. The medical examiner says it might have mattered a little, by the way." Penelope looked around to see if anyone looked nervous. What she saw was that everyone was waiting for her to continue.

"Until a couple of days ago, that would have been the whole update. But it's funny how things happen sometimes. The other night Marika wanted some company and invited me to spend the evening with her. I'm a new teenager in town spending the summer in St. Georges, so you know I didn't have any competing plans." Everyone smiled.

"It was supposed to be a super fun girls night but this ginormous dude broke into Marika's house, home invasion style. It was terrifying." It seemed like everyone had heard the story but they all tried to look appropriately shocked and concerned. "The crazy big dude knocked the snot out of me, to the point that my memory of what really happened is a little fuzzy. What I did remember, do remember, is the conversation Marika and I were having just before the action started.

"Somehow, while I was out cold, or when I was recovering in the hospital later that night, a bunch of seemingly random things came together in my head. I had an idea. I think Sheriff Phillips indulged me and did the research I suggested just because he knew I had a bad night." She smiled at the Sheriff and he blushed ever so slightly.

"So here is the update we brought you together to hear. We know who killed Harry and we know how."

"Tell us, please." Yelena spoke up, which triggered a chorus of similar murmurs.

"I've told you most of what you need to know. You see it came down to listening very closely to things. Bud, you're the bartender who hears everyone's secrets. You listen a lot. Maybe you should tell us who killed Harry." Penelope looked across the room at her friend Bud.

"Miss Penelope, I'm sorry, I don't think I was listening closely enough to solve your little riddle. You know sometimes I only pretend to listen." He flashed his trademark grin.

"I know. And I know sometimes you hear things you wish you hadn't. You told me that once. Do you remember that, Bud?"

"It's true. I hear a lot of things that make me sad for people. No one has confessed about Harry to me, if that's what you mean."

"Not quite. Maybe I listen better than you do, Bud. Remember when you told me what you thought of Marika? You said you bet she hurt people sometimes without even knowing it."

"I'm not sure. I guess I could have said that."

"You did. I didn't think much of it at the time. We were just chatting about Marika and how I was jealous of the attention she was getting from Bags.

You made it a point to tell me you didn't really know her. Do you remember that?"

"Now wait a minute-"

She cut him off. "That wasn't true at all, was it, Bud. You're the boyfriend with the alibi in our story, aren't you?"

"Ok, yeah, that's me. Of course I lied to you about knowing Marika. It was really important to both of us to keep our relationship a secret."

"I know. Marika told me that just before our evening was interrupted. What she said, in fact, was that Harry never knew about you and you never knew about Harry."

"That's what I'm saying. I didn't know about Harry, so why would I be mad at him. And even if I was mad at him, I wasn't around that night. I was working another job. There's video of my car sitting in a hotel lot for four hours for God's sake?"

"Because, Bud, you're the bartender. People tell you things. People tell you things they shouldn't. Sometimes they tell you things you don't want to hear. Marika might have done a good job of hiding you from each other, but in doing that, she withheld an important piece of information from Harry. So when he broke down at the bar one night and told you about Marika, he had no idea what damage he was doing. Actually, I bet he never used her name. But something he said, some detail, told you he was talking about your Marika.

"Marika was pretty clear that she ended things with you because you had become too possessive. For the month or so before she broke things off, you knew something was up. You knew there was another guy. You found the socks. They could have been from a long time ago, so you didn't confront her. It wouldn't have mattered anyway. But you took one just because you knew it would annoy her. Based on what you saw around the club, you suspected it might belong to Bags. Didn't matter."

"I'm sorry, Miss Penelope. You're crazy, just plain crazy. Sheriff, do I have to listen to this?"

"Same as I told Mr. Sturridge. Your choice, but you know my recommendation." The Sheriff responded.

"For some reason, when Harry told you about Marika you went a little crazy. Maybe he shared details you didn't want to hear, intimate details. Who knows? For whatever reason, you couldn't get past it. You wanted to hurt Marika but you were still in love with her. So you decided to kill Harry instead. You knew from being around the club when Bags and I were working out details for the Gala that Harry would be in the perfect place for you to get at him.

"You already had the sock. You probably liked the irony of using his own sock to kill him and it also would throw suspicion toward people with better access to Harry's sock drawer, like Yelena. All you needed was a big rock, which you knew would be waiting for you on the ground right outside. So you waited there for Harry to be alone on the veranda to change out of his dead guy costume. You whacked him on the head really hard. You're a big guy so it probably was easy for you. You knew from Marika his head might be particularly susceptible. People might even think it had been a freak accident if you made it look like one blow.

"What you didn't count on was me hearing you. See teenagers have way better hearing than old people. You were planning to hit him a few more times maybe, walk casually over to the dock, and lower the sock into the water. I ruined that for you. Instead, you had to toss the sock into the water and hide in the bushes until everyone was distracted by Harry's body and my screaming. Then you slipped behind all the houses between the club and Jerry and Joan's house. You didn't know about Ricky or the other drug wannabes so you had no way to know they would hear the big sploosh that would lead us to the murder weapon. It didn't really matter, you figured, because it would be really hard to connect it back to you. You were the dark clothed figure that showed up on Jerry's camera."

"But Sheriff, you know I was working at a hotel up the road all night. I couldn't possibly have killed Harry." Bud protested.

"I know that's what you told us. And I know you really wanted us to look at that video of the employee parking lot where your car was sitting. I also know that the camera covering the valet section of the lot set up just for that big event shows a man with a small duffel getting into a silver sedan and driving off, then returning later with no duffel. We also know your job that night was to deliver room service while the regular staff covered the event. We checked on a few of the tickets for your deliveries. There were a couple of customer complaints about how long they waited for their food."

"I don't know anything about a silver car or a duffel bag and I can tell you the kitchen was the problem that night, not me." Bud defended himself. "And if there was a silver sedan pulling into St. Georges that night, I guarantee it wasn't me."

"That's interesting, Bud, because you're right, there wasn't a silver sedan on any of the video I watched. I knew you could fake your alibi pretty easily. I was actually surprised how quickly Detective Benton started finding holes in it. What I couldn't figure out was how you got in and out of St. Georges. And then I was driving around with my dad this morning and it hit me. The answer was just a little up the road from my front door. The golf cart gate to Sunset Point was right there in front of me all along. You knew the Sheriff would do everything possible to identify who came and went through the St. Georges gates and probably even over the water. But why would he think to check with the security folks at Sunset Point?" Bud was holding up better than Penelope expected. She basically had one card left to play.

"It comes down to listening again. I remember you telling me that you had a lot of different gigs around town. Looking at your tan, it wasn't much of a guess that some of your jobs are outside. The people at the tiki bar on the beach at Sunset Point confirmed that you work there and that you would have an employee ID. We checked with the guards at the gate. Anyone who flashes an employee ID doesn't have to sign in. So you took your silver sedan to Sunset Point, flashed your ID, and borrowed a golf cart. We looked around this morning. A lot of the residents are very sloppy with their golf cart keys, just like the folks here at St. Georges. You slipped through the gate, parked just out of sight of Jerry's driveway, and walked along behind that row of houses to the back of the club. After it was done, the golf cart went back to Sunset Point and the silver sedan went back to the valet lot, well before the end of the party there, and in time for you to finally deliver those cold room service orders. The dark clothes you wore and the duffel are no doubt long gone but we have the rock and we have a picture of you on Jerry's camera."

"Wow. That is one elaborate little story. I did all that because Harry stole my girlfriend. You know, Miss Penelope, I'm not even mad at you. You're just a kid. I'm sure it all makes sense in your head. But Sheriff, you should know better. I may not be rich like all these people at St. Georges but that doesn't mean I'm stupid. You don't have any real evidence or you would have made an arrest. This was a sad little trick that you only bought into because you're desperate. I didn't do any of those things. That is a fairy tale concocted by the overactive imagination of a teenage girl. So if you want to arrest me based on that fairy tale, go ahead. I'm right here."

A long silence followed. Penelope's heart sank. She had underestimated Bud. It was embarrassing. This trick always worked on TV. The killer always made some little mistake. Bud wasn't just a killer. He was a stone cold killer. His plan was solid. He carried it out flawlessly. And now he was sticking to his story perfectly. She wanted to cry or yell at Bud, neither of which would make things less embarrassing.

"Sheriff, I think we are done here. Penelope and I are going home now. Mr. Billings has laid down the gauntlet and we will look to you to decide how best to proceed." Her dad looked coldly at Bud, rose from his chair, and extended a hand to Penelope. She could tell he was seething. Nobody else would recognize it and Penelope had never seen it before exactly. She just knew what he sounded like when he was not seething. His tone scared her a little. There was just a hint of badass about it. Maybe he was channeling Raglan Dunne. Whatever the source, she was glad to see it. He was coming to her rescue the only way he could, by extracting her from the kill zone.

They were out the door before she could hear the Sheriff's response to Bud. Penelope felt bad. She put him in a bad place and like Bud said, he was the Sheriff, not some teenager. That night was horrible. The more she thought about it, the more she realized what a total goober she was; so cocky about her little story, so sure Bud would crumble in response to her logic. It hadn't occurred to her that anyone able to plan such an elaborate crime would be hard to break. It only now occurred to her how high the stakes were for Bud. There was a selfish part of her that wanted him to get away with it. She liked

Bud. He was likable. The thought of sending him to prison for the rest of his life made her sick to her stomach. The trouble was, the thought of him getting away with killing Harry, whom she liked even more, made her sicker still. The only good news was that it was all very clearly out of her control at this point. It would be a long time before the Sheriff would talk to her again.

Chapter 32

Penelope didn't sleep much after the debacle in the bar. It made her sad to think that was the last time she would be in that bar. There was no way she would set foot in the club again, let alone the bar. She finally gave up her fight against the morning light around eleven and checked her phone. She found several texts from Bags stacked up. He wanted her to run errands with him. It was a sweet gesture. He knew she would need distracting. Bags was about the only one who could really understand her right now, so she agreed to go with him after lunch.

The "errands" turned out to be completely fabricated and consisted of Bags tooling around St. Georges in his golf cart visiting people. He tried to keep clear of anyone likely to know about the events of the prior afternoon, although they did check on Ander. He was trying kick his heroin habit without doing an in-treatment program. It sounded like Bags had been checking on him pretty much every day. Ander seemed in good spirits and knowing that Bags was so attentive made her think even more of her adopted grandfather.

They stopped at a few other houses. Penelope met some new people. More precisely, she matched names with faces she saw around St. Georges all the time. The last stop on their circuit was Mr. Brownfield -- Brad. He was last for a reason. Brad, as Bags predicted, spent a great deal of time talking about his quest to prove there was a panther roaming the alleys of St. Georges. It wasn't as crazy as Bags made it sound. St. Georges bordered a small wildlife preserve on one side. Actually, parts of the community were completely surrounded by its dense woods and mangrove swamp. The Brownfield's house was right at the edge of the preserve and when you looked out from the patio around their pool, it seemed like the trees and vegetation were about to swallow the whole property. It wasn't a very big patch of wildness, and everything around it was heavily developed, but there were definitely critters living there. Penelope could understand why Brad might be a little twitchy about unwanted visitors.

Bags couldn't really complain about Brad's panther update. He was the one who brought it up by asking if Brad had any good pictures from the wildlife cameras he had around his house. That was all the invitation Brad needed, apparently, and Bags had to know it was coming. It took every bit of fifteen minutes to get a final answer on the camera question. "No," there were no good pictures to show Bags and Penelope. The specific discussion of the cameras was, by itself, good for a solid five-minute monologue. This guy knew a lot about hunting and using cameras to find game.

As an aside, Brad mentioned being down to three cameras for the summer because he had loaned one to Chuck Fabregas to help Chuck figure out whose cat was crapping along the side of his house. Penelope was barely listening at this point. The subject of what might be lurking in the wildlife preserve next door was marginally interesting. Talk of cameras and cat crap was less so. What got her attention was how Bags reacted. Thankfully, he asked Brad to repeat himself, which at least gave her a clue.

Before they could escape the panther conversation, Brad insisted on a demo of his $500 cameras. Penelope struggled to feign interest. "They're triggered by motion sensors, you see." Brad waived his hand in front of the camera on the side of his house so Penelope and Bags could see the little red light go on.

"Very interesting. What about at night?" Bags asked.

"Same thing at night. They have the most current generation of night vision." Brad launched into another geeky description. Bags was in trouble for egging him on like this. Penelope turned in the direction of the sound of an approaching car.

"And with the night vision images, you can also set it to do this," Penelope heard Brad say just before there was a little button click and a flash. "And the nice thing is, here at the house I don't even have to check the cameras to get the pictures. They upload right to my laptop over wifi."

"Wifi, very fancy, indeed." Bags kept him going.

"Wait," Penelope turned back toward the camera. "Was that a flash? Do that again, please." She turned away, closed her eyes, and waited. The camera flashed again.

"What do you think, Penelope? Pretty cool, huh?" Brad asked proudly.

"Yeah, it's great, Mr. Brownfield. Thank you." She said politely. "Bags, where does Mr. Fabregas live?"

"Next to the club." He grinned. "Maybe we should go and check on Mr. Brownfield's camera."

"I think we should go right now, Bags. Like, right right now!"

Bags said the polite goodbyes for both of them. Penelope was already in the golf cart. Two minutes later they were walking to the back of the Fabregas house. The camera was gone. It had clearly been right where Brad told them to look. They could see where someone had broken the straps holding it to the trunk of a small palm at the back corner of the house.

Penelope stood by the tree and faced the club. The veranda was not in her direct line of sight. It was slightly around the corner and obscured by some shrubs. That was exactly what she expected to see. "Crap Bags. It was here. That camera has a picture of Bud on it. I know it does. He's just too smart. He probably came back the next day and took the camera, one step ahead of us again."

"For someone who prides herself on listening, I think you missed a fairly important thing back at Brownfield's." Bags grinned.

"What do you mean?"

"These cameras can do wifi."

"Seriously?" She blurted.

Bags was dialing his phone even as he said the words. "Brad, yes, hello. Say Brad, you know that camera you loaned to Fabregas? You didn't help him set it up on his network, did you? Uh-huh. Very good . . . no, no, I think they are out of town . . . you say you have the keys . . . no, the code, my apologies . . .. Actually, Brad if you could come right now, that would be wonderful." Bags ended the call and looked up. "We should know soon enough."

"Don't play with me, Bags. Not today." Penelope responded, not daring to get her hopes up.

"He is on his way. He will help us look on Chuck's computer. If there are any pictures, we will see them."

The ten minutes it took for Brad to arrive felt like hours. Penelope could barely speak as they opened the door to the house and walked up the stairs to the den. Brad seemed familiar with the computer. It didn't have a password, which was just stupid these days but suited their immediate needs. There were a couple of times Penelope wanted to rip the mouse out of Brad's hand and beat him with it. He was moving so slowly.

When he found the folder for the camera images, Penelope thought she was going to hyperventilate. Click, click, click, and images started opening up.

"Well there's Chuck's nemesis, right there. Looks like a raccoon, not a cat. See how clear the picture is with the flash?" Brad observed proudly. "Say, these images are all a couple of weeks old at least. What is it we are looking for?"

"Just open the more recent pictures, I think." Bags redirected him.

"Ok, there you go. These are the last two." Brad clicked a few more times. "Hey, what the heck is the bartender doing back there?"

"Say 'cheese' Bud!" Penelope blurted as she jumped up and down grabbing Bags by the arm.

"What's that next one, Brad?" Bags tried to remain calm.

"Looks like the very next day. Bartender again. What's all this about, anyway?"

"We have been trying to catch our own nighttime prowler, Brad." Bags smiled at Penelope. "And now we have."

"We got him, we got him, we got him!" Penelope repeated, hugging Bags as hard as she could.

"He won't be so smug next time he sees the Sheriff, will he?" Bags hugged her back.

Brad printed copies of both pictures for them. He was happy to have someone show interest in his geeky camera stuff and didn't seem to mind being left in the dark about the significance of the moment.

As soon as they had the pictures in hand, Bags called the Sheriff. Penelope could tell from the one side of the conversation she could hear that Sheriff Phillips was less than thrilled to hear more from them. That all changed when it became clear exactly what Bags was describing. In fact, he wanted to send one of the detectives to St. Georges immediately to collect the evidence.

As soon as he was done with the call to the Sheriff, Bags was dialing again. He agreed to try to contact Mr. Fabregas so the Sheriff would have official permission to take digital copies of the pictures. It took a few minutes for Bags to explain enough background so Chuck understood why they were snooping around on his computer and why it was so important to give the Sheriff what he needed. Penelope suggested asking if they could use the Fabregas email account to mail copies of the pictures to the Sheriff, and to Penelope and Bags, of course. Bags asked and Mr. Fabregas agreed to let Brad send the emails.

Her epic fail the day before seemed a distant and tiny memory as she stared at the image of Bud's face staring back from her phone. The time stamp was perfect. It placed him fifty feet away from Harry's body at the same moment Bags and Doctor Patterson opened the dining room doors in response to Penelope's screams. The actual picture was perfect. Not only was it a clear image of Bud's whole face, lit perfectly by the camera's flash, it also had a delicious comic quality. In his haste to get away from the crime scene, presumably driven by Penelope's unplanned appearance on the veranda, Bud stumbled. At the moment he triggered the camera's flash, he was on all fours staring right into the camera with open mouth and wide eyes. Penelope only felt a little guilty for relishing that stupid look.

They would have checked on the borrowed camera no matter what but the reason Penelope was certain it would give them a picture of Bud was the flash. That night it barely registered because the timing was so perfectly coordinated with the bright light suddenly pouring out of the doors in front of her as Bags opened them. She might have forgotten all about it if Trip and Blair hadn't described something vaguely similar in their account of that night.

When Mr. Fabregas tripped the flash on his camera to show Bags how it worked, Penelope knew in an instant it was the same thing she had experienced the night Harry died.

The second picture, the one from the next day, was gravy. Clearly it was a case of the camera reaching back from the grave to tell them who killed it. Bags said they would never find the camera. Bud ripped it off the base of the tree and made sure it would never be found. He was probably smart enough to melt the memory card and might have known to smash the GPS transmitter. Based on his attitude the day before, Bud was pretty confident he had disposed of the only direct evidence tying him to the crime. Bags said "smug." She knew what the word meant in theory. Until yesterday she didn't have a real life example. Bud had been smug. She would not forget how it looked in the flesh. She wanted to see Bud try to be smug when he saw his "oh crap" face staring back at him during his next little talk with the Sheriff.

Chapter 33

Still riding the high, Penelope had the chance to tell the tale of Bud's unwanted portrait to a larger audience that night. Somehow she had gone through the last week more or less oblivious to the fact that it was almost July 4th. She vaguely recalled the Commodore's invitation to go out on his boat and watch fireworks. Her mom and dad were planning on it. Doctor Patterson and his wife would be there too. Bags was also invited and it was hardly a shock when Marika showed up with him. What surprised and pleased her was they way they were behaving decidedly date-like. It was about time. The effort required to push the two of them into each other's arms had been fatiguing.

It was a big boat, fifty feet, Penelope guessed. As they were leaving the marina, the Commodore joked with Penelope that she was the designated driver. Ha ha. She had been around big power boats just enough since moving to St. Georges to know her only role on one should be to look fabulous in her sunglasses with the salty breeze blowing her hair around like she was in a photo shoot.

Once they were situated in the flotilla of other boats -- "flotilla," a word she had only recently learned -- drinks were poured and Penelope was given the stage. It wasn't quite as good as the gotcha moment she really did believe would come at the end of her performance at the bar. Still, she enjoyed the retelling. It was the definition of a captive audience. The boat's bridge, where they gathered to drink and wait for the fireworks was only just big enough for their group. She held everyone's attention, even Bags, who had lived through it with her.

The only wrinkle, and one she found out about only because her teenage hearing was better than Bags and her dad thought, was that the Sheriff had not yet arrested Bud. Bud had gone missing. Until he was actually behind bars, Penelope would not feel fully vindicated. The Sheriff was afraid he was on the run, which meant Penelope might not get the closure she so badly wanted. But that was a small blemish on an otherwise awesome day. For the first time in several years she actually enjoyed the fireworks.

Everything started to catch up with her on the way back to St. Georges. With all the boats out watching fireworks, the water highway was congested. It was taking forever to get home and Penelope was suddenly having trouble keeping her eyes open. She dozed on her mom's shoulder for a good part of the trip, waking up only as they pulled into the marina. As usual, backing the big boat in to its slip was a bigger and longer production than Penelope liked. She was glad to step onto the dock, one step closer to her bed.

Uncharacteristically, her dad accepted the Commodore's invitation to stay on the boat and play poker for a bit. Mother was clearly happy to see him volunteering for more social interaction and ignored the fact that Marika's plan to join the game was probably the reason. She smiled and agreed to take Penelope home.

It was a busy day in the tiny marina parking lot so they were parked across the street in the lot by the tennis courts. Penelope leaned on her mom as they walked in silence. As they approached their cart in the darkness, Penelope became aware of another set of footsteps behind them. As she turned to look, her mother's arm was ripped from her grasp. In the darkness she could see her mom slump to the ground.

Penelope tried to scream. Nothing came out. She was frozen, watching as their attacker turned to face her. Before she could move, one arm was twisted behind her, jammed up into the bottom of her shoulder blades. A big, rough hand clamped over her mouth.

"Ok, you little bitch. Let's see how you feel about being on the victim end of a murder investigation."

It was Bud. He was dragging her across the parking lot to a beat up Mustang. She was pretty sure her left arm was out of its socket. The pain had her struggling to remain conscious. She was headed for the trunk of Bud's car and probably the bottom of the Gulf after that. She had to think of something.

"Just so you know, I'm going to cut you up and feed you to the gators."

Any sympathy Penelope might have harbored for Bud was definitely gone at this point, not that it was likely to matter. Her only chance was right before he put her in the trunk. He would have to use one hand to open it.

258

"Why did you do it, Bud? Why?" She mumbled through his clamped hand.

"Ok, I'll tell you why." He said as he pushed her toward his car. "I don't care about money all that much. They can keep their fancy cars and houses and yachts. I didn't care about anything that much until I met Marika. She was the one thing I had in my life. Harry had everything but he couldn't be happy. He had to use his money to take my Marika too. That's why I did it, Penelope. It's not right to take away the only thing a man cares about just because you can."

For just a split second Penelope felt sorry for Bud. He sounded so pathetic. Her sympathy wasn't enough to let him kill her, though. As they approached the car, Penelope felt Bud's grip on her arm loosen. He used the other to pull her head back hard into his chest. When he finally let go to fish keys from his pocket, Penelope stamped hard on his foot and tried to wriggle free from his other hand. Bud yelped a little in surprise but didn't let go. He leaned forward sharply, slamming her into the top of the trunk lid. The shock combined with a new jolt of pain in her wounded shoulder caused the light in her eyes to dim and then go black.

Chapter 34

Penelope opened her eyes, or so it seemed. She was back in the strange gray room on the little cot. It was the dream again. She was aware it was a dream and there was nothing she could do. "Open your eyes for real," she said under her breath. Penelope closed and opened her eyes several times trying to will herself out of this weird lucid dream state.

The door opened. "Good afternoon, Penelope." A woman entered the room.

"I forget, are you Agent K or Agent M?" Penelope decided it was her dream and she could be obnoxious if she wanted.

"Agent K." The woman answered. "The last time we talked, you were having trouble remembering what happened last night. Is your memory coming back to you?"

"Last night? Sure. Bud the bartender tried to stuff me in his trunk." Penelope answered.

"Good. Do you remember anything about why that didn't happen?"

"Not much. He tried to break my arm. He slammed me into the top of his trunk. I blacked out. Then I woke up in this dream with you." Penelope was trying to make sense of what was happening. "Hey, my shoulder still hurts."

"The pain medicine is wearing off. We can give you a little more." The woman looked over her shoulder and whispered something. "Penelope, how much do you remember about the few weeks before last night?"

"You mean Harry's murder, the investigation, all of that?"

"Yep, all of that. Also, the night Marika was attacked."

"Everything. I remember everything. That's how my brain works. I can replay it all back like a movie." Penelope explained.

"That sounds almost like a superpower, Penelope. How would you feel about doing that for us in a little bit?"

"If you tell me who you are and why you have me here." Penelope was still convinced it was a dream. She was hoping she could guide it to a point where she could force her eyes open.

"We are investigators working for an insurance company that wants to be certain who killed Mr. Cumberson before it pays on a life insurance policy."

"You mean they want to make sure they aren't giving the money to the guy who killed Harry."

"Something like that, yes." The woman nodded.

"If you say so. When do we start?" The insurance thing was a cover Penelope wasn't buying. It was a good story and one that might make sense in the hazy reality of dreamland. In the real world, insurance investigators didn't use made up names and didn't hold witnesses hostage in little gray rooms. Also, they would just ask the police. Duh.

"There are some of your clothes on the table. Why don't you get dressed and we'll go to a room where we can sit and talk." The woman pointed to a stack of clothes Penelope hadn't noticed. It was more proof she was dreaming.

She put on the clothes and Agent K led her to a room filled with a utilitarian metal table and matching chairs. The woman invited her to sit on the side opposite a wall-size mirror. It looked just like the interview room at the Sheriff's Office. She was definitely dreaming.

Agent M entered the room and sat quietly next to Agent K, hiding behind a pair of moderately tinted glasses. For the next hour Penelope retold the whole story of the investigation, starting with the night of the Gala. Agent K asked a few questions along the way. She seemed particularly interested in the night at Marika's house, which was annoying because that was the only part of her memory not crystal clear in Penelope's mind. Actually, her memory was clear but it wasn't in sync with what everyone else said happened, which caused her to doubt herself.

She waited and waited for her eyes to open, signaling the end of her very weird dream. It never happened. When there were no more questions, Agents K and M stood and walked to the door. As she left, Agent K told

Penelope her father would be in to get her in a few minutes. Penelope wondered the whole time she was talking who might be watching from behind the glass. Maybe it was her dad.

Chapter 35

Axel watched his daughter staring back at him through the glass. He wondered if she knew he was watching. The door opened and a woman entered. "So 'Agent K' and 'Agent M.' Interesting. I guess that makes me Agent H." He said without taking his eyes off Penelope.

"No sense using real names." The woman responded.

"So, what do you think?" Axel asked.

"She doesn't know what happened to Bud last night. That's pretty clear."

"And the night at Marika's?" He followed.

"Her memories of that night are vivid enough but she doesn't trust them. I think you're safe."

"What does 'Agent M' say?" Axel pressed.

"She agrees. Your daughter isn't trying to hide anything from us. She believes this is a dream."

"And what about the larger question?"

Agent K paused. "She shows promise. Her memory is an asset. More impressive is the way she can sort through everything in that memory to put together the right little bits."

"And her temperament? I've always thought she was very much like her brother in that respect."

"Well, we would have to test her but she appears to have handled herself very well in two life or death encounters. It seems only fair that she inherit something from you." Agent K smiled at Axel.

"I will take that as a compliment. Thanks."

"I have a question for you, Axel. Do you feel our work here is complete?" She asked.

"No. I believe we have only seen the beginning. Things will get worse, I fear." Axel responded earnestly.

"Then we agree. I think things around St. Georges will continue to be interesting for you. Make sure you take care of your new family."

"That is why GSC put me here." Axel smiled before adding. "I think we will go now. Thank you for coming all the way from Denver. I know you are a busy woman."

The woman smiled. "It was a pleasure to finally meet your daughter. We will be keeping an eye on her development." She offered. "I'll stay here until you are gone."

Axel nodded and left the room.

Chapter 36

"Dad!" Penelope had never been so happy to see him. She stood and threw her arms around him, wondering if she was, once again, imagining his presence.

"Whoa, good to see you too." He replied.

"Mom?"

"She has a knot on her head but she's fine."

"Can we leave?"

"That's why I'm here. Time to go home, I think." He smiled.

Penelope gripped her dad's arm in silence as they walked through the drab hallways to the front door of the building. Outside, it took her eyes several seconds to adjust to the harsh sunlight. She looked back over her shoulder. From the outside her prison was a big, nondescript warehouse in the middle of scruffy Florida pine forest.

Once in the car, Penelope remained quiet until they were out of the parking lot, off of the side road leading to it, and back on a main road. "That wasn't a dream was it?"

"It was not."

"And Harry . . . he's really dead, right?" Penelope asked hoping he might not be.

"Yes, that was all real."

It was now dawning on Penelope what had happened. The first dream with Agent K was not a dream at all and it had happened hours ago rather than weeks. The time in the middle when she thought she dreamed of waking up in the gray room and then dozing again also hadn't been a dream but an interruption in her sleep. The real dream had been one long replay of the events after the night Harry died. And now she was awake again. At least she hoped this part was real. She still had questions, though.

"Are you going to tell me what that was really all about with Agent K and Agent M?"

"I thought they explained about the insurance investigation?" He said without taking his eyes off the road.

"Really, you let them hold me hostage at a remote location to ask insurance questions? Not buying it."

"You weren't a hostage. You were a guest. I agreed because they offered to make a very nice contribution to your college fund."

"Sports car fund, I think, and I'm still not buying it. If it was all about insurance, why were so many of her questions about that night at Marika's?"

"I can't answer that for you -- curiosity, maybe. That kind of thing doesn't happen every day, you know."

"It seemed like more than curiosity."

"And we can talk about what to do with your reward later." He interrupted. "For now, I will just say you earned it and I'm proud of you." This time he looked over at her and smiled.

Well that was no fair. She wanted to be mad at him for lying to her and now she couldn't. "I'm just happy to be alive. Bud was a whole lot crazier than I thought."

"Yes he was. We all misjudged him."

"What exactly happened last night? I was sure I was dead. What stopped Bud?"

"I did, actually. Can you imagine? We sat down to play poker on the boat and I realized my wallet was in the car. I ran to catch the two of you before you were gone and got there just in time to surprise Bud after you stomped on his foot."

"Wow! That's pretty cool. How did you stop him?"

"I just cracked him on the back of the head with both fists as hard as I could. I didn't really think about it. It just kind of happened."

"So Sheriff Phillips has him, right?"

"Yes, we're all safe now, Pea."

"Good. Thanks for saving me."

"Anything for you."

"Both times." Penelope looked over to see his reaction.

He smiled. "I think the pain medication is making you silly, Pea."

"Maybe so."

Penelope looked out the window. They were somewhere north of Ft. Myers. She decided her dad was not going to tell her the real story. That was ok. He didn't have to. It was all in her high-def memory. She hadn't imagined any of what she saw that night at Marika's. Penelope suspected the mystery of her dad's real story would be just as complicated as the one she and Bags just solved. She looked over at him, smiling behind his sunglasses and looking down the road toward home. Somehow he looked very different to her.

This was not the summer Penelope expected. She expected extreme boredom made tolerable only because it would be a break from high school drama. Instead, she got a very real dose of drama. Bring on the mean girls and stupid boys. Penelope was pretty sure her new high school scene could not be more high school than what she had experienced so far at St. Georges.

Made in the USA
Middletown, DE
30 April 2015